———

KILLING THE GOOSE

———

D. Michael Flanagan

KILLING THE GOOSE

———

S-CLUB PUBLISHING
1631 Alhambra Blvd. — Suite 120
Sacramento, California 95816

PRINTED IN THE UNITED STATES OF AMERICA

ISBN-13: 978-0-578-50189-5

To Mom…
who always loved a good ghost story.

———

"Your sons and daughters will prophesy,
your young men will see visions,
your old men will dream dreams."

(Acts 2:17)

———

CHAPTER ONE

—— October 6, 1971 ——

An acid trip can be a beautiful thing. A journey you embark upon, quite unlike any other. One that takes you, willing or not, into an unexplored new world of sound, texture, and deeper understanding.

It often starts softly, delicious, moving over you like a warm bath as you relax into it, colors rich, dancing and increasingly vibrant. The voices of those around you become strikingly resonant, more meaningful, causing you to think about each word as they reach down and touch a part of your soul that has never been touched before. Everything begins to intensify, resulting in a weightless state of complete euphoria. Most of the time it's wonderful. Most of the time.

But once the door opens and you step through... the journey begins. Be it good or bad. It can shift at any time and take you anywhere it wants to. You are no longer in control. And there is no turning back. Thus, the term trip. For Howard Perkins, it became nothing short of a nightmare. And the trip lasted for almost forty years.

He was just seventeen years old. Not that it mattered. When the chemicals begin to float into the bloodstream, age becomes meaningless. LSD doesn't care who you are or what you look like. It takes everyone. Especially at a concert.

Leaving his job as a hardware stock clerk a little earlier than usual, he had driven alone to San Francisco in the heat of the afternoon. Lydia Carter and Purple Crow were playing Winterland and, pumped full of adrenalin, Howard wanted to get as close to the stage as he could. It would be better that way.

Despite arriving early, parking had proved impossible, leaving him no choice but to stash his beat up old Volkswagen in a neighborhood that made him nervous. Walking back at night was going to be a problem as well, but with the steady stream of other kids doing the same thing, he figured everything would be OK. They were everywhere, kids, hippies, flower children, and everyone was already flying as high as you can fly, flowing like a steady moving river of lava down towards Winterland.

Everyone swarmed around the front, flowers in their hair, smiling and hugging each other. It was so good. There were the drug dealers, not so subtly selling their wares. Artists selling handmade earrings and roach clips. Those selling or looking to buy an extra ticket. Howard already had his ticket and this time it came with a free hand-drawn poster.

This was not his first concert. He had been to quite a few already for someone his age. He knew the drill now. There was no time to hang around out front as he pushed through *the door into the hall. The sooner you wedged your way through the crowd, in the direction of the stage, the better chance you would have of getting up close to the stars. And tonight, he needed to be close. He desperately wanted to see Lydia eye to eye.*

Ever since her first album came out in early '68, when he was a pimpled fourteen, he had been out of his mind in love with her. There were posters and photos of her stapled into the plaster and covering the walls and ceiling in his bedroom back home. His record collection included each one of her albums, purchased the day it was released. As the self-proclaimed biggest fan in his high school class, he had seen her in concert only once before, a year earlier, but had shitty tickets and was shoved way in the back, up in the rafters. He had barely been able to make out her face. Her sweet, sweet face.

Tonight was going to be different. Not only did he want to see her, he wanted her to see him. To notice him. To know that he loved her. He was going to touch her.

The crowd parted easily, as he forced his way continually toward the stage. Nobody seemed to mind. The house system was blaring Country Joe songs and everyone was smoking and dancing. Howard's mild interruption lasted only for a moment, on his way passed, then melted into the crowd again as it closed in around him.

The stage was about five feet in front of him when he decided he could go no further. It was surrounded by a group of drunken Hells Angels that would not take kindly to him trying to push passed them. Guys like that were like rabid animals, loved any form of conflict and waited hungrily for it, hoping for the chance to tear somebody's head from their neck. They were a vicious breed driven even further towards violence with a stable diet of hallucinogenics and amphetamines.

There was pot everywhere, too. The air was thick with the sweet smell as joints were passed through the crowd. A bizarrely tall guy, much older than Howard, stood next to him for about twenty minutes, just looking at him. Howard assumed he was gay or something until he eventually tapped him on the shoulder, holding out a joint for him with a smile.

"It's really good shit," he said. "Don't pass it along. Hold onto it for a few hits."

Howard accepted the gift with a grateful nod of his head and placed the joint to his lips, taking the smoke into his lungs. At such a naive age, he had no idea that it was heavily laced with Orange Sunshine.

LSD was the drug of choice and it was everywhere. A chemist in Berkeley, Owsley somebody or another, had whipped it up in his lab back in '66 and spread it through San Francisco like a plague. It was still lingering and stronger than ever. People spiked the punch at parties with it or put it in the food at concerts. It wasn't a bad thing, it was just what they did. Everybody was tripping. And everyone was very much in love with each other.

Winterland was their church. And they had come to pray. Thousands of kids in their teens and twenty's, dancing and seeing colors that were not even there. And tonight they had gathered, this congregation, in unabashed worship to their deity; Lydia, the goddess of rock and roll.

When the lights finally went down, Howard was flying. Pressed in by the bodies all around him, he imagined he was a small carrot floating in a gigantic bowl of vegetable soup. In his way of thinking, if there was one vegetable more important than all the rest, it most certainly was the carrot.

A person could probably live their entire life eating only carrots.

The house music died down and the crowd went berserk, screaming out Lydia's name. Over and over they yelled it. In the darkness, behind the amplifiers, Howard could make out the silhouetted figures of the band as they came up the back stairs and out onto the stage. He waited, his head spinning. Then, in a sudden explosion of color, the entire stage came to life.

She stood, directly in front of him, microphone raised defiantly toward the heavens, bathed in a pool of purple and blue, encircled with a vibrant halo of crimson. A lone guitar wailed painfully beneath her as she moaned heavily, erotically, moving slowly forward, a lion upon its prey, toward the crazed audience writhing at her feet. These were her faithful. They loved her. She held out her hands to them, palms up, beckoning them to become one with her and the music kicked in.

The lights shifted to an amazingly bright sea of yellow and blue. The drums pounded, relentless, sending everyone including Lydia into an animalistic frenzy. Like a rogue wave, the energy mounted until it filled the entire auditorium, smashing violently from the floor to the rafters high above. The place was on fire. And everybody was in ecstasy.

To Howard, it was absolutely sexual. A full release of all the beautiful, raw energy, built up deep inside him, coming directly from the woman swaying there in front of him. Dancing from one side of the stage and back again, she laughed, as clothes were torn from bodies and thrown upon the stage before her. They were spent, screaming for her. Howard closed his eyes. And together, making love to her, the masses around him moved seamlessly to the music, a school of fish, deep in her ocean.

Lydia turned, dancing toward the back of the stage and lifted a bottle of Jack Daniels from a stack of Marshalls with her name spray-painted in white along the sides. She tilted the bottle back recklessly, emptied it and threw it to the floor, returning to the congregation before her. She swung her long, famous hair in wild circles, and began tearing at her own clothes. Howard screamed as she shoved her hips repeatedly outward, a personal offering of herself only to him.

Other members of her band danced around her beneath the lights, like pagan priests of old circling their ceremonial fires centuries before. But it was she who controlled the show. Lydia. The people below worshiped her. And as each light blazed brightly above, bathing her in her kingdom of color, she would never let them go. And they did not want her to.

The music softened suddenly and transformed into a slow, defiant beat of simple bass and drums. A haze of white smoke swirled seductively throughout the dimly lit auditorium. To a completely mesmerized audience, Lydia began to sing.

For the first time since she had bounded onto the stage, the people lost their voice, their own silence heightening the intensity of the moment. She was not of this Earth, this woman. So taken in was everyone, by the sweetness and intensity of her voice, by her beauty, that nobody fully realized what had just happened, so suddenly, down there in the darkness of the audience, only five feet in front of her.

A series of three small, silent bursts of bright yellow flame leapt rudely out from the crowd directly in front of the stage. The people watched in a sort of unbelieving stupor as, in slow motion, three brutal holes appeared defiantly upon Lydia's chest. Her eyes squeezed shut, tightly against the pain, as an immediate spray of red assaulted her beautiful face. She fell violently backward onto the stage into a rapidly growing pool of blood, turned a beautiful shade of purple by the cascade of blue lights overhead.

The music stopped. The other band members could not make sense out of what they were seeing. It wasn't real. It could not be real. Everyone stared. Silence fell over the auditorium like a heavy black sheet. The crowd came slowly to life, pushing back, away from a single kid down in front. A hysterical Howard Perkins, standing in front of the stage, screaming and holding a gun in the air.

Lydia's eyes, seeing nothing, struggled, rolled back, and slowly shut forever.

CHAPTER TWO

—— May 21, 2019 ——

(Forty-eight years later)

"Father, it's been about, um… a hundred years since my last confession," the man said, through the small wicker screen separating him from Father Bernardo. His breath smelled of rank cigarettes and quickly dominated the already musty smell of the darkened confessional, causing Father Bernardo to pull back with a little instinctive jerk of his head. It was as though a disease had suddenly entered.

"Sorry," he laughed. "Just kidding. I didn't exactly come to… you know, confess my sins."

"Oh? And what did you come for?" Father Bernardo asked.

"I was referred to you. I guess I need your help."

"What kind of help?"

"OK… well, it sounds sort of stupid, I guess, but I was told you wouldn't think so. It's… of a spiritual nature. You see, there's this old house, up in the Palisades, huge place, and…well it's got a history. Like, I don't know, ghosts or something."

Father Bernardo breathed in deeply. The Catholic priesthood had not exactly been kind to him over the last 50 years. In the course of service, he had lost the use of his left eye, acquired some twenty-three odd stitches here and there, as well as most of the muscular skills on the left side of his body. A severe stroke had exploded some time in his late sixties. That alone would have done enough damage to discourage most men from continuing, especially his particular calling, as it might be. But not Bernardo. An old-world Italian man of the Cloth would never allow himself such a luxury. Retirement, however well deserved, was an American concept.

Due to his age and condition, he no longer held mass. Supposedly the right of every priest, it had not been his decision. He did, however, still hear confessions on a regular basis, thankful, believing it kept him grounded, firm in the faith. His faith. He was a man of little humor and took his church, her sacraments and her adversaries very seriously.

An awkward silence followed. The visitor became uncomfortable, fumbling for words that would somehow absolve him of his foolishness and just as quickly excuse him from the confessional. He himself did not fully believe what he was asking and was given over to the fact that he had made an obvious mistake.

"I don't do that anymore," Bernardo muttered. "Whoever told you that I did… was mistaken."

"Do what anymore? So… you can help me," the man blurted. "Please sir… uh, Father, I really need your help. There's a ton of money at stake here."

"Money? Money is not my concern," Father Bernardo said. "Please, if your penitence is not at issue here, I ask you to leave… There are others waiting their turn."

"OK, I get it," the man said. "So, if I confess something, like my sins or something, will you help me then?" he pleaded. "That's what priests do, yeah?"

Father Bernardo took another deep breath and allowed the air to escape slowly from his lungs, closing his eyes.

"OK, I'm married… see?" the man continued, not waiting for Father Bernardo's response. "And I sort of banged this waitress chick last night. I can tell you shit like that, right?"

"I'm sorry," Father Bernardo interrupted. "I really cannot help you."

"You've got to," the man pleaded. "Nobody else knows about this stuff. You do."

"I simply do not deal in the supernatural any longer."

"C'mon Father. You gotta help me. This thing is causing real trouble. Has been for a long time. Just ain't nobody ever done anything about it. One guy almost died. Went to the hospital. I swear on it."

The man was suddenly silent, drumming his fingers against the wood beneath the small window, searching now for words that would help close the deal. "See, the way I figure," he continued, "if I can deal with this, if we can deal with this…then I can slip in, sell the house and make a fuckin'…sorry, I can make a bundle. Whaddya say, Father? It's just a house. Take a quick look. Say a prayer. That's all I'm askin'."

Father Bernardo did not answer. He simply leaned his head against the dark cherry wood of the confessional and rubbed his thumb deep into his right temple.

Over the centuries, Rome had never actually condoned actions such as his. Not publicly anyway. Doctrine supported it fully, but the realm of the supernatural… witches, demons and ghosts… was handled quietly in the back room. Few priests had the desire to pursue a road that would bring them nothing but trouble and if so, lacked the courage. And those that did, too often would be left standing alone in the time of need, so as not to tarnish the good name of the church. But that was understood. It was an accepted part of the job. Dabble in the supernatural and you left the supreme safety of the fold. Protection ceased.

Finally, there was the unspoken understanding, a cold, cruel warning most priests fully accepted and obeyed. A kind enemy Satan was not. Once you crossed the line, you were never able to return. He would forever hunt you.

"As I said, I'm sorry. My work is here, now," Father Bernardo offered with a deep sigh. "Please leave."

The shuffling of paper was followed quickly by a folded business card, slowly sliding back and forth through a small crack beneath the confessional screen. Bernardo lifted the card and unfolded it, squinting in the dim light.

Ronald Stenton, Realtor.

"You help me on this, Father, and I give one percent of my commission to the church. One percent. We're talking close to five hundred grand. Five hundred. That's a promise."

The sound of creaking wood and the swoosh of a heavy curtain thrown aside left the compartment across from Father Bernardo empty. The stench of a nightclub ashtray remained momentarily as the old priest pushed the palm of his hand, wiping the perspiration from his forehead, back across a thin layer of silver hair.

CHAPTER THREE

Father Bernardo pulled his 1972 Chevy Impala to the side of the road and rolled to a stop in front of a rather foreboding wrought-iron gate. It was heavily rusted from years of neglect, protected only by a layer of green ivy and weeds. The gravel on the roadside crunched painfully under the weight of his tires. He studied the gate, shoving the gear shifter into park and turned the ignition off.

Ronald Stenton, the realtor, stood patiently leaning against a shiny black BMW. Perhaps it was instinct, but Father Bernardo knew it was the man in the confessional. The salesman-like grin and signature cigarette dangling from his mouth spoke volumes.

As though on cue, Stenton smiled and motioned through the old gate toward the house. Father Bernardo took it all in, examining the six gables on top of the roof, several castle-like spires pushing upward further still, all evident victims to years of decay. Fifty years ago this house had been a Gothic masterpiece. Four stories of medieval architectural angles and dark leaded windows rose defiantly above a half-century of untended trees and foliage. A towering wall of deep green vines had grown thick up the north side, crawling across the roof, ripping at the shingles and forcing several sections aside, aimlessly making their way somewhere deep into the dark recesses of the attic. Remaining splinters of tired white paint held on desperately to the gray wood. Bernardo removed the keys from the ignition, eyes fixed upon the house, and pulled himself from the car.

"Hey ya, Father," Stenton said, through a cloud of smoke, extending his hand. "I knew I could count on you, man." Bernardo reluctantly shook it and continued to stare up at the ominous estate.

"Quite a beauty, ain't she?" chided Stenton, as he reached into his pocket, withdrawing a key and holding it out. "I hope you don't mind… But I prefer to keep my distance from the place. I've been in it once before. No desire to go back in, if you catch my drift."

"Oh, I catch it," grumbled Father Bernardo. He took the key and turned toward the gate. It was unlatched and groaned reluctantly, dislodging the rust as he shoved up against it.

Four angular stories of chiseled stone and wood, protected only by the blanket of overgrowth, rose threateningly above him. A massive, forgotten treasure, the house had remained virtually untouched, seemingly forever.

Bernardo studied the architecture. It belonged in a magazine. The very structure appeared to bear down upon him, threaten him, warning him to retreat. Why he had ever agreed with Stenton to bless this property was against the very boundaries set by him almost three years earlier. He was too old for this type of work and had most likely suffered the stroke because of it. And yet, here he was again. Fool. Perhaps it was for the money. His Parish certainly needed it, that was for sure, and in comparison to some of the spiritual battles he had fought, this was easy. If the place sold because of him, wonderful. A few unfortunate city kids would have better lives for a couple of years. And on the off-chance that there really was something supernatural taking place here, well, he couldn't pass that up either.

Stenton, however, had conveniently failed to mention certain details. Specifically, that many prospects in the past had shown genuine enthusiasm in purchasing the property, but always pulled out, some sooner than others, but all inevitably losing interest. So much so, that every real estate company in the area had long since given in to the fact that it was not a viable property for sale. It had been black-labeled. Unprofitable. Abandoned.

Unaware of this piece of information, Bernardo proceeded, naively, over the raised cobblestone and clover driveway. The mansion loomed even larger over him as he proceeded, wrapping him in its shadow. A crumbling fountain, green with ancient rainwater, stood directly in the center of the circular entrance, two cherubs intertwined, gazing up toward heaven through empty eyes of stone. Heavy steps of roughly hewn granite, now at odds with each other, chipped and tilted with age from the tree roots beneath, led up to a massive, arched oak door. A thick layer of cool moss spread like a disease up across the stones and out, infecting everything beyond into the surrounding army of untamed sycamores hanging high above.

The door itself was an impressive piece of ornate carving, imported Italian or French perhaps, solid oak stretched between three broad, rusted iron hinges. The shadows from the trees danced slowly in unison across the threshold to a ceremoniously soft breeze. Welcoming. Taunting.

Father Bernardo slipped the single key into the lock and twisted it several times before it yielded, the door swinging inward with the breeze. It was dark inside and the odor of decay hit Bernardo like an insult.

Stenton watched from the behind gate, leaning against the hood of his leased car. The commission on this property alone would snag him a nice piece of Hawaii. A condo, if nothing else. No time-shares. He had actually sold a few of those in the beginning of his career. Legalized crime. Time-share properties were designed for suckers lucky enough to still have a few dollars left over after the rent was paid. Stenton was ambitious enough to demand something with a little more return on investment. A lot more return. And this particular deal was his stepping-stone. Like destiny or something. Let everybody else be superstitious. Now was the time that this gem had waited to fall into his lap.

He removed the pack of Winstons from his jacket pocket and examined the remaining three. He frowned slightly, wrinkling his nose, ashamed that he had just purchased the pack before coming up into the hills.

The old priest had long since disappeared into the house as he placed the cigarette in his mouth and paused instinctively, waiting for something to happen. Nothing did. Staring up at the fogged glass panels of the French windows jetting gracefully, yet defiantly out from the roof line, Stenton clicked his lighter several times before lighting the end of the cigarette and inhaling. Smoke swirled around him, like incense in a church, as he allowed it to escape from his lungs through his nose. If he could do what no other real estate agent had been able to do over the last forty to fifty some odd years, sell this monster, he stood to literally make a small fortune.

He was determined to unload this place. He loved it. And he certainly hated it. Only last year, he had ignored the warnings of fellow agents and had tried to show the house to a prospective buyer from New York. He had entered the house early, to get a lay of the land prior to his client's arrival. The meeting never took place.

Stenton had been standing in the living room, staring down at the ocean from a large wall of windows in the grand room. He had just begun to light up the customary cigarette when his match blew out. He lit another and it too blew out leaving a wisp of smoke swirling around his head, when he realized suddenly how cold he was. He distinctly heard the rapid whispering of a woman's voice. Threatening. All around him, like a swarm of angry insects. He had dropped his cigarette and run for the front door.

Although embarrassed by his cowardliness, Stenton was not the sort of man who would let his own fear stand in the way of money. He respected what he did not understand, in fact, found a way to ignore it, take it less as a warning and more as a challenge. He never told anyone what he had experienced. But he knew better than to step foot in that house again.

Father Bernardo was a solution, perhaps. A means to an end. Stenton was anything but a religious man, but knew this was an area he was not qualified to judge. Plus Myra, his pious nut of a mother-in-law had highly recommended

Father Bernardo. She had read something about him in an article somewhere, said he knew everything there was to know about the supernatural realm and that if anyone could deal with… a ghost, or whatever… it was him.

Stenton tossed the remains of his cigarette to the ground and crushed it ceremoniously under his heel into the gravel. He looked at his Korean Rolex, shrugged his shoulders, and reached for another cigarette.

The front door to the house flew opened and slammed against the inside wall with a shower of dust and plaster. Father Bernardo appeared in the archway, gasping for air like a fish that had just been pulled from the water. Clutching at his chest, he staggered painfully down the steps, spun and collapsed onto the stones.

The cigarette dropped from Stenton's lips as he watched in stunned horror. He lunged forward instinctively and then stopped short, looking up at the house. He froze as though welded to the ground just outside the wall of ivy. Father Bernardo lay motionless on the steps. Stenton backed up slowly, turned and managed to reach through the open window of his BMW, grabbed his cell phone and jammed his finger at the keys, dialing 911.

———

From Oregon to the Mexican border, the California coastline twists and turns through some of the most beautiful countryside in the world. The road often winds radically away from the raging ocean, searching desperately for a sign of civilization, leaving huge pockets of raw scenic beauty to those with either the means to afford it, or simply those who have somehow held it firmly in their possession since the first missionaries claimed it well over a hundred years ago.

St. Augustine was such a place. A crumbling old monastery, it was a humble retreat of meditation and prayer, hanging precariously, yet majestically over the ominous cliffs of northern California. A private sanctuary for the Catholic clergy who so desired or required it. Father Shawn Kennedy was of the latter.

He sat on a small handmade, oak bench wedged between two large stones, overlooking a deep aqua blue cove. He tossed what was left of the pinecone he had picked apart over the edge of the cliff, unable to see where it landed far below. In the bay beyond, massive rock formations, standing firm like obedient soldiers, defied a never-ending attack from the ocean waves, sending pearl showers of salt and foam into the sky. Greedy seagulls kept a watchful eye from above, moving in slow, constant circles around Father Kennedy in the undying hope that, surely this time, he had brought them something to eat.

Like the stones that gripped it, the wood of the bench was cold and hard, weathered mercilessly by the damp ocean air. The unforgiving elements had long ago produced dull splinters that were, by their very nature, working their way through Father Kennedy's thick black hassock. The key was to sit as motionless as possible. Strangely, though, the small amount of pain brought on by a simple piece of wood, acted as a reminder of the God he was supposed to love. Not so much in the obvious form of the cross and the crucifixion, rather, the blunt pain he endured by his religion itself.

Today had been a particularly dark day for him. He wasn't sure why, but things seemed to be getting worse, not better. He felt not the slightest amount of hope anymore. His faith had been trying to leave him for some time now and just recently been extinguished almost entirely. He could not stop thinking about Father Bernardo and how disappointed he would be in what he would have rightly labeled Kennedy's selfish juvenile disposition and general doubting Irish ways.

In fact, repeated flashes and disturbing thoughts of Bernardo had weighed heavy on his mind since early this afternoon. It frightened him, because he knew all too well his strange ability, like a curse, to know things unknown. It had been quite some time since the two had spoken, face-to-face, and Kennedy worried about him.

His head fell into his open palms, allowing his hair to cover them completely. At forty years of age, and all that had taken place, he had given up and no longer cared to keep it cut.

The sun dipped into the ocean, turning the sky into a kaleidoscope of continually changing pastels... orange, peach and purple. A daily performance of which Kennedy took no notice. The rhythmic smashing of the waves on the rocks below somehow lulled him into a state of unconsciousness that, as the sun sank, kept him from feeling the drop in temperature. He ignored the biting sea wind, swelling up from the bottom of the cliff and whipping at his black garment like the torn flags of an ancient pirate ship.

The distant clang of an old steel bell, signaling the 6:00 Mass, dissolved somewhere in the back of his mind, woven seamlessly into the tapestry of his dark thoughts. Even the seagulls, one by one, began to give up, searching elsewhere for satisfaction. Small pieces of a shredded pinecone lay at his feet. He was alone.

In a sudden flash, a brilliant white light burst throughout his head and he glimpsed Bernardo lying on several stone steps. Just as quickly, it was over. He had learned many years ago, as a child actually, not to become overly alarmed by these sudden occurrences. He saw things others could not see. Perhaps were not meant to see. He had no understanding of the visions or if they even meant anything at all. They had increased with age and, if he allowed, would drive him mad.

He lifted his face onto the endless ocean, roused by the empty sound of the bell long after it had finished. He turned, a man slowly waking up, and looked off towards the distant church now shrouded by the gathering ocean mists.

Rising, he kicked at the remains of the desecrated pinecone, covering it with a thin layer of dirt. He felt somehow embarrassed by his simple act of destruction. But it made no difference. Like all things beautiful, the pinecone was a meaningless part of nature. Sooner or later, everything yielded to death. The distant sound of singing monks annoyed him. Appealing in some way, perhaps, but equally meaningless.

Father Kennedy turned reluctantly. He studied his feet, one in front of the other, making their way, obediently, down the crude dirt path in the direction of the old church.

He had not come here willingly. Not exactly. He had given in to the urgings of his Diocese after a rather disturbing incident involving the death of a young girl. It wasn't his fault, but he should have been more careful. He could have prevented it. He had publicly embarrassed the Church and now she had quietly hidden him away, asking him to lay low under the guise that he needed it. It would serve as a much-needed time of spiritual replenishment and an opportunity to humbly seek God's will.

What did God's will, if there even was such a thing, have to do with any of this? Like the priesthood itself, Kennedy was simply wasting time.

He entered a long musty corridor that ran the length of the compound. To his left was the church where all the monks gathered twice daily to sing and to worship. To his right were the dormitories, small plainly appointed cubicles consisting of a chair and desk, a dresser and a small bed. He chose not to attend the Mass and turned instead, down the hallway towards his room.

His footsteps fell heavily on the polished tile floor. He walked slower in an effort to remain unnoticed. When he finally came to his room, he lifted the latch and opened the door as quietly as possible and closed it carefully again behind him, leaving him in total darkness. He quickly fumbled for a book of matches left on the nightstand, lit a match and placed it against the wick of a fat brown candle sitting there. He blew the match out and placed it in a small glass dish next to the candle.

Pulling a black rosary from his pocket and clutching it between his fingers, he sat down on the foot of the stiff bed and looked at the wall. He was not planning on praying. Years ago, prayer had been something he enjoyed, but now it served only as a source of guilt. As a priest, you are expected to pray. But it's painful and stupid to continually attempt to carry on a conversation with someone who isn't listening. He played with the Rosary, swinging it back and forth like the pendulum of a clock, unaware of the sound of hurried footsteps echoing in the distance down the long corridor outside his door.

A gentle, steady rap on the heavy wood of his door finally pulled him to the surface.

"Come in," he responded, rising to his feet.

The latch lifted and the door creaked open allowing a flood of warm, yellow light from the hallway to fill his darkened room. A young monk stood, black, like a specter against the brighter wall of light behind him, struggling to see into the room.

"Father Kennedy, I apologize for the interruption, but there is an emergency."

Kennedy already knew. He had known the moment it happened, but had ignored it, purposely, not wanting it to be true.

"It's Father Bernardo," Kennedy said. "What has happened?"

"Yes. He has suffered a…heart attack, Father," the monk answered. "He has asked that you come."

———

Flight 502 to Los Angeles lifted off the runaway on schedule. It was the last flight that evening out of San Francisco and Kennedy had barely made it. One of the Monks, brother Tom had driven him in rather shabby Ford Taurus through the dark winding roads of the coastal hills and nearly killed them both on several occasions. The car was falling to pieces and Brother Tom was not exactly a skilled driver. He talked non-stop and forgot to keep his attention on the road in front of him. It had taken just over three hours to reach San Francisco, but by the time they pulled into the airport, Kennedy was grateful to be alive.

He was the last to board the plane, but had purchased first-class, so his seat was waiting for him as he threw his bag in the overhead compartment and settled into the comfortable leather seat next to the window.

Earlier in the evening, while staring off into the ocean, he had never imagined he would be sitting here right now. The truth is, it occupied his mind and kept him from feeling sorry for himself, something he had grown weary of over the last several months of solitude up at St. Augustine's. True, it was indeed the perfect place for deep contemplation, but that sort of thing can drive you mad after a while.

The engines roared outside the window, lifting the massive 737 off the pavement with a lurch and directly up into the air. Several jaded rabbits, ignoring the explosion of the engines, sat fearlessly in the field below, watching as the plane grew smaller by the second. They had seen it so many times, day after day, night after night. They were most likely deaf by now and it provided no sense of threat to them.

The lights of San Francisco and all around the Bay twinkled below, competing with the stars above Father Kennedy. The contrast brought a small smile to the corner of his mouth. Bernardo was just such a man, he mused, that would never forget to take pleasure in small wonders such as this. The stars, God's celestial quilt... a gift to man. And a sea of city lights... man's defiant challenge to stand on his own in the darkness.

In moments, the city fell away as the plane increased speed, boldly penetrating the empty blackness ahead of them. It would take less than an hour to reach John Wayne Airport. Perhaps another half hour to the hospital depending upon LA traffic. Nighttime would be better. The truth was, however, it didn't matter what time of night or day it was. In Los Angeles, there would always be traffic.

A rather interesting, young stewardess approached holding a bottle of champagne in her right hand. She lifted her eyebrows, asking the question with her eyes alone. Kennedy smiled in return.

He felt no compunction for his decision to fly first class. None. Even for the ridiculous price of a last-minute ticket. Cost was irrelevant. In fact, he had grown accustomed to not caring about matters of money over the past five years. His church worshipped luxury perhaps more than God Himself. Who was he to tell them they were misguided?

He refused to wear the traditional Roman collar of a priest as well, thereby blending seamlessly with the others in first-class. Fat businessmen and their lovers, everyone here had little or no inhibitions regarding spending money. Like Kennedy, it really wasn't their money they were enjoying anyway.

The Church paid his bills consistently, without question. His finances and expenditures were actually part of an arrangement made long ago, not by him, but by Father Bernardo. The arrangement, in fact, was much older than that, centuries perhaps, but he knew that Bernardo had demanded it on his behalf when he joined the ranks. What a mistake that had been.

While the few remaining priests of his Order were in no way heralded publicly by the church, they were regarded with a certain respect by those on a much higher-level, deep inside the church. Demon chasers. He hated it. It was embarrassing.

His work or spiritual missions were kept quiet, so as not to disturb the common believer. In return, few questions were ever asked. Financial excesses were of course, the smallest concern. The church was a whore and he knew it. Spending Her money came without a shred of guilt. It was actually an addiction now. Unfortunately, like sex to a prostitute, it brought increasingly little pleasure.

In the beginning, when he had first met Father Bernardo, he had believed in the supernatural. It was unknown and as compelling as God Himself. Bernardo was a raving lunatic in his war against the Devil. His fervor and faith were intoxicating. As just a child entering the priesthood in his twenties, Kennedy had been seduced. From the start he had loved Bernardo and everything about the Church. But love fades.

Now, like the church Herself, he had all but given up on his own beliefs. Outwardly, he feigned faith, often even attempting still to pray. Going through the motions kept the flood of fear and guilt somewhat at bay. But faith had become a distant friend. The result was a dark bitterness growing like scum, thick on the surface of a pond. His religion, like his heart, was empty.

The supernatural was a lie as well, exaggerated stories invented to frighten children and keep adults entertained. There was a logical answer for everything he had seen.

He lifted his finger slightly, acknowledging the stewardess as she swooped in with a well-paid smile.

"Um, no champagne. Jack Daniels, please. No ice."

"Oh, that sounds perfect, I'd like one too," interrupted the woman sitting next to him. "In fact, make mine a double." She giggled as the stewardess retreated politely. The woman tugged at the rather large earring dangling from her left ear. Diamonds. Faux. She offered her small hand to Kennedy.

"Jackie Powers, how do you do?"

Kennedy shook her hand politely, smiled and looked out the window into the darkness. He'd experienced so many women like her. A few men as well. Being hit on was nothing new to him. It had long ago become part of life and he incorporated it into his way of dealing with people. He'd learned how to read them, how they would approach him, and how best to fend them off without purposely offending them. Unless he had to. He wasn't mean or hateful. Just tired. They were all the same.

From the reflection in the window he saw Ms. Powers quickly undo the top buttons of her rose-colored blouse. "I'm an associate producer for FineLine Pictures," she offered. "We're beginning a new production, Hurricane Factor…very big. Principle shooting starts this weekend. I actually discovered the writer. First-timer. Very talented," she continued in an effort to impress him. Kennedy smiled politely.

"No ring, huh?" she giggled pointing to his finger. "You're either very smart or just…very playful," she laughed, impressed with her own quick wit. Kennedy turned and purposefully examined her chest, looked up at her and smiled, saying nothing. She smiled back, somewhat startled by his boldness, but equally aroused. Strong, silent type.

The stewardess brought their drinks and placed them on the extended trays. Kennedy grabbed one of the little airline bottles, unscrewed the lid and poured it, slowly over the ice, into her glass. She giggled. He looked at her again and grinned like a movie star, raising his left eyebrow rather suggestively. "Forgive me. Chauvinistic little something we do… from where I come."

"Really... Well, I certainly like it," she mused, calculating her next move. "I hear a trace of an accent. It's nice. Where exactly, do you come from?"

Kennedy chuckled under his breath and lifted his whiskey bottle from the table. With one swift motion of his thumb, the cap spun from his bottle, flying carelessly onto the floor. He grinned again, impishly, then tilted the bottle to his lips and drained it.

"Ireland, originally," he stated, raising his empty bottle to the stewardess as obvious evidence. He smiled at Jackie and winked.

"But I was ordained in Italy."

CHAPTER FOUR

A confusing variety of overly expensive machines hummed rhythmically, beeping every now and then, lights blinking impressively, keeping track of every little physical detail that took place deep inside Father Bernardo. His heart rate. His blood pressure. His breathing. Everything.

His eyes opened as he struggled anxiously for a moment, trying to adjust to the darkness of the hospital room. He had no idea where he was as he fought to breathe, taking in as much oxygen as permitted by the small plastic mask strapped to his face. Panic washed over him. He remembered the house and walking in to it. How cold it was. He remembered being afraid. And he remembered seeing her face. Her voice. He remembered hearing her voice…

The lights on the machines next to his bed flashed in unison as his pulse quickened. His eyes rolled back in his head as his chest heaved once again in severe pain. He would not survive a second time and he knew it instinctively. A pen lay on the table next to him, on top of an unopened Hallmark card. His hand thrust out like a striking cobra, grabbed them both and began scribbling, desperately, despite the violent eruptions of pain pounding his chest.

The pen faltered suddenly, coming to a stop, then dropped to the floor and rolled quietly against the wheels of the stainless steel bed. The get-well card lay motionless atop his chest. His eyes remained open, fixed, lifeless and empty upon the ceiling above him. On cue, the machines changed their song, signaling the nurse at the front desk just twenty feet away. Father Bernardo had passed.

But unlike the sad, scripted situations often seen on television, Sylvia, the on-duty nurse, did not jump into a panic-driven mission of life and death. She was far too seasoned and had seen this so, so many times before. Simply stated, it was not her emergency and so, she responded accordingly, finishing her last sip of Diet Pepsi before making her way casually toward his room. It wasn't callous. People died all the time in the hospital. It was part of the job. The weak quit. The strong got used to it. That was how you survived.

———

Kennedy's plane had landed almost twenty minutes prior. He had no baggage to speak of, other than his small carry-on, and had slipped into the first taxi without consequence. It was easy in Los Angeles. Everything was easy. Everyone was polite to you, too, treating you with love and the utmost respect, even if it was fake. Nobody ever knew who was riding in their cab or to whom they were serving dinner. You could be an agent, a producer or even the next Tom Cruise. The result was a thin, faux kindness. Unconditional love. It had become the one true religion in Hollywood. A very effective means to an end.

When Bernardo stopped breathing, Kennedy was just three and a half blocks away, stuck in traffic. Almost 11:30 at night and he was stuck in traffic. Welcome to Los Angeles. He thumped the edge of the open taxi window impatiently with his thumb. It was warm despite the hour. The stars in the sky were gone now, hidden beneath the constant haze and Kennedy knew he was too late.

"How much further to the hospital?" he asked.

"Could be fifteen minutes. Could be an hour, fifteen," snorted the driver, a stand-up comedian in the making. "First time in LA?"

"No. But hopefully the last," Kennedy smiled.

"What, you're not here with dreams of making it big on the silver screen?"

"Sorry. Not today."

"You're the only one," the driver laughed, choking slightly on the ever-present phlegm collected in his throat. He puffed on the remains of his wet cigarette stub, tossed it out onto the street and smoothed his sweaty, black hair back across his head. "Someone you know in the hospital?"

"Yeah. Know him well," Kennedy mused. "Very well."

"I'll get you there as quick as I can, my friend," the driver assured, looking back at Kennedy in the mirror.

"I'm from New York originally," he continued. "Speed is the name of the game, I'm tellin' you. And this place?

Well, hang on, my friend. This place is butter. Melted butter."

He jammed his foot against the accelerator and his hand on the horn at the same time, edging within inches of the cars around him. Brakes screeched, leaving stretches of black rubber on the pavement. Middle fingers raised all around in defiance. The cab driver smiled, burying his chin into his chest and gripping the wheel firmly. Everyone was speaking his language now. Horns and curses. A New York Symphony. Heaven on Earth. To him, driving a cab was an art form. And he was a self-ordained master.

––––––––––

Sylvia sat at her post as two young doctors exited Bernardo's room. She had seen them pull the sheet over his face. He was dead. Truth is, she knew it the minute they wheeled him in. Not the first time. She had a sense about these things and played it like a hand of poker, who would keel and who would walk. If it were legal in Vegas, she'd be quite wealthy by now.

She pulled a new Diet-Pepsi from the small refrigerator under the desk and popped the top, sucking the quick burst of foam so that it wouldn't ooze over the edge and onto her computer keys. She examined the personal articles left in Bernardo's room, his wallet, a key and the strange message written on the unopened card and quietly slipped them together into a large Manila envelope.

Outside, Kennedy slid from the back seat of the yellow cab and stepped safely onto the sidewalk in front of St. Elizabeth's Memorial. He leaned forward with two twenty-dollar bills and locked eyes with the driver. "Thank you," he said. "You're a man of your word. I owe you more than this." He shoved the money into the driver's hand and smiled, closing the door.

The cab pulled away as Kennedy turned and looked up at the hospital. Seven floors loomed above him. Bernardo was in there somewhere. The doors spun, like a wheel waiting for a hamster, allowing him to enter a nondescript lobby of gray and maroon, certain to offend no one. A small corporate flower shop offering last minute gifts and cards sat to the left of the lobby for those unfortunate souls who had forgotten to pick up something a little more affordable on the way. Scalpers.

Kennedy proceeded directly to the elevator, skipping formality and completely ignoring the old woman stationed at the front desk. She never saw him. The sign to the left of the elevator gave Kennedy all the information he needed. Intensive Care. Floor 4.

The elevator doors slid open and Kennedy instantly apologized for attempting to enter the small space before the occupants had departed. Nasty habit of those in a hurry. He entered. Looking up at the numbers as the oversized, polished doors shut, sealing him in a tomb of silence. The fluorescent bulb above him struggled to maintain, sputtering a little every few seconds. He wasn't even sure if the elevator was moving, and in fact, it wasn't. Jamming the button repeatedly with his thumb, the old elevator engaged finally with a lurch and began one of several thousand daily journeys from one sad floor to the next.

Kennedy closed his eyes and placed his head against the cold steel of the elevator wall as it slumped to a halt, indicating his final arrival. The doors opened unceremoniously onto a lonely stretch of hallway.

He exited, looking in both directions and saw Sylvia sitting obediently behind the hallway desk. Approaching, he looked directly at her. "Father Emil Bernardo," Kennedy said before even reaching the desk. "He called for me."

"All right, well… you're family of Mr. Bernardo?

"Father Bernardo. He has no family," Kennedy stated flatly, furrowing his brow. "I am Father Shawn Kennedy. He called for me."

"Oh, I'm sorry. Forgive me. These matters are difficult," Silvia managed, looking suddenly very uncomfortable.

"What do you mean?" he asked.

"I'm sorry, Father Kennedy. Your friend passed away about a half an hour ago." Kennedy turned and looked down the long hallway. He walked slowly over to a small row of chairs against the wall and sat down. He wished he had not already known, but perhaps it had eased the pain somewhat. His gift of knowledge was a curse in his eyes. He examined his fingernails and picked at the skin around the edge of his index finger. Bernardo had been his confessor. His mentor. Despite 20 some odd years of age difference, they had shared a deep friendship. He should have stayed in touch and he knew it all along. And now Bernardo was dead.

The name Kennedy rang a sudden bell in Sylvia's mind. She had seen it scribbled on the card.

"Um, Father Kennedy…I think you might want this," she said picking it up the manila envelope containing Bernardo's belongings. "There might be a note or something for you, too," she offered, holding the envelope up. Kennedy rose and reached for the envelope, turning it over.

"May I see him?" Kennedy asked.

"I'm afraid they've already taken him downstairs," Sylvia stammered.

Kennedy nodded, tucked the envelope beneath his left arm, thanked her and proceeded back to the elevator from which he'd just come. Sylvia pretended to work, quickly shuffling a small stack of empty forms from one side of the desk to the other. She only wished the phone would ring, giving her the excuse to answer it.

Back on the sidewalk in front of the hospital, several pigeons were still awake, wandering aimlessly, searching for anything that resembled food. They fluttered lazily out of the way and landed several feet away as Kennedy exited the revolving doors. He pulled his coat closer to his chest. It had finally begun to cool down, although it was nothing like a night up on the northern coast. Same state. Different worlds.

He approached a cab sitting at the curb and climbed inside. " The Waldorf, please," he said, looking up at the hospital again. The driver grunted something and studied Kennedy for a brief moment in his mirror. Kennedy glanced back down at the envelope as the cab pulled into traffic.

He unlatched the little metal clips on the back and opened it, sliding the contents onto his lap. The old black leather wallet was thin and contained Bernardo's driver's license, a credit card, a small laminated verse from St. Paul and about ten dollars in cash. There was a crumpled business card, too, from a real estate agent named Ronald Stenton that sat loosely between the two sides of the wallet. He examined the card, then the house key house that was in the envelope as well, wondering if there was any correlation between the two, then turned his attention to the hastily scribbled note.

"Father Shawn Kennedy. Lydia…"

He slid them all back into the envelope and resealed it. Like the Spanish song that played on the cab's radio, he had no idea what the note meant. The name Lydia meant nothing.

The never-ending sea of traffic swallowed the cab. Kennedy gazed out the window at all the people struggling on their way somewhere. The city had no idea he was there. Just one more face in the crowd.

The Archdiocese of Los Angeles would take care of any funeral arrangements, but Kennedy thought it best to stick around for a few days to make sure his body was treated the way he would have wanted. Even though the church changed its viewpoint on cremation as far back as 1963, he knew Bernardo was old school and would never have agreed to such a thing. Because he had no family, other than Kennedy, the Church would foot the bill for his burial and Kennedy didn't trust them to spend money they didn't have to. He would ensure that they did.

CHAPTER FIVE

In Los Angles proper, *Coldwell/Banker* has several hundred real estate offices and several thousand agents. Ronald Stenton, however, had steadily risen to the top and had been honored in the Top 100 Ambassador's Circle for the last five years straight. He had long ago learned it took just as much work and just as much time to close a deal on a small property as it did the larger deals…the homes of movie stars. Because of it, he had earned the reputation in the company as the "agent of the stars." He was always at a party of some sort, rubbing elbows, working his magic, keeping the doors open and doing deals. It kept him busy and in direct connection with his love for cocaine.

He tried to light a cigarette, but the lighter was out of fuel. Tossing it into the wastebasket next to his desk, he withdrew a small box of matches from his drawer and lit the cigarette dangling impatiently from his lip. He placed the lit match into the ashtray where it eventually died out with a final wisp of white smoke. He glanced at his watch. At 8:30 in the morning, he had already been at his desk for almost two hours and was making fast work of finishing his first pack of cigarettes for the day. Even he was a little disgusted by it.

The phone rang as he exhaled, quickly waving the smoke away from his eyes so that he could see. He put on his best face and grabbed the receiver.

"Ronald Stenton. Ready and… Action!"

Father Kennedy sat on the edge of the bed in his hotel room. Unmoved by Stenton's apparent enthusiasm, he reread the business card for the hundredth time.

"Yes, my name is Kennedy. Father Kennedy…I'm a friend of Father Bernardo. I believe you may have known him…"

Stenton sat back in his chair and placed the cigarette on the rim of the ashtray. "Father Bernardo… yeah, how's he doing?" he asked. This was not a phone call he wanted. The whole situation, convincing an old priest to come out and bless a haunted house, was more than a little embarrassing and he wished it would all just go away.

"I'm afraid he's dead," Kennedy offered.

"Holy shit," Stenton muttered.

"Would you mind if I ask how you knew him? What I mean is… before he died, he seems to have tried to tell me something. He had your business card. I just thought maybe you might know something that would help."

"You a priest?" asked Stenton, changing his mind, thinking suddenly that he might have another shot at selling the old house.

"I am," said Kennedy. "Can you tell me if the name Lydia means anything to you?"

"Shit," Stenton said again. "Yeah, you could say that. Why?"

"Father Bernardo wrote it on a piece of paper, along with my name. I don't know what it means."

"Yeah, well… Father Bernardo, he was sort of helping me. You see, I'm trying to sell this big old mother of a house, up in the Palisades, beautiful place, right on the ocean… Belonged to a Lydia. Long time ago anyway. Lydia Carter. Name ring a bell?" Stenton mused, reaching for his cigarette.

Kennedy ran his hand through his hair and looked out the sliding glass door, over the balcony and across the hazy city skyline. "Lydia Carter… the rock star?" Kennedy asked.

"The one, the only," Stenton laughed, drawing the smoke into his lungs. "She died or something back in the 60's, 70's, I don't know, and some say… she still lives there, if you catch my drift."

"And Bernardo was helping you."

"We had a deal of sorts. He does his thing, whatever, and I compensate him… the church, whatever. I never thought this would happen."

"What exactly did happen?" Kennedy pressed, standing to his feet, moving toward the window.

"Look, I don't know," Stenton offered, a little too defensively. "The man just came out of the house and dropped dead, I guess. That's it. I don't really know what happened. That's the God's honest truth." He stamped the remains of his cigarette into a warm pile of dead soldiers in the ashtray as proof that it was over and certainly not his fault.

"I see," Kennedy mumbled, stepping out onto the balcony. The cars below him swarmed like hungry insects, each going about their business, uninterested in each other except to avoid collision. The sidewalks were packed with people moving steadily in either direction. The Hollywood hills were barely visible in the distance beneath the constant blanket of brown and gray fumes. "This house," Kennedy continued, turning the old copper key in his palm, "where is it, exactly?"

Like any hungry real estate agent, Stenton had offered to show Kennedy the place, but he had refused. He had other pressing things on his mind and didn't have time for some greasy salesman to take him on a ridiculous tour. With the directions Stenton had given him, he thought he might drive up later, after the funeral and take a look.

He arranged with the concierge to rent a small Nissan sedan and drove the short distance to St. Francis of Assisi Catholic Church just north of Venice. Even though it was not that far, it took him the better part of an hour to reach it. A quick funeral service had been arranged for Father Bernardo in which he would receive the allotted sacraments, before being tucked quickly away in a nearby Catholic cemetery. All very neat and tidy.

There had been no quarrel from the Archdiocese in regards to his wishes for keeping his body intact. The priest, Father Baxter, whom Kennedy had spoken to over the phone had said he preferred it himself as well and the issue was settled. They had also arranged a brief viewing time prior to the funeral in a smaller sanctuary just off the main sanctuary.

Bernardo had no family remaining and few friends. Several of the older parishioners had stopped in to pay their respects, but when Kennedy arrived, the room was dark and empty, somber, the only light emanating from a rack of candles in blue glass votives rising up along the wall like a pyramid. Bernardo lay in a simple black casket lined with white silk, the light from the candles dancing softly across his pale, sleeping face.

Kennedy stepped forward respectfully and stared down at the man responsible for bringing him to America. They had met in Italy so many years ago and had been reassigned to California together; a little political footwork that Bernardo had engineered. Kennedy had become his chosen protégé and he wasn't going to leave him behind to get swallowed up by the Church. Over the years they had developed a unique relationship and Kennedy knew that, although it was never said, Bernardo viewed him as a son.

Kennedy had never known a man with such an unusual relationship with God. He had believed in Him with his entire heart, but often spoke to Him, out loud, as though they were sparring partners in a boxing ring. It was not for a lack of respect, on the contrary, it was simply that he felt he could. There was no lack of love, just a rather bizarre way of communicating with one's God.

It had caused problems on occasion, especially in the early days back in Italy and he had been accused by some of the older priests as being a blasphemer. He had laughed at them and told them to go back to bed with their old nuns. That hadn't exactly gone over very well either. He was branded a rebel and looked down upon by some of the older more conservative clergy and was probably the reason he was eventually assigned to California. Where else would he have fit in better?

Kennedy laughed silently at the thought of Bernardo being considered a rebel. Compared to Kennedy himself, the man was about as conservative as a priest can get. He often would chide Kennedy for refusing to wear his

Roman collar, saying that it served as an outward sign of their commitment and oaths to God. It should be considered a blessing to wear. Kennedy had just found it uncomfortable and resembling a penguin. He couldn't see any reason a priest needed to look like an idiot.

Kennedy stood there staring down upon Bernardo. He wasn't sad. Bernardo was at peace now. He had lived a rough life for a priest, often dodging bullets, working with the gangs in East Los Angeles. And they were tame compared to some of the paranormal entities he had challenged. Bernardo was what might be considered a spiritual warrior, standing in the face of Satan with fists raised. He had encountered things that most people only want to see in a dark movie theater. His courage was based on his faith, but it had not come without a cost. He had paid a severe price for it on more than one occasion.

His eyes, closed now, did not reveal that only one remained. An old black woman had been found by her neighbors, sitting in the far corner of a dark basement, mumbling strange words, with a demented voice that did not belong to her. Bernardo had been called in because nobody wanted to go down there and deal with her in that state. He had boldly, or stupidly, placed his hand on her head to pray when, like a bolt of lightening, she had reached out and yanked his eyeball straight from the socket and shoved it in her mouth, chomping down viciously, then swallowing. Kennedy knew this was not an exaggerated story. He had been there with him and seen it himself.

Bernardo had taught him how to pray and fight against evil. He said it was everywhere and all you needed to do was turn over a stone to find one of Satan's underlings squirming in the mud. Most people, even priests, have no

50

stomach for such things, nor the courage, and prefer to look in the opposite direction or call it foolishness, laughing at those who would suggest that such things even exist. Kennedy knew that they did. He too had seen enough to scare the shit out of most people. It was God he was not sure about. No matter how hard he had tried, he could never seem to find him. It became his joking frustration with Bernardo, that God had abandoned the world ages ago and left it to the devil to wreak havoc on. They were just two stupid priests left to fend for themselves behind enemy lines. And now Bernardo was gone and Kennedy was left all alone.

He shoved his hands in his pocket and felt the old tarnished house key that Bernardo had left behind. He pulled it out and looked at it again, then down at Bernardo. He thought about placing it in the coffin with him, then decided against it, knowing Bernardo too well and that there was a reason he had wanted him to have it. And if that was so, he needed to see the door that it unlocked. And perhaps even, what was behind it.

The funeral itself was short and sweet, Bernardo's final Sacrament. Only Kennedy was there along with the parish pastor who gave the final blessings and shut the coffin. Bernardo was gone and a part of Kennedy's life was as well. He said goodbye and genuflecting in front of the altar, turned and walked down the long stretch of silent, deeply padded carpet, out the sanctuary doors and into the bright sunlight of a hot Los Angeles day.

He thought of his conversation earlier that morning with Ronald Stenton. He was glad he had not taken the agent up on his offer to show the old house to him personally. Stenton had actually become sort of giddy at one point, perhaps at the prospect of having Bernardo replaced and regaining his treasure. The incident with Bernardo must have shaken him pretty badly, but you would never know by his continuing enthusiasm. And so it was reluctantly, that he had given Kennedy some basic directions on how to find the place. Since it was only a few minutes off the coast, a single turn off Highway 1 was all that was really required. There were a lot of mansions up in that area, but only one that matched the description.

It was actually quite a pleasant drive. Further up, on the northern coast line of California, the sun and blue sky could be, and often were, replaced without much warning with thick, rolling waves of fog. Gray skies came and went throughout the day and caused your energy to become much heavier. Not in a bad way, but in a deeper introspective way. Kennedy liked it. It helped him to retreat inside of himself when looking for answers.

But here, on southern coastline, it seemed brighter, more animated, and came at him like an invitation to a college party. Even the ocean seemed friendlier and urged him to pull his little car over and dance with it. He had the windows rolled down, letting the wind whip his hair into a frenzy as he drove. He didn't care. It felt good.

He thought about Bernardo. Was his life worthwhile? Had it mattered? Did he make any real impact on this stupid world? He had sure been beaten up by it. Did any of it really make a difference or had Bernardo simply been the brunt of a cruel joke? Couldn't he have had a simple, pleasant, more selfish life, bought a small sail boat and some brandy and drifted lazily away to some distant port?

Had God ever spoken to Bernardo? Did they know each other? Did He leave him dry and empty in return for his years of undying dedication and service? His unquestioning faith? What was Bernardo's reward? Heaven? Eternal life? Well, if it was anything like his life here on Earth, it was a complete rip off. Kennedy didn't want anything to do with it anymore. It seemed to him that Bernardo had been given the lousiest deal possible. It was true what they say, you work your ass to the bone and then you die. As much as he loved and respected him, Bernardo had played the fool. And like a love-starved puppy, Kennedy had followed him.

He gripped the steering wheel in his right hand, navigating the demanding curves of the road. With his left, he held back his hair from his face, resting his elbow on the edge of the door. The sun warmed him, gently urging him not to drive straight off into the ocean below.

There has to be a reason to live your life and it can't simply be to serve someone else. To do their bidding without question? Especially if that someone doesn't even know you exist. That is not a life with purpose. That's stupidity. How many men and women, throughout history, gave their lives, literally gave their very lives, to a God that didn't care and never really wanted it in the first place? This whole idea of answering "The Call," living a life of faith and service, was nothing more than a man-made solution for a much deeper fear that life truly is empty and meaningless. Wine, women and song… maybe that was a better road to take after all. It was just as meaningless, but at least you were not alone along the journey.

The road began to pinch left and right, twisting back on itself and demanding that Kennedy give it more of his concentrated attention. His mood lifted and he smiled using the brakes and the accelerator in tandem, pushing the four little cylinders to their limits. Despite having just come from the funeral of a friend, he was actually enjoying himself. The idea crossed his mind, that maybe he would take a quick look at this house and then just keep right on driving, all the way back up the coast to St. Augustine's. Maybe he would even stop in for week or two in San Francisco. Maybe he wouldn't even go back at all. Maybe he would just stay and get a job on a fishing boat. Rent an apartment. Find a girl. Fool around. Get married. Have kids.

Pine Hills Lane was just up ahead and Kennedy slowed to make sure it was the name he had scribbled on the little pad of paper from the Waldorf. He turned right and crunched through a small drift of sand and gravel as he pushed the little car almost straight up the steep incline. The road began to turn and spiral its way up to the top, then straightened out and dipped into a dark green tunnel of moss and pine trees. Wet and much cooler, the damp smell of forest mold and mushrooms swept through the open car. It was beautiful, still, and except for the sound of his engine, very quiet.

Two deer, startled by the intruder, looked up suddenly at him, then in a flash, darted across the road and disappeared just as quickly into the black depths of the trees on the opposite side. He pressed down on the accelerator again and followed the road as it narrowed, leading him further into the woods. A light mist had gathered, hanging above the ground, swirling and disappearing like a ghost as he pushed through it.

He approached a large, stone wall up ahead on his left, covered in moss and pine needles, aged and blending almost seamlessly into the forest floor. As it curved down a small drop in the road, he followed it to the gate Stenton had described, sitting closed, a chain wrapped through the bars, but unlocked. He checked the address and pulled the Nissan over to the edge of the road and shut it off.

Sudden silence flooded through the open car windows and smothered him. He could hear the ocean now, softly in the distance, blowing in on the breeze, and then it was gone again. As he sat there, adjusting to the strange sensation, he looked up at the mansion, looming just past the gates. It was magnificent.

"What have you gotten me into, old man?" Kennedy said out loud as he opened the door and pulled himself out of the car. His legs ached from the drive. He stretched them out, ran both hands through his tangled mass of hair and studied the house, windows high above, broken and dark. It must have been four stories, he thought, and obviously, nobody had lived there in quite some time. How does somebody let a place like this just crumble and die? But then he knew.

Unlike Father Bernardo, Kennedy felt her presence before he even stepped through the gates. Nobody had to convince him of the reality, the supernatural reality, of the situation he was now facing. He was quite used to being found alone across enemy lines. He knew the old feeling, subtle at first, that travels almost instantly from your neck down your spine, signaling to those that are paying attention that all is not well. Most people ignore it, if they even feel it at all, when it happens. Kennedy was different. He felt it in ways few ever could. It was one of the reasons he and Bernardo had hit it off in the early years. They had many things, intuitions, premonitions, abilities, in common.

Over the years, Father Bernardo had called upon Kennedy to assist him, or simply relied on his insight and counsel. It sometimes felt as if they were the only two humans on the planet who were aware of the existence of the unseen forces that ruled it. They leaned on each other that way. Only Bernardo had not called on him this time and he should have. The presence here was so strong. It was aware of him as well. Of that, he was sure.

He stood outside the stone walls and continued to take in the entire house. Sitting directly over the ocean, he guessed, the mist from below formed thicker patches of fog that moved quickly up the steep walls of the cliffs and passed up over the gables and cathedral spires on the fourth floor like spirits on their journey home. Each window, hundreds it seemed, were dull and black, covered with years of seaside grit, hiding anything on the other side. Many were shattered leaving only empty holes. Kennedy imagined there was a good thirty rooms in a house like this and wondered how long it had been since anyone living had wandered through them.

As he proceeded, cautious, through the old rusted iron gates, he approached a stone fountain, running his finger along the edge. He turned, looking up at the windows again, high above him, and carefully moved up the stone steps where Bernardo had fallen. He took the key from his pocket, but there was no need. The door was open. He hesitated, and laughed quietly to himself, amused at the obvious. Perhaps it had simply remained unlocked since Bernardo had been here and the wind had jarred it loose. Perhaps.

The presence was even stronger now as he stood in the open door, made the sign of the cross, and passed over the threshold. A large marble entry with four pillars on each side opened onto a massive grand room. Four white marble steps, once polished to a mirror-like sheen were now covered in decades of dust, leading down into it.

Kennedy proceeded slowly, taking each step while adjusting to the lack of light. The wooden floor of the grand room creaked painfully under his feet as he stepped into it, making his way deeper inside the house.

"Who are you?" he demanded in a soft yet firm voice. "In the name of our Lord, Jesus Christ, I command you…" He stopped suddenly, hearing a voice. Whispers. Ramblings. Anger. Like a swarm of angry insects fluttering past his ears. He grabbed at the Rosary in his front pocket. Confusion penetrated his mind. He pressed forward, concentrating, determined to confront whatever this thing was that had caused the death of his friend.

The ceiling, three floors above him, circled wildly over his head. He felt a mounting pressure on his mind, could not concentrate, stumbled and fell, ripping the knee on his pants against the old blistered wooden floor. He resisted the urge to crawl back for the open door and instead, stood defiantly and raised his fist above his head. "I am a soldier of the Living God!" he yelled. "None shall stand before me!"

A sudden violent blast of wind moved through the room, rattling the windows about him, knocking him from his feet and dashing him hard against the side wall. His vision blurred as he clutched his ribs, gasping for air.

At the top of the stairs she stood, in a swirl of flowing crimson, looking down, directly at him. Her eyes, ice-blue and empty, penetrated his heart like a blade of cold steel.

He felt consciousness slipping quickly away as her mouth opened wide, filling the house with the deafening roar of a rushing wind.

Everything went black.

Then, music... Extremely loud music.

It filled Kennedy's head. His eyes fluttered, jerking open wide. In awe and wonder, he stood, shoulder-to-shoulder in a crowd of people, dancing to the music blasting through their ears. Row after row of colored lights were spinning and flashing overhead, flooding a stage directly in front of him. It was dark where he stood. Someone next to him was holding a gun. He could not see them clearly, but the lights bounced off the long shiny barrel as it was raised, pointed directly at the young woman up on the stage.

Lydia Carter.

Like a dream where you cannot run, you cannot talk or scream, Kennedy stood motionless, unable to do anything as the gun jumped three times. And she fell.

The music stopped.

Silence first, followed by the increasing screams of terror of the people as they began to realize what was happening. Lying there on the stage, blood flowing from her chest, her head rolled to the right and, eyes still open, she stared directly at Kennedy.

"Help...me," she whispered, then closed her eyes. Someone shoved Kennedy hard from behind and he fell to the floor beneath the crowd as they began to kick at him, screaming.

He awoke alone. The wooden floor was chilled against his skin as he struggled to remember where he was. The sun was already half way through its daily habit of dropping lazily behind the wide expanse of sharply bronzed ocean, outside a wall of neglected, dirty windows, just beyond the grand room. Kennedy had not had the time to notice the overall grandeur of the house. And now in fact, found himself ironically, appreciating its neglected charm and architectural beauty while lying prostrate upon the floor.

Warm light filled the back of the room with a glow found often only on the beach itself at sunset. The calming, reassuring sound of the ocean waves outside the windows, beating ceaselessly on the sand below, brought a sense of peace and relaxation over his entire body.

He moved slowly, as though drugged, using the palms of his hands to lift a body that seemingly weighed four thousand pounds. With a sudden shudder, Kennedy forced himself into fuller consciousness. Like a night after too much drinking, his mind was foggy, a slight throbbing in his head.

He stood awkwardly, with the legs of a newborn calf, looking helplessly around him. Studying the old home, he became aware of the more obscure details that had escaped him before. Despite the light from the setting sun pouring through the back windows, it was difficult to see very far into the house and down its darkened corridors. Everywhere, the light fell off into shadowed pools of black. He was able to make out a defeated, oversized Victorian fireplace on the opposite wall of the grand room, a small chunk of blackened wood and ash still remaining, possibly from fifty-some odd years ago. Her last fire. The walls around it were bare, but revealed the faded telltale signs of such impressive paintings that had once hung there in place. Odd pieces of furniture, couches and chairs here and there, for one particular reason or another had never been removed and had been covered, for their protection, then forgotten, with various selections of randomly available sheets and blankets. Along with the years of dust and sediment, a heavy layer of sadness also covered the room.

His mind cleared, storm clouds separating, allowing the light to shine through. In an instant, everything became clear. Kennedy knew all too well what he was dealing with. But it had never been this strong before. He was shaking now. As best he could, he ran for the door and the safety of the outside world.

Perhaps Bernardo had experienced the same turn of events. It explained the terror racing through his heart. He ran for the gate, resisting the urge to look back at the windows. Feeling as though someone was directly on his heels, pulling at him, he made it to the Nissan parked on the side of the road, slipped in the deep pine needles and went down. He pulled himself up, grabbing the handle on the door and threw himself into the front seat, slamming the door closed behind him. He breathed heavily, searching for more air. Only now, did he allow himself to look back at the house and up into the threat of the shattered windows. He turned the key and shoved the car in reverse.

The massive house, grew steadily smaller behind him as he pushed the little car quickly over the thin mountain road. The trees once again enveloped him, bringing with them a welcome sense of protection and safety. The further he got from the house, the more the tension in his limbs began to recede. But the thoughts, relentless, pounded his mind. She had been it that house, this Lydia, a woman who died, murdered in the worst possible way...she had been in that house. And for so long.

His pants were torn on the knee and he became aware of the sting from the palms of his hands where he had scraped them, falling next to the car. He looked at himself in the mirror and saw the scratch, bleeding now, down the left side of his cheek.

———

CHAPTER SIX

St. Augustine's was probably a good ten-hour drive. Maybe more, far up the coastline. Kennedy was not tired though, and the time would do him well, allowing him to further examine his fears and his actions. The monastery would become what it was designed to be, for him, a sanctuary. A place of escape, where he could hide peacefully behind the high adobe walls.

This whole thing was exactly the sort of bullshit he had been trying to put behind him. Permanently. The mystery and spiritual nature of it all was not compelling to him in any sense of the word. He knew all too well that nothing but pain and misery were attached. Bernardo served as the perfect example. Kennedy had come to Los Angeles to visit a friend. As a result, he ended up having to bury him. But it was over now. He had said goodbye. His responsibility there was fulfilled and he was not going back.

The sun had slipped away finally and the scenic beauty of the California coast was lost in darkness. The steady winding of the highway became too much work and Kennedy decided to make his way over to Highway 101, just passed Santa Barabara, for a straighter, less demanding drive. It was a good decision.

It brought him passed Monterey and Santa Cruz and into the south San Francisco bay area around 1:00 in the morning. His adrenalin was gone now and his energy worn thin. His stomach growled and, strangely, he thought a burrito sounded rather decent. Not much else would be open this time of night anyway, so he began to search the off-ramps for the telltale neon signs of fast-food.

It was a Taco Bell that pulled him off the freeway. The kid running the drive-thru window was not surprised to see someone at that time of the morning. It was the burrito hour after all. Usually, it was a couple of guys, far younger than Kennedy, but the kid didn't seem to notice. Only Kennedy felt awkward.

He pulled out of the parking lot, turned right and realized he was had made a mistake. He was lost within half a minute and, while peeling back the paper and tin foil from his chicken burrito, scanned the street signs for any indication of how to get back on the freeway.

He came upon a large park to his left, with a large wood, sand-blasted sign establishing it as Buena Vista Park. He was dead tired now and having a difficult time navigating the dark streets while attempting to eat his food. The park afforded the opportunity to pull in, shut the engine off, relax and eat in peace. He had not realized just how tired he was at that point and, pushing his seat back, reclined for a few minutes, allowing the chicken and grease to do their work. It seemed the perfect remedy. He slept the remainder of the night, sitting there in the Nissan, parked beneath the oaks of Buena Vista Park in the belly of Haight-Ashbury.

The warmth of the sun, beating down through the windshield woke him gently. He laughed at himself, the remains of a burrito sitting on the passenger seat next to him. The need for coffee became his immediate rally cry and he decided to take a little stroll around the park. Picturesque Victorian houses stood proudly, up and down the street, peppered in between with small shops and cafes. The thought of pancakes and maple syrup crossed his mind.

He tossed the stiff burrito in a bent, green can sitting conveniently in front of his car and stretched himself out, yawning, his arms held above his head. He walked slowly, around the outside of the park and down Haight Street. It didn't take him long to decide upon a comfortable little place called The Hippopotamus, with its little square tables and the irresistable smell of fresh, dark coffee pouring out the open front door.

He walked in and the man behind the counter greeted him with a genuine smile and motioned for him to select any table that suited him. He chose one closest to the window and sat down. There were only two other people in the café, both alone and Kennedy watched them for a moment as they enjoyed their food. He noticed the black and white photos decorating the walls and realized they were all musicians; Jimi Hendrix. The Who. George Harrison. Janis Joplin. Hundreds of photos from the early days of rock and roll, all signed by the stars themselves. Probably a small fortune hanging on these walls, Kennedy thought as he picked up the menu from the table. But before he could examine the faire, a cold shiver shot straight down his spine as his eyes caught hold of a large photograph of Lydia Carter staring directly back at him with those same chilling eyes he hat witnessed back at that house.

She was really quite attractive and it suddenly dawned on him. He had not noticed before, in his vision, what a strikingly beautiful woman she was. The photo was signed in black ink.

Dale, my little brother.
Love you for eternity.
Lydia.

The waiter came up to the table carrying a fresh pot of wonderful, life-changing coffee. He was a rather chubby old hippie, his gray hair long, twisted into a single braid hanging dow the center of his back. His beard was gray too, and competed with Santa Claus in length. He smiled at Kennedy again and noticed he had been looking at Lydia.

"Gorgeous, ain't she?" he said with a wink.

Kennedy saw that he wore a name badge, indicating that he was Dale, evidently the owner of the café as well. He looked back at the signature on the photo.

"Did you actually meet her?" he asked.

"Meet her?" Dale laughed, filling Kennedy's cup. "You could say that. Lived with the girl for almost two years. See that big old green house over there," he said pointing out the window, down the street at a large, lime green Victorian, now beautifully restored. "That's where we used to live, upstairs. The good ol' days. Me, Lydia and my brother. We all came to the Haight together back in '65.

We saw it all, man. Even the Summer of Love. But that was a thousand years ago. Not too many of us left around here."

"Your brother?" Kennedy asked, sipping his coffee, genuinely interested. He found Dale to be a living piece of history, like an old man, still alive, who had fought in the Civil War.

"Oh, Bobby died. But you don't want to hear that one. It's too nice of a day out there."

"Sorry," Kennedy said looking back out the window at the crisp sky.

"No problem. Those were some wild times. A lot of freaks doing a lot of freaky things. If the drugs didn't get you, then the cops would. If you lived through that, then there was always good old Viet Nam. Lost too many friends that way. And of course, we all know what became of our sweet Lydia."

Dale shook his head slowly and scratched his beard.

"Sorry. Your hungry, " he said. "What can I get you to eat?"

"What's good?" Kennedy said, picking up the menu for the first time.

"It's all good at the Hippo. But my favorite is and always will be, bacon and eggs ala Dale. I like a little cheese on my eggs. A nice smoky Gouda."

"Interesting. Maybe a couple of pancakes on the side?"

"I like your style," Dale said, a big grin across his face. He looked like he took his eating pretty seriously and Kennedy liked him. He was honest, had traveled a hard road, and had managed to find the brighter side of life. His happiness was part of him and it filled the air around him.

Kennedy looked back up at the photo of Lydia as Dale retreated back to the kitchen to place his order. She wore a dark velvet choker around her neck with a gold heart on it. Her make-up was part of an era that placed her undoubtedly in the 60's, but she had the kind of face that didn't need any at all. She was, as Dale had put it, gorgeous.

But, sitting there, looking up into her eyes, he could not stop seeing her lying on the stage, looking back at him. She was haunting him, sitting here in a coffee shop hundreds of miles away. She had reached out to him, asked him to help, and he had said no. He looked across the little café at Dale, a man who had wrestled his own demons and, for the most part, won. He was a good man. Kennedy felt dirty inside, for running like he had. He didn't feel like he was a good man.

He drank his coffee, but Lydia just kept staring down at him. She would not let him go. Kennedy almost got up the courage to switch tables, to escape her eyes, but would not have been able to explain his actions to Dale. He tried to watch the people outside, strolling up and down the sidewalk passed the window, but always she was there, calling to him.

It didn't take long and Dale was back at the table holding two large white plates of steaming art. He set them down in front of Kennedy and stepped back with his wonderful grin.

"If you don't fall head over heels in love with that, it's free," he said.

"I love it already, just looking at it," Kennedy said.

"I know. Only ever had one person take me up on my offer and that was this prune of an old lady who had some sort of lactose intolerance thing going on. Didn't much care for the cheese. Gave her gas, she said."

By now, the other two people in the café had paid up and moved on, leaving Kennedy to enjoy his breakfast alone in the place. Dale, too, had moved back toward the kitchen, cleaning a few dishes behind the bar area.

Every so often he would carry his grin across the planks of the wooden floor to refill Kennedy's cup, but allowed him the time to eat in peace. And it was delicious. Kennedy had never tasted melted Gouda cheese and eggs together. But now he'd been spoiled and regular old plain eggs would never be quite the same. With difficulty, he managed to keep his attention on the food before him and not look at Lydia.

But as soon as he finished, sitting back in his chair, drinking his coffee, she was right there again, with him. Dale came out of hiding once more and plunked the check down on the table, picking up the empty dishes.

"Well, how was that? You feel like paying for it?"

"I can't lie. That was incredible."

"Excellent. I'm a rich man. Can I get you anything else?"

"No, I'm good. I wouldn't mind hearing a little bit more about Lydia, though."

Dale looked around the empty café and laughed.

"As you can see, I'm a very busy man. But, you get me talking about my girl and I can't stop."

He placed the dirty dishes on the table next to them and grabbed a clean cup. He filled it with coffee and then pulled up a chair next to Kennedy and settled in with a pleasant moan.

"Lydia was the real deal," he said. "Me and Bobby, my brother, met her up in Redding where we grew up. She was a runaway and we hung out for a while together, playing guitars, making up songs, before coming out here. But even as a kid, you could see she had a gift. Something special you just don't see in other people. And man, could that girl sing you a song. It'd make you cry. Everybody was in love with her. Everybody. Even the other chicks. You couldn't help it. She'd just smile at you, put her hand into your chest, rip your heart out and keep it. And you'd be grateful for it."

Kennedy listened quietly as Dale leaned back, his chair groaning, cradling his ceramic mug and looking up at the ceiling.

"Yeah, she was a treasure. People like her, they come into this world with a purpose. I mean, we all have purpose, right? We're all supposed to do something with our time here. But hers was to change the world. And she did."

Dale leaned in and took a healthy gulp of coffee, looking over at the photograph. "And she still is," he continued. "Her voice is as strong today as it was way back then. Everybody still loves her."

"Why would somebody want to kill someone like that?" Kennedy asked.

"Well, now that's the real question, isn't it? It's like good ol' Jesus. The Son of God himself comes down into our little dirt patch, does all these cool miracles, heals people, and what do we do to him? Hey, let's kill the poor guy! Let's nail him to a board and watch him die. That's what people do, I guess. There's the good ones and then there's the one's that can't stand having them around for whatever reason and feel it necessary to kill them. It's the strangest thing."

"The kid that shot her was spaced out on more acid than you can imagine," he continued. "But that's no excuse.

Trust me, I've done my share of LSD, and of all the crazy shit that's gone through my head, I never once thought about killing someone because of it. Drugs don't make you kill someone. That kind of stuff comes from somewhere else, deep inside the person. It's got to."

"Take my brother Bobby," he said. "There was no reason for him to die. None. It was just plain stupid. A bunch of Hells Angels thought it would be fun to end his life one night and so they beat him to death. No reason at all. And the police, they didn't care. Hippies were dying all the time around here. They hated us anyway. We were blight on their society. The less of us there were, the better, as far as they were concerned."

He looked up at Kennedy and laughed. Kennedy had been sitting quietly, soaking it all in.

"Sorry, I told you, when I get going, there's no shutting me up. Should have been a politician."

Dale stopped for a moment thinking about what he'd been saying. He scanned his tidy little establishment and smiled, motioning with his arm in a wide arc at the other photographs on the wall.

"I knew all these people. We were this great big family of traveling children, looking for answers, looking for peace, for love. And we found it in each other. Little Janis over there, she lived right down the street from us on 635 Haight. She lived all over this place actually. I won't tell you some of the things I know about her. It's personal, if you know what I mean. Weird Joe McDonald, from Country Joe and the Fish, he lived on Ashbury. Graham Nash up on Buena Vista by the park. Jefferson Airplane had their weird place over on Fulton and Willard, which is down a bit around the other end of Golden Gate Park there. It was painted all black and everyone thought that was so cool. The boys from Grateful Dead had a crazy house, too over on Ashbury. Even the Master himself, old Jimi, when he was in town anyway, had a place around the corner on Central."

"Yep," he said rubbing the curve of his belly and patting himself, "this was quite the neighborhood back then. Me, Bobby and Lydia and a bunch of other people. Just hanging out makin' love and makin' music. That's what we did."

"You miss her?" Kennedy asked.

"Every day. There was a time there, where she had gotten so famous, she sort of drifted away from us, me and Bobby, but she'd always come back home and see us. Even after Bobby died and she had this great big Mansion down south, she never forgot about me. She used to have me down for these great parties. I'd stay with her for a month or so and it would be just like we never missed a beat. Even though she was like a total star, she never acted like it. She never looked down her nose at me or anybody. No, that girl was something special. Something very, very special. Yeah, I miss her. I miss her bad. I would do anything to have her back. I would even have taken those bullets for her. In a second. And that's no lie. That's what a true friend does."

He took the photo of her off the wall and held it, his eyes moist around the edges. Kennedy still had a difficult time looking at it as Dale handed it to him. Up close, her eyes gripped his heart and tore at it.

"But, like I said, that was a long, long time ago," Dale said. I have no doubt, she's in a much better place now. Probably up there somewhere, singing away in some rockin' angel band. Bringing down the roof of heaven."

Kennedy smiled, but his stomach twisted inside under the weight of the knowledge he kept concealed. Lydia was not in a better place. She was not at peace. She was in torment and had been since the night she died. She was not singing. For her there was no music, only pain. And with each passing second, Kennedy felt more and more guilty, like a coward who knows the truth but is too afraid to stand up for it.

"I'm going to be on my way," he said and handed the photo back to Dale. Dale smiled and hung the photo back on its hook and turned to shake Kennedy's hand as he pushed his chair back and stood.

"If you're ever back on the Haight, you make sure to stop in. I've got a million other stories and the coffee's always hot."

"I just might take you up on that. Thanks for the breakfast. And the advice."

"What advice would that be?" Dales asked.

"The thing you said about being a friend. A wise man once said, 'No greater love than this is there, than that a man lay down his life for another."

"Amen to that," Dale said with a firm nod of his head. "You be good and have a safe drive wherever your headed. Next time your in, the pancakes are on the house."

They shook hands again and Kennedy opened the front door. A small string of copper bells, hung around the knob, jingled as he waved and walked out onto the sidewalk. Dale stood there in the center of his café and watched him walk down the street a ways. He looked back over at the image of Lydia, sighed deeply and went to search for a broom.

Under the shade of the thick oaks in the park, Kennedy slid into the front seat of the Nissan and sat there, thinking. God would not judge him either way. It was his decision to make and his alone. He did not feel required to do anything.

He watched out the front windshield, up the hill in the park. A young boy and his lover sat in the grass strumming guitars and laughing. She leaned forward and kissed him. Kennedy placed the keys in the ignition, started the engine and backed up. The couple in the park were singing now, as he put the car in first gear and headed back down to Los Angeles.

——————

CHAPTER SEVEN

Back in his hotel room, Kennedy switched on his laptop, sitting at a large, polished Queen Anne desk that complimented the décor of the rest of the suite. It was a little over the top, but Kennedy barely took notice. The blue light from the screen illuminated the outlines of his weary face in the darkened room. It was about 11:30 and he had not eaten since earlier that morning at the Hippopotamus where he'd met Dale. Talk about interesting characters.

But even now, he felt no real hunger. Food was not a concern at the moment. In a suite such as this, at the Waldorf, he would be able to get something to eat around the clock if he so desired.

Earlier in the evening, he had wandered the streets around the hotel, trying to clear his mind and figure out what he was supposed to do, and found himself in a small used-vinyl record store thumbing through copies of old CD's. Lydia's specifically. Purple Crow. He was familiar with their music, but had never really been what you would call a fan. It was just a little before his time. He enjoyed it whenever it came on the radio, but had never actually purchased one of their records. Until now. There were several there, Flowers at My Feet, Tin Roof, Whispers, even Purple Crow Live. He wasn't sure which one was best, not that it mattered, and had simply chosen the one with a large photograph of Lydia on the back. It moved him. Those eyes.

Back in his room, he listened to the entire CD while nursing a glass of Maker's Mark. Her voice really was incredible. It was actually rather haunting after what had taken place earlier in the day. Despite the violent attack, he had a twisting feeling in his gut that the spirit in that house was not evil. Vindictive, angry perhaps, but something told him there was another side to it. There was a strong reason for a spirit to hang on like that. It had been, what…almost fifty years now.

As the last song faded out, Kennedy listened more intently as the sound of live voices in the studio could be heard. There was some sort of commotion going on, doors slamming and scuffling. It was all recorded on the CD, for a more personal affect perhaps. Then her voice, quiet and in whispers could be heard.

"Love me, baby. I'm so tired." "Don't you ever leave me. Don't you…"

The CD ended and Kennedy felt a shiver race up his spine. That's no doubt how they had come up with the name "Whispers" for the album.

He logged on to the internet and thought about Bernardo again. He had no doubt endured a very similar experience as he had. And he was dead now because of it. Kennedy felt no anger, however. Bernardo had not been attacked by an enemy, Kennedy knew that. He had been approached, perhaps the same way, for help. And given his age and poor physical condition, he simply had not been strong enough to deal with it. His heart had given out.

Lydia Carter – the internet was filled with thousands of pages of information, fan clubs, lyrics, photographs and more. Although she had been brutally murdered in the beginning of the seventies, according to her current popularity, she was still very much alive. Photographs showed a strikingly beautiful woman, small, full of contagious smiles and laughter, often donning a different pair of bizarre sunglasses, evidently her trademark, and peering out from beneath a wild mass of dark hair. The classic 1960's rock star. Without argument, she was as they called her, Sweet Lydia.

Seeing her face, Kennedy's pulse quickened suddenly as he recalled the vision of her at the house. It was indeed, the very same Lydia.

He quickly pushed the images aside and guided himself to several pages recounting her murder. They too had photographs.

One in particular, had appeared on the cover of Life Magazine. It was a large black and white photo taken of the gunman at the concert. He was a wild-haired kid and several people around him were swinging their fists at him. He had shot Lydia only seconds before and was still holding the gun. The same gun Kennedy had seen in his vision.

Kennedy paused, then stood and walked over to the mini-bar. He removed another small bottle of Makers

Mark, twisted the cap, breaking the seal of smooth red wax and poured the contents into a waiting highball glass. There was no more ice in the room, but he did not require it. He lifted the glass to his nose and smelled it for a moment, then sipped gently, filling his mouth and swirling it around, before allowing it to burn its way down. He sat back in the chair amazed and looked at the photograph of that stupid kid and the gun.

He had stayed up until almost 3:30, soaking up as much information about Lydia as he could find on the internet. While he remembered her music and stories about her from when he was much younger, he never really knew all that much about her. One thing was quite evident; her fans had never forgotten her. They still adored her.

In his search he had come across several articles about her murderer as well. He was just a crazy kid. He didn't look all that vicious. Not like a murderer. Kennedy remembered what Bobby had said about LSD and that it wasn't the drugs that made people want to kill each other. It was just something inside them. It was this piece of the puzzle that confused him.

Before ending his unusually long day and crawling between the sheets, Kennedy decided he could go no further without talking to him. Exhausted, he yawned, picked up the phone and booked a flight to Sacramento to pay a visit to the kid, now a man, responsible for ending it all. Harold Perkins, Jr.

By 10:30 the following morning, he was driving down Brown's Ravine Road headed for Folsom State Penitentiary. Perkins had been just over eighteen years of age when he pulled the trigger three times. Tried as an adult, the jury was not impressed with his attorney's defense; that two hits of windowpane had placed him in a state of temporary insanity. They saw it as nothing less than pre-meditated murder and had seen fit to give him three life sentences, one for each bullet, without possibility of parole. He would be in his fifties now and most likely wouldn't remember much outside the familiar towering stone and cement walls.

Folsom State Penitentiary, a maximum-security prison, was home to some of the most vicious killers in the States. Nestled innocently up in the brown hills above Folsom Lake, it was conveniently hidden out of sight, from the daily thoughts and concerns of miles of newly developed family neighborhoods, just on the outskirts of Sacramento, California.

As a priest, Kennedy had no problems gaining entrance to the prison. Father Dennis O'leary was the prison's full-time Catholic priest. Although they had never met, it took only one phone call, and the massive steel doors and barbed-wire gates that remained sealed shut, both to those on the inside as well as those on the outside, swung freely open to Kennedy.

He maneuvered smoothly up the twisted two-lane road, toward the prison gates. Guards watched stoically from the towers above, looking down upon Kennedy as he approached. He was on their clipboards for the day, so they were not overly concerned, simply aware of his arrival, M-16 rifles cradled in their arms. He came to a slow stop at the small booth before the gate and rolled his window down.

"Father Kennedy," he offered politely to the approaching guard. Without a comforting word, the guard examined his paperwork, then nodded from behind mirrored sunglasses and pointed forward through the gates. A small, wiry guard on the other side opened the tall, wire-mesh gates, and immediately closed them again as Kennedy passed through. Inspecting a visitor at the gate, verifying his identification and crossing his name off the clipboard was likely the most excitement the young man had seen all week. It was a vital job, opening that damned gate, and it made him feel just a little taller.

Kennedy pulled into a small gravel parking lot, marked in small but bold black letters for visitors. He shut the engine off and stepped from the vehicle, stretching his back and looking up at the emotionless guards on top of the high gray walls all around him. He felt like waving, to see if he could gain any kind of response, but knew better. This was not a place for friendliness or, God forbid, humor. He proceeded across the gravel towards the entrance doors to the prison office.

A brief meeting with Father O'leary, an introduction more or less and the appropriate exchange of pleasantries was all that was needed. O'leary made sure that Kennedy was taken care of and given the access that he required before shaking hands and going about his own busy schedule for the day. With O'leary's blessing, the guards would treat him accordingly.

The prison, or at least the outer offices, didn't appear all that intimidating. Not like in the movies. Deeper inside the prison might prove a little more foreboding, but few were allowed that far without actually having killed somebody. Kennedy was shown into the meeting area, which consisted of a series of green, padded chairs on opposite sides of a thick glass wall. Communication took place by means of an old black telephone hanging on the wall in each semi-private cubicle. There were ten in all, but he was the only one currently in the room.

A guard opened a large solid steel door, banging it against the wall on the opposite side of the glass. He looked over at Kennedy, then ushered Perkins in. Kennedy was surprised at the man's lack of presence. It was not quite what he expected. He did display a variety of prison ink, embedded into his flesh. But he was amazingly gaunt, not quite six foot, with eyes sunk into dark circles of flesh. His hands shook as he removed a crumpled pack of Marlboros from his pocket and turned to the guard for a light. From the corner of his eye, he studied Kennedy through the glass across the room. He and the guard shared a few unheard words followed by a short burst of laughter. As his cigarette took hold, he inhaled deeply and moved toward Kennedy, sliding his chair back and sat down. Kennedy removed the phone from its hook and placed it to his ear. Perkins remained still on the other side of the glass, looking at Kennedy and enjoying his cigarette.

"What can I do you for?" asked Perkins as he finally lifted his phone.

"You're Howard Perkins?"

"And you're a priest, Father somebody, so they tell me," Perkins replied still sucking on his precious cigarette. "Have you come to bless me, Father? Or just forgive my sins… 'cause that might take a long fucking time."

"Let's just say this is not a casual visit," Kennedy responded. "I was told I could have as much of your time as I like."

"Well, ain't that a funny one," Perkins replied, scratching his forehead. "It just so happens time is the one thing I got a lot of." He bit his lip nervously and stared defiantly through the scratched glass at Kennedy, studying him, fingering his cigarette. "You go ahead, take as much of it as you like."

Unmoved, Kennedy looked back through the glass barrier at Perkins. "Tell me about Lydia," he stated.

Perkins demeanor changed instantly, as he took the cigarette from his lips, holding it tenderly between two fingers. He looked down at the edge of the counter in front of him and placed his arm against it, bracing himself, thinking. He flicked the ashes onto the floor, ignoring the ashtray next to him. Leaning back, he slowly unbuttoned his shirt and violently yanked it open to reveal a rather large, detailed tattoo of Lydia's face across his chest. Cherubs flew gracefully above her along with a flowing banner of purples and blue, circling her head containing the words, "God Save The Queen."

"You mean this Lydia?" Perkins teased, a small grin wrinkling the corners of his mouth.

"Yeah. That Lydia," Kennedy replied. He sat for a few seconds scrutinizing the large tattoo. It was quite impressive. And it was without a doubt, Lydia Carter. Perkins sat on the cold metal stool and looked at Kennedy defiantly, as if he was from another world.

"Please," Kennedy said. "There are things that have been buried for too long. I don't know what. But I want to help."

"What is it you want to know?"

"I don't know. I just want to help her."

"Help her? Uh, Father O'malleyboy, it's a little late."

"Maybe. But what made you want to kill her?" Kennedy asked.

Perkins clenched his fists. The guard standing across the room was watching him closely. Perkins did not know whether he should give in to the emotions now swelling up inside him, and scream like a madman at Kennedy. He sure as hell wanted to. The guard would jump at the opportunity and it would end this meeting in a heartbeat.

On the other hand, Kennedy was sincere and interested in his side. He might just be the first person in a quarter of a century that would listen and who actually might be able to understand. The result was a small, crumbling wall somewhere deep inside him. His teeth, clamped against each other, relaxed slightly as a small bead of perspiration made its way down the side of his left temple and dampened his thin gray sideburns.

"You listen to me, Father. I loved her, OK?" Perkins managed through a thin mask of smoke. "I loved her. What of it?"

"Then why did you shoot her?" Kennedy asked.

Perkins looked up at him with the innocence of a martyred saint. "I've been living in a 6-by-10 cement room with iron bars for half a century since somebody asked me that question. Funny, isn't it, how my answer is still the same? I didn't."

"You're saying…you're innocent?"

"Look, it doesn't matter what I say. I ain't never getting out of here. Never. What difference does it make to them whether I'm guilty or not?"

"If you didn't shoot her, who did?" Kennedy pressed.

"Now there's the real question. That's the one I wished they would have asked a long time ago," Perkins laughed, the smile almost instantly replaced with a heavy frown.

"She was an angel of God. I'm standing there watching her one minute, the next, some fucker shoves a blazing hot gun down the back of my pants. I screamed and yanked it out. The damn thing burned the shit out of me. I had fucking burn marks on my ass… You think anybody gave a shit about that? Hell no. They got Lydia, lying dead on the stage and some punk tripping on something, holding up a gun and screaming like a maniac. That's good enough, huh?"

"How old were you?"

"Nineteen stupid, fucking years old. I didn't know what was going on. I had smoked something. Some crazy shit that was passed around. I was like on Mars or something. Everyone looked like these monsters, you know? Standing there. Looking at me. They like started growing, up off the floor. With these huge fucking teeth. And I had this gun. This hot gun. I didn't even know what it was at first. Then this one guy, big fat biker, takes a swing and down I go. Then somebody else. Everybody around me starts kicking. I can't really remember much else. I know I laid in that hospital for a month or so afterwards. They broke my fucking jaw. By the time I could talk again, I was already proved guilty."

"No trial?

"Right. If you want to call it that. The courts appointed a lawyer. Some flat-top, crew cut, ex-Marine or something. Classic hippie-hater. Called me a sorry little faggot after it was all over. Said I got what I deserved. How's that for legal representation?"

Perkins sucked deeply on the remains of his cigarette and smashed the butt into the glass ashtray. Small spirals of white smoke swirled from his nostrils.

"So what's it to you?" Perkins said. "If I get to ask any questions. You're a priest. Are you writing a story or something?"

Kennedy dropped his eyes to the floor. He had no real answer. Not even for himself. He wasn't even sure until now that he was doing something. But here he was, face-to-face, talking to the man convicted of killing her.

"I don't know," he responded. "I don't know."

Perkins sat back in his chair and stared at Kennedy, perplexed. He couldn't figure him out. Especially now.

"I guess we're done then?" he said. "You let me know if you need anything else, for no particular reason. I'll be right here if you need me."

He slid his chair back and looked over his shoulder at Kennedy as he walked back towards the guard standing next to the open door that would lead him back to his cage. Kennedy sat motionless in his chair, empty, wondering exactly what he was doing and why he had come.

———

CHAPTER EIGHT

It was sometime after midnight when Kennedy got back to his hotel room in Los Angeles. He had purposely not checked out, leaving his belongings in the room. He wasn't so sure he would come back if he didn't. This way, there would be something he had to come back for.

Ghosts are troubled spirits. They don't hang around for no good reason. Lydia had asked for his help, but he wasn't anywhere near sure what that meant. None of this made sense. Unless Perkins was actually innocent, which seemed pretty unlikely.

Kennedy thought about Lydia, up there all these years, in that old rotting house. This beautiful woman. Sweet Lydia as Dale had said, suffering, alone…in that house. That house.

Ronald Stenton's business card sat in the ashtray next to the phone. Kennedy sat down, picked up the phone, punched in the numbers and got him out of bed.

"Stenton, who owns that house?" demanded Kennedy, pacing his hotel room now like a half-crazed panther.

"What house? Who is this?" Stenton returned. "It's passed midnight."

"Who owns the goddamn house? Who is your client?"

"None of your business, that's who. Is this Father Kennedy?"

"Yeah. She was murdered, Stenton. Lydia was murdered."

"Yeah, well duh." Stenton scoffed. "Where have you been hiding for the last fifty years?"

"I think the guy in prison is a scapegoat."

"He's a goat?"

"You want to sell the place or not, Stenton? I need to know."

"Fuck! AMI Records. That's all I know."

"AMI," repeated Kennedy.

"Yeah. That's all I know. Some bitch, we never even met. I drop off the paperwork, she signs it… boom. I sell the place. I'm rich. That's it. That's the deal."

"Give me a name."

"I don't think this is legal."

"Give me a name, Stenton. The sooner you give me a name, the sooner you cash the commission check."

"Jessica. Jessica Burton."

Kennedy hung up the phone and sat down on the edge of the bed. He cracked the red wax from another single-size bottle and poured it into the glass sitting on the night stand. He stood again and looked out over the twinkling Los Angles skyline. Traffic still streamed steadily below.

He lifted the bourbon to his lips and swallowed most of it. With a second gulp, it was gone.

He was exhausted. But there would be no sleeping tonight. He had been in the presence of a powerful spirit. Not a demon, not some Satanic foe…but the ghost of a person who had died so many years ago. An innocent person. A woman. There was no road map here, and he was lost. No question, the apparition he had witnessed was Lydia Carter. It was her and she had tried to communicate something to him.

His head was spinning and he felt as if he would pass out. Disregarding the fact that Father Bernardo had died because of all this, he had blindly stepped into her world. His entire life, he had sought God, asking, searching, pleading… never getting an answer, leaving him an empty shell without hope. It was no use turning to him now. Why this? Why her? What could he possibly do to help?

And all the time, his mind reeling, only reminding him… she was so beautiful.

———————

AMI Records was like a castle built out of glass and steel. A brother to the other skyscrapers that have the nerve to reach up into the toxic Los Angeles skyline. The building disappeared into the haze over Kennedy as he stepped from a taxi. He took a package of gum from his coat pocket, unwrapped a piece and placed it in his mouth.

Inside, the lobby was from another planet. It wreaked of incense, money and fame. Kennedy had the feeling that he had walked into a nightclub more than a professional business. In fact, *Angie*, by the Rolling Stones was pumping through speakers tastefully hidden within the walls. He wondered if people were expected to dance their way to the reception desk.

A young woman behind the desk looked at him, but was evidently carrying on a conversation with somebody else. She wore one of those microscopic telephone headsets that give the impression that the person is talking to themselves or perhaps you, if they happen to be looking at you. In this case, Kennedy knew she wasn't speaking to him. He couldn't have been expected to know anything about a Ricky and the fight at the party last night. He waited for her to finish, which she reluctantly did, apologizing to the person on the other end as if Kennedy had somehow rudely interrupted them during an important piece of business. She promised it wouldn't take long and she would call right back.

"I need to speak with Jessica Burton, please," Kennedy said.

"OK. You have an appointment?"

"No, I don't," he answered. "But I really need to see her. It's about a house she is selling."

"A house." She punched a few numbers on her keyboard and waited. "Ms. Burton, sorry to bother you. There is a gentleman in the lobby who needs to speak to you about your house." She placed her hand over the microphone and looked back up at Kennedy. "Who are you and what do want to know about the house?"

"Tell her, I am a priest and I am trying to help her by exorcising the original owner of the house," Kennedy said with a smile. "She was brutally murdered."

The girl's face changed instantly. She grinned and nodded in approval. "Cool," she said. Kennedy had at least one new friend at AMI records.

In most cities, people pay big bucks to locate their offices in a swanky high-rise. It gives the dramatic feeling of wealth and superiority to be able to look out over the land at those poor laborers far below your feet. But here, in a city built on entertainment, all that was visible 32 stories up was a brownish glimpse of some of the neighboring buildings. It was like being inside a cloud of mud.

A second reception desk awaited Kennedy just outside the elevators. He moved toward it, but never reached it. A short woman was bobbing down the corridor, like an elf, directly toward him with the gratuitous Hollywood smile. She shot her hand at him.

"Jessica Burton. How can I help you?"

"Well, this is rather complicated," Kennedy said. "Is there a place we could sit down for a moment. I really need to talk to you about the house."

"Of course," she said, again with the gratuitous smile.

He followed her back down the floor-to-ceiling glass corridor, passed office after office of people yammering on the same telephone headsets that the girl in the lobby had worn. They all appeared to be crazy, carrying on heated conversations with nobody. Each office had hundreds of photographs of recording stars and gold records framed behind glass. Kennedy was indeed on another planet, but it struck him how similar it was to his own. There were no statues here, no candles, but if there were, they would have fit in nicely.

"Lydia Carter. She was the original owner of the house," Kennedy said, after he'd been seated in Jessica's office. He wasn't exactly sure what Jessica did for AMI, but by the size of her office, he knew it was fairly high up in the ranks. It was at least twice the size of many he had glanced into on his journey down the glass corridor.

"Yes, she was," replied Jessica. "I take it you're not interested in buying it."

"I actually sort of inherited the job of getting rid of her ghost."

"Stenton? I apologize," she said. "The man is supposed to be a very good realtor. But, what can I say? Welcome to Hollywood."

"That was pretty much my take when I first met him," Kennedy said. " But it got a little crazier right after that. You see a friend of mine suffered a heart attack after going into the house. And I know why. I've been in it myself. Everything you've been told about that house…is true."

Jessica had put away her pleasant smiles. Kennedy had her full attention. "I spoke with Howard Perkins, the man in jail for killing Lydia. He says he didn't do it. I believe him."

"You believe him?" Jessica asked, shaking her head. "Why? Everyone in prison says they're innocent, don't they?"

"That's what I hear." Kennedy took a moment and gathered his thoughts. If he wanted this young woman's help, he couldn't hold back now.

"Look, I realize this must sound absolutely crazy," he confessed, "but I experienced a presence…her ghost. Lydia's. You don't have to believe a word I'm saying, but…it was real. And if it was…her ghost…there's a reason she is hanging around. If this Perkins guy is telling the truth…well, then somebody else killed her. And that might be a pretty good reason."

"I'm sorry. Back up. This is all a little much," Jessica said. "I'm not really sure what to make of it. A ghost? It's a little out of my league."

"I'm not exactly sure about any of this either," Kennedy confessed. "How did AMI come into owning the house in the first place?"

"I have no idea," Jessica said. "Really, I don't. That was in the late 60's, I think. I wasn't even born yet."

Kennedy looked up at her. They both laughed. "I was," Kennedy continued. "And I can't even remember that much."

He ran his hand through his thick hair and looked out the window at nothing. Jessica quickly ran her eyes over his entire frame, then followed his stare with nothing more to offer. She quietly thumped a pencil eraser on the desk.

"So, AMI is somehow connected to Lydia, then?" Kennedy asked.

"I suppose," Jessica answered. "She's been on our label ever since I started here."

"Lydia Carter is on AMI's label?"

"Oh, yeah. I'm sorry, I assumed you knew. She still sells like crazy. Better than most of our living artists, unfortunately."

Jessica bit her lip nervously and pushed a cold coffee cup away from her. "Um, Father... I want to help you, trust me, I need to unload that place... Like you, it somehow became part of my job. But honestly, I am not really sure how I can help you. And right now, is not a very good time."

An uncomfortable silence followed. What more could be said?

"Look," she said, taking a business card from a holder on the front of her desk and handing it to him, "if you need anything or have more questions that you think I might know the answer to…call me. I know I haven't been much help…but I will make myself available to you."

Again she smiled and stood up. Kennedy shook her hand once again and thanked her. She showed him back down the glass corridor toward the elevators.

"You know, I noticed," Kennedy said as he pushed the elevator button. "There are photographs of stars everywhere around here, musicians I imagine. You mentioned Lydia was one of your best-selling artists. I don't see any pictures of her.

"Huh. Yeah, you're right. I know I've seen them around here. Lots of them. Most of them are probably hanging in Mr. Hampton's office. J.W. Hampton…he's the CEO. Gets first dibs on all the vintage stuff," she laughed.

The elevator slid open and Kennedy shook her hand goodbye. The doors closed between them and Jessica stood motionless for a few seconds, then glanced over at the reception desk. Nobody paid any attention around here. Good. She didn't have to explain any of this. All the same, Mr. Hampton should probably be made aware. It gave her the opportunity to appear as though she was on the ball, at least in regards to the house.

She turned on her heel and with the same energy as before, made her way back toward her little throne room. She entered and closed the door, pulled back her chair and sat down officially behind her desk, ready to do business. She immediately picked up her head set, placed it over her ear and punched in three digits. She practiced her professional voice in her head.

"Mr. Hampton, good morning. Jessica."

"Jessica," he answered. "Good news on the old house? I only want the good news today."

"Um, no sir, no sales, but I do have something, regarding the house, I thought you might want to be aware of."

J.W. Hampton stood in his office behind closed double doors, just down the hall, looking out over what could still be seen of the Los Angeles valley below. He puffed on a cigar and listened to Jessica over the speaker on his desk. He had built his kingdom and did not have time for people who could not deliver what he wanted, when he wanted it.

The sound of Jessica's voice irritated him. She had always irritated him, but she had put out. The truth was, she wasn't all that bad at her job, in fact, probably did a better job than most, but that wasn't why he had promoted her. Like the smart ones before her, she had agreed to a simple business bargain. She'd upheld her end of the deal, several times in fact, and Hampton had no particular reason not to uphold his. It had been business as usual, LA style. Even so, there was a quality in her voice that bit at his ears and he simply preferred it when she stayed quiet.

He was a stout man who loved spending too much on his clothes. And even though suspenders were no longer the style, he wore them every day. They were much more comfortable than a belt, due to his waistline, and he felt they continued to give him the air of pompous superiority he deserved, style or no style.

Despite his enormous success, his jowls had fallen over the years, cemented now into a permanent frown. He was not considered by anyone who knew him, to be a happy man. He even admitted it, laughing at the foolishness behind the notion. Happiness was not something he was even remotely interested in. Happiness was something left for peasants to struggle toward. His fulfillment came in the form of power. In that sense he was extremely successful and proud of it.

"I just had a very strange visit," Jessica continued. "From a priest. He wanted to know about AMI's involvement with the house."

"A priest? Goddamnit!" he blurted. "That's all I need. Some whacko drumming up more goddamn ghost stories."

Hampton was well aware of the urban legends circulating about the house. Over the years it had caused him far too much grief and served as nothing more than an embarrassment to his precious label. He did not believe the stories, of course, but feared the damage they could do if it ever got out of control.

"I hate that fucking house."

He seemed particularly interested in the fact that Lydia was on our label."

"Did he?" Hampton said, a dry statement more than a question. "Well, I'm sure it's just another ghost chaser, Jessica. Just sell the place. Please. I am tired of these interruptions. It's just an old fucking house and it's costing me a lot of time and money."

"Yes sir, of course."

"Was there anything else?" he asked, shoving his cigar in his cheek.

"Um, no sir. That was it. I just thought you…"

"If this priest bothers you again, call security for Christ's sake," he said and jammed his finger on the speakerphone, abruptly ending their conversation.

Jessica sat at her desk, humiliated. It had not gone the way she had hoped. Hampton made her nervous and she could never manage to do things right when he was around. The fact is, she despised the man. But he held the keys to a place she was destined for. She took his advice and decided the best way around this mess was to make sure she did everything she could to get that house off the books. She removed Ronald Stenton's business card from her rolodex.

The phone number blinking on Stenton's cell phone was quite familiar to him, if not down right depressing. He rolled his eyes, trying to quickly invent some sort of excuse as to why things were taking so long. As always, she wanted an update on the property.

"Jessica. Hey, perfect timing! Good news…" Stenton lied.

"Good news…or just pretty good bull shit," she responded. "What's up with the priest?" she demanded, cutting to the chase and ignoring his usual plastic approach.

"Oh, him… He called you?"

"No, he didn't call. He stopped by and paid me a visit. We had a wonderful little chat. What the fuck are you up to, Stenton?"

"Goddamn him. Look, I'm sorry about that. I had no idea he would do that. I hired a fucking priest, OK? I had to hire a goddamn Catholic priest. Two of them!"

"What the fuck for, Stenton?"

"Look, you work for a swanky record company. You live in the fake world. I'm a real estate guy. I sell fucking dirt. Stop jumping on me! You do what you do, I do what I do… I went out on a limb on this one."

"Uh, yeah. I'd say so."

"Come on, Jessica. We're on the same team here. This is not exactly an easy property to unload. You guys have been sitting on this fucking monster for a hundred years and suddenly I'm supposed to be Mr. Miracle man… and get rid of it? Zippety zam? Hokus pokus?"

"So you hire a priest? The tabloids would kill for this kind of shit. Look, Miracle Man," Jessica responded, unfazed by his practiced aggressiveness, "I've got three thousand guys who are promising me daily that they can sell it… "this monster." So you come on… Give me something I can tell my people. Something good, OK? I'm not the bad guy here. You with me?"

"Yeah. Yeah, I'm with you," Stenton offered. "But you wouldn't believe what I've been through on this one."

"No, you're wrong. I do believe you," Jessica responded. "This house has been on the company's books for quite some time. There are too many stories. But they're just bullshit stories, Mr. Stenton. It's time to unload it and move on."

"That's precisely what I'm trying to do," Stenton said. He paused to collect his thoughts and inhale his cigarette. Silence flooded the phone line. "Look, you and I both know, nobody has been able to sell this piece of shit," he continued, filling the gap as he had been trained to do. "But I will. And that's a promise. You just tell your people to relax and back-off a bit."

Another brief moment of awkward silence followed. Stenton could hear her rhythmic breathing through the phone's small speaker.

"Ok, fine. I understand," she replied. "But here's the real thing, Mr. Stenton. And please, listen closely. Personally,

I trust that you can do all that you say you can do. Seriously, I do."

Again, more painful silence followed. Neither of them spoke. Men in general disgusted her. She had to do what she had to do with the ones like Hampton, but she was not going to be pushed around by a snake as vile as Stenton. Fine, he was the Realtor to the Stars, but he worked for her.

"Results are everything around here," she continued. "Immediate results. So let's not discuss the property's so-called history. It makes little difference. Just sell it. Sell it and sell it right now," she stated coldly. "Oh, and if I didn't make it perfectly clear in the beginning, a cardinal rule if you will, Mr. Stenton…it is not wise to tell my people to… 'back-off a bit.' "

Stenton was silent, struggling for the response that did not exist. Besides, it was too late. Jessica calmly hung up the phone, leaving him alone with orders he could not refute.

With a dull reluctance, Stenton placed the phone down. It seemed terribly unfair. Arguably, he was the King of Los Angeles. The man who could sell homes. Everyone knew that. It even said so, in gold leaf, on his business cards. IMA Records had contacted him. Besides, this was a problem property. It had been forever. If anyone could sell it, he could. Obviously, that's why they had offered him the whopping twenty-five percent commission. They knew he was the King. This fucking piece-of-shit property was causing them thousands each year in taxes alone. Ronald Stenton was their last resort. He was their savior. Their last chance. Who the hell did she think she was, talking to him like that? If it wasn't for the money, he'd have told her to go fuck herself.

He picked up the phone again and, rummaging through the bits and scraps of paper on his desk, found Kennedy's hotel room number and proceeded to dial.

"Listen there, Father," he started after getting the voice mail box, "I ask you guys a pretty simple favor and the whole things turns into a major mess. I certainly never asked you to go harassing my client. So, if you don't mind, I changed my mind. You're gonna get me fired. So please, don't go messing around any more, Ok? I got way too much money to lose with guys like you and Father Bernardo playing ghost hunters. Sorry, but the deals off."

He hung up the phone and grabbed his car keys and jacket. Goddamn people didn't know shit about selling real estate. He would show them a thing or two. True, the whole priest thing was a little embarrassing. Nobody was supposed to find out about that part. But that was the difference between him and the next guy, Stenton told himself. He was willing to go to extremes.

———

CHAPTER NINE

With a piece of old wire he had found in the trunk of his Beemer, Ronald Stenton attempted to reattach the personal nameplate on the for sale sign in front of the old mansion. It had broken loose on one side during a recent storm and had been dangling for about a week, making the house look even more haunted. And it certainly didn't need any help. He didn't really believe it was haunted, but still didn't have the guts to go inside. Especially now. It was getting late. But he was determined to sell this dump, even if it killed him. He had to. His reputation demanded it.

Nobody would have imagined that a high-school drop-out like Stenton would have been able to achieve the level of success that he had. If ever there was a self-made man, it was Ronald Stenton. And he told himself this every morning when he looked at himself in the mirror. There were the years before he fell into real estate, where he tried selling insurance, or before that, several stints at auto dealerships. He had made some money, enough to pay the bills, but not real money. It wasn't until he took some classes in real estate and got his license that everything began to fall in place. It was like he had finally found out what he was supposed to do with his life.

Then, on a stroke of luck, he had been invited to a party where he ran into Olivia Darworth, the star of a recent trilogy of thriller films about a female British spy, like the female James Bond sort of thing. She had been just drunk enough to find Stenton's rude humor entertaining and had taken him home to play with that evening.

The awakening must have been rather rude the following morning, for her anyway, but Stenton had somehow managed to get some business out of the deal when she told him she was selling her home. She probably agreed to use him as the agent in an effort to get him out the door.

The rest sort of fell into place. He sold the house within a week, for more than the asking price, and although he was never able to sneak back into her bed, she did refer him to another one of the actors from her films. He hustled and hustled and it wasn't six months before he had bought and sold almost ten homes for some of Hollywood's biggest and brightest.

Right place. Right time. Plus, as he told himself, he was the right guy. He was trying to convince himself of this very fact as he twisted the stiff wire together, fixing the sign. His thumb suddenly slipped and the sharp end of the wire sliced open the tip.

"Fuck!" he shouted into the wind. He shook his hand trying to ward off the biting pain and looked down at his thumb. The gash was about half an inch in length and deep enough that blood was now starting to run down and pool into his palm.

He walked over to his car and opened the door with his good hand searching for a napkin or anything to stop the bleeding. Blood dripped off of his wrist and onto the tan leather of the drivers' seat. "Goddamit! Mother freaking… shit!" he swore and tried to wipe it clean with his hand, only serving to smear the blood across the seat. He swore repeatedly to himself and kicked at the dirt, then gritting his teeth, popped the trunk and went to the rear of the car and lifted the lid. Quickly rifling through some random things in a box, he found an old white gym shirt. There was good amount of blood now, running down the length of his arm as he used the shirt to clean himself and stop the bleeding from his thumb.

Out of the corner of his eye, he caught a glimpse of someone, a woman, wearing a long red dress, disappearing into the overgrowth around the side of the house. A small iron gate leading toward the pool creaked in the wind and slammed shut.

"Hey, hello!" Stenton shouted, hoping someone might possibly be looking around the house with the intention of actually buying it. He tossed his cigarette into the dirt, threw the bloody shirt back in the trunk and straightened his tie.

Looking up at the house, he swallowed his fear. He moved through the main gate into the courtyard and quickly passed the fountain in a sort of anxious jog. The latch on the little gate leading toward the back of the house had long since rusted and broken, allowing the gate to swing in the breeze. Stenton pushed it aside and swept at the tangles of ivy growing overhead. A grey stone walkway lay beneath decades of leaves and weeds and wound around the side of the house down some stairs and opened onto a immense stone patio behind the house. Stenton moved cautiously, whistling as he ventured toward the back.

"Hello?" he yelled. Nobody was back there. He didn't like being here at all, but knew he had seen someone enter the gate. His thumb still dripped and was throbbing painfully. He stood directly next to the pool, although he had no idea it was there. He had never seen it. The years of leaves and debris had covered over it entirely, blending it seamlessly into the rest of the overgrown property.

In fact, he had never even seen the house itself, not from this perspective. He had always been too afraid to venture this far, and with good reason. But now, in the broad daylight and with the possibility of a sale, he felt much braver than before.

The structure was a magnificent piece of architecture, even in its current state. As he scanned the long roofline from left to right, he imagined for a moment how much it might cost to buy and fix the place himself. He knew guys that had done that and almost doubled their investment. Something caught his attention and he looked down from the rooftop suddenly. She was standing six inches in front of him, here eyes of blue fire, staring directly into his.

Stenton jumped back instinctively with a gasp as his foot slipped on the wet leaves, shooting straight out in front of him, sending him toppling backwards. His head smashed violently against the hidden cement edge of the pool, his vision instantly going dark. For a moment, his body hung precariously on the edge of the pool, then collapsed suddenly under his weight as he slipped through the camouflage layer of old leaves and sunk slowly, disappearing into the burbling green and black slime beneath.

———————

The report of a "missing person" was called in a few days later. Stenton had no family, to speak of, nobody who missed him anyway, except the staffers at the *Coldwell Banker* office. He had a reputation for taking a bender now and then, but only a day here and there. After two days and no returned phone calls, they had sent someone to his residence, only to find it empty.

The police took down the information and slid it into a file folder along with too many others. Los Angeles was overflowing with missing people, mostly young girls who disappeared right along with the empty dreams that had brought them to the city in the first place. There certainly was nothing particularly interesting about an older, washed-up, real estate agent that should cause for expediency, so it was no small miracle that detective Blakey even noticed the folder in the pile placed on his already messy desk, much less pick it up and look at it.

During a casual conversation about a recent body, bludgeoned to death and dumped in the canals, he just happened to open Stenton's file and found himself slightly amused by the description "Realtor to the Stars." It looked like he might have been trying to sell a significant pice of property up in the Palisades. Big money there. Maybe there was a little foul play and it turned the wrong way. Worth a look. Could be interesting.

At least, in some small way, Stenton had finally stood out in somebody's mind. If this was his only real claim to fame in life, then it served him well, as Blakey closed the file, but kept it aside from the others, deciding for one reason or another that he might just take a look into it.

Kennedy stood on the threshold of the old house once again. He had received the message Stenton left on his hotel answering machine. For two days, he had tried to reach him. After his tenth phone call, the woman who answered his phones said he had not shown up at work for the last two days, nobody could reach him and that they had notified the police. With a little too much pleasure, she divulged that the last time she had seen him, he seemed pretty upset and had stormed out of the office, mumbling something about an old mansion.

The door was still unlocked as he turned the knob. Kennedy had seen Stenton's BMW outside the gate and thought perhaps he had actually gotten up the nerve and gone inside. He feared what he might find. But the house was silent inside as the door swung slowly open under its own weight, leaving a cavernous black hole as an entry.

Even though he knew what waited inside, he was somehow less afraid now. Less afraid, not unafraid. The sweat formed at the sides of his temple. He entered and looked around, his eyes adjusting to the darkness. The electricity had been shut off long ago but he tried the light switches to the side of the door anyway, simply out of habit. He knew they didn't work from his first visit so he relied on the flashlight he had retrieved from the trunk of his car.

"Stenton! You here? Stenton," he yelled out. Gut instinct told him he was alone as he moved carefully into the house. "Lydia," he said on impulse, swinging the flashlight beam around the room. I am here to help you. I apologize for my arrogance last time. I didn't know. I want to help you."

It was dead silent, as trails of dust swirled in front of the narrow beam of light. It smelled heavy, of must and mold, like an ancient tomb. He moved on further into the house and, intending on making his way toward the back, he hesitated at the foot of a massive staircase. The steps were made of a cream-colored marble. The layer of dust now covering each step proved that Stenton, nor any other living person had been upstairs in this house for quite some time and he realized it as he placed his foot on the first step leaving the perfect mark of his shoe imprinted in the dust. He shone his light above. The staircase spiraled three floors above him. A large glass chandelier loomed in the center. The stairs were silent and cold as he stepped slowly upward, his hand firmly grasping the iron railing. The higher he rose, the colder it got.

At the top of the second floor, he stopped. He was finding it difficult to breathe and it dawned on him that he had been holding his breath. He filled his lungs and peered down a long corridor that split the house in two and disappeared in either direction. He decided to continue upwards for some reason, perhaps to explore the house backward from the top down. It made no sense, but he wasn't really thinking about his reasoning. He was drawn up the stairs.

When he reached the landing at the top of the third floor it seemed actually lighter than below. The sunlight filtered in through the shutters covering the dormers in the roof, allowing small shafts of light to fill the hallway with a dim overall cast. There were paintings on the wall. It was called modern art at the time. Bizarre. Drug induced nightmares of wild color. Nudes that more resembled a child's scribbling than works of art. Someone would probably pay handsomely for them today. Kennedy ignored them.

He moved cautiously down the long hallway toward a closed door from which a bright light glowed beneath the bottom edge. He opened it slowly. The room was filled with sunlight that poured through an open window. The gauze drapes blew lightly in the breeze. It was her bedroom. Kennedy knew instantly.

A large canopy bed with silk sheets and a thick maroon down comforter sat majestically in the far corner. It looked like something designed for a princess piled high with too many pillows. He entered the room, turned off the flashlight and placed it on the edge of a dark wooden dresser. His reflection greeted him from a perfectly polished mirror. In fact, the entire room was spotless. It smelled of fresh roses. The marble floor was covered with a brightly colored Persian rug that filled almost the entire room. It too had no sign of dust. She was here, in the room with him.

He saw her, standing near a desk on the opposite side of the room, her back to him. She was draped in a long red robe made of silk that fell down around her and onto the floor. Her hair, dark and thick, fell in waves over one shoulder.

"Lydia," Kennedy spoke softly, "Lydia…I want to help you." She turned, lifeless, like a mannequin on a spindle, looking directly at him. Unearthly, crystal blue eyes, large and wide, pierced his soul. His heart pumped wildly in his chest. Even in her death, she was the most beautiful woman he had ever seen. The blackness of her hair framed a perfect white face as though masterfully sculpted from ivory. She had the innocence of a child, but the full mouth and shape of a woman.

She reached for a small, leather-bound book lying on the desk at her side. Her face showed no emotion whatsoever. She just stood there, as did Kennedy. His entire body was shaking as she lifted her arms toward him, allowing the front of her gown to fall open. Kennedy felt a sudden surge, an increased fear, as three ghastly holes formed in the center of her naked chest.

The wounds gaped, vicious, and the blood began to flow, coursing down to her stomach. She glared at Kennedy, pain and rage in her eyes, then down at the book in her hand. She turned and walked toward the bed, bent over, and tucked it between the mattress and the box spring below. She stood, her eyes piercing Kennedy again, turned her back to him, and faded into the wall.

Kennedy gasped and felt his knees weaken beneath him. He steadied himself on the dresser there next to him and gulped at the suddenly rancid air. He was alone in the room, but it was not the same room. Not at all. In fact, the entire bedroom now appeared as the rest of the house, dusty and forgotten. The drapes were old and torn, falling into pieces. The furniture, the dressers, the bed, all were there, but covered in decades of dust and mold. The desk sat still on the far wall, a host to a thick collection of cobwebs. Her bed was covered entirely with an old, stained sheet.

Kennedy pushed himself forward to the spot where she had stood. It was so cold now. His vision seemed to close in around him and he felt as though his consciousness was escaping again. He banged the side of his forehead with his clenched hand, fighting hard to remain present. The house was still and quiet. He could hear the distant crash of the ocean waves somewhere outside beyond the cliffs in the back yard. A seagull flew past the window unaware that a living person was inside, just behind the dark window.

He wondered what had become of Stenton, then, on impulse, plunged his hand deep beneath the mattress, pushing it inside, and felt a small book. He yanked it out and lifted it towards the light from the windows, revealing the name Lydia, etched in gold into the old, leather cover. He opened it carefully and beheld the words, scripted elegantly in her own hand.

MY DIARY
January 4, 1966

My name is Lydia Elaine Carter. I'm in a rock and roll band. Purple Crow. I sing. I play guitar, too, but I don't think I'm all that good. Eddie, now that boy can play. My manager, Jack, says we're going to be famous. He bought me this diary. He said it would be worth a million bucks some day. That's OK with me. I've never had one before, so I guess it's kind of cool. I'm not real sure how to begin or what I am supposed to write about... so I guess I'll just write about everything. Whatever floats around in my head, which is a ton these days.

Let's see...I was born in Tacoma. That's in Washington... on March 23, 1947. My father was some sort of an Air Force pilot, but I never had the opportunity to meet him. Annie, that's my mom, said he was a great man, but he died somewhere over Korea while she was pregnant with me. She raised me all by herself, and I know it wasn't easy.

I don't remember a whole lot from when I was real little. I remember I loved kindergarten a lot. There was one boy there, Jacob Klein, I was so in love with that boy. Even kissed him once on a dare. But then I went to another school for first grade and it just wasn't the same. Not as much fun. I pretty much hated school after that. Got in a lot of trouble, too, I remember. I was always trying to kiss the boys.

I think I was about nine or ten, when Annie took a job at Parkers' Music on the main stretch by the A&W, answering the phone when it rang, paying the bills, balancing the books and dusting all those beautiful pianos, keeping them glowing for anyone who might pass by the large window in front. She loved those pianos. She knew how to play a bit and got to give a lesson or two on the weekends for the extra money, but mostly for fun I think. She could never afford a piano for herself, so I guess Parkers' Music was the perfect place to work. I liked it, too.

It was Annie who encouraged me to try music. She gave me lessons. I'm not sure if I was any good, but I remember how much I liked just sitting next to her and smelling her clothes. They were always clean smelling. We laughed a lot, too. I remember that.

I think Annie figured something was up with me when I just started singing one day. Real loud, too. That's what she used to tell me. I made up all the words. It probably didn't make a whole lot of sense, but Annie loved it. So did old Mr. Parker. He used to ask me to sing when customers came in. He said I was a better salesman than he was.

Annie said I had a gift. I don't think she knew what she was doing or where it would take me. In fact, if she knew how I turned out, she would have burned down the music store. She was a pretty religious lady. I'm not. Not any more. I mean I believe in God and all, but I don't go to church.

Every day, on my way home from school, I would stop in to Parker's and spend the next several hours hopping from piano to piano. Then one day, Mr. Parker got in a shipment of guitars. I don't even know if I'd really even ever seen one before and all of a sudden there was about ten of them hanging on the wall by the front door. Nobody, not even Mr. Parker himself, knew how to play one. But he said they were becoming increasingly popular. So I just taught myself. It was a lot like the piano in many ways and besides, Mr. Parker got some guitar music books, too. They had these big black and white photos of how to put your fingers on the neck of the guitar. They didn't say really much about strumming, but that part wasn't really all that hard. I just sort of knew what do, I guess.

Christmas of 1965, Annie scraped enough extra money together from giving lessons to buy me the Gibson acoustic that was my favorite. Mr. Parker gave her some special deal, I think. I just know it was expensive. I think she would have rather gotten me a piano, but they were real expensive. Plus I could always go to the store and play them whenever I wanted anyway. Besides, she knew I loved the Gibson. It was a light blond maple with a rose color pick guard. It had these little inlaid pearl-like squares along the edges. I loved it.

Annie died right after that. She was in a car accident. She was headed to work I guess, in the morning after dropping me off at school. The fog had rolled in as it always did that time of year. It was like these huge gray wool blankets. There was a big truck headed the opposite direction. They told me she probably never even saw it.

I was seventeen by then. Mr. Parker, he was too old to take care of me and I didn't have nobody else. He tried adopting me, but the state people wouldn't let him. I know he was crying when they came and took me. I never saw him again. I think he's probably dead too by now.

I became what they called a ward of the state. When they told me that, I remember I thought I was going to jail. I thought maybe they thought I killed Annie.

I had some clothes shoved in my father's old military duffle bag and the Gibson. I think they sold all our furniture, but I don't know. I don't think they were even going to let me keep my guitar but I screamed like a crazy kid when they tried to take it away.

After a bit, I was placed in a foster home. And looking back now, I thought they were nice people and all, but I never really stayed long enough to find out. Wallace and Bernice or something... I can't remember their names... but they were nice.

I sneaked out the window one night and just started walking. I wasn't even sure where I was going. I hiked forever through these huge cornfields and cow manure before I found the Interstate. There was a Texaco station. It was all lit up even though it was closed. That's where I slept that night. I didn't mean to, I just sort of fell asleep. A truck driver woke me up the next morning. He tried to talk me into going home, but gave up after awhile. I told him my mother was dead and I had an uncle in San Francisco. I don't really have an uncle, but he believed me and said he'd take me as far as Redding, California. That's where I met Bobby and his brother Dale. I was in love with both of them. They were a year or so apart, but they looked like twins. It was Bobby's idea to head for San Francisco. That's when we met Soldier and everything changed.

It was 1964 going on '65, I think. San Francisco was what was happening. If it was going on, it was going on in San Fran. An incredibly groovy place. So many people, just like me. Cast out. Thrown away. Forgotten. Experiencing life. From the minute we got there, we all just sat in the park, every day, smoking, loving the world and playing our music until the sun went down. For some reason, the world hated us for it, but we just loved them in return.

There was this club, off Sutter Street, the Avalon. They had bands in there all the time. We met Jack some time right around then. He was so cool. Always had something going on. Bobby told him I was a singer and he asked me to come play, up on the stage with this band that was in town. Purple Crow. That's pretty much how this whole thing started.

That was a year and a half ago. So much has happened since then. It's like this blur. I joined the band and it went crazy. We packed the Avalon every single time and started to play bigger places like the Matrix. We had to move on to something even bigger after awhile and opened for The Doors at Winterland. The whole thing just kept growing.

————

Floating far away now, lost in a blurred world somewhere between reality and dreams, Kennedy saw himself, as though watching from above, standing on the side of the road, his thumb out, cars passing him by, one after the next, pretending he was not really there. And yet, he was there. How could he be there?

He was cold and unprepared for the weather, wearing only a pair of well-worn jeans and a thin green army shirt with peace signs stitched upon the sleeves. He was much younger, too. Somewhere in his twenties, maybe. He had not shaved in weeks and his long hair was pulled back and tied in a ponytail.

An old Volkswagen van approached, down shifted and pulled over to the side of the road. Kennedy waved and ran to catch up with it as it passed him and stopped.

Two scruffy guys who looked a lot like him sat in the front seat and greeted him with a genuine smile and a sign of peace. He thanked them, pulled at the door handle and the side door slid open. He threw his pack into the van and climbed in.

And there she was. Lydia… She lay sprawled on the far back seat, round purple sunglasses covering her eyes, grinning at him. She held a joint pinched between two fingers and raised it up, offering it to him.

Welcome stranger," she said. "We're going to San Francisco. I'm Lydia. That's Bobby and Dale… Where you headed?"

"Anywhere," Kennedy answered.

"Anywhere is cool," she nodded.

"Anywhere is everywhere," Bobby laughed, and pulled the van back onto the road.

"And everywhere is always where we will be," continued Dale. They all burst into laughter as Kennedy reached for the joint and placed it to his lips, inhaled deeply, and passed it on to Dale.

"And I don't want to be anywhere else," Kennedy continued, holding his breath. Again they all laughed, causing Kennedy to yield to the pressure of the smoke in his lungs.

Lydia watched him, smiling. Bobby glanced at them in the rear view mirror and just grinned. It was all about love and if you were open to it, everybody could love anybody. Just five minutes ago, this cat in his army shirt, standing on the side of the road, was nobody to them. Now he was with them and he was part of them and they all loved him. Such a cool thought.

It was so cool, in fact, Bobby thought about it for the next half hour as he drove onto the onramp and headed down Interstate 101 South. Dale soon was lost, too, counting the clouds overhead. They just kept changing up there and, each time, he gladly started over.

"You're beautiful," Lydia said. "I like your shirt."

"Thanks." I think I made it, sort of."

"You're like a soldier or something, aren't you. Can I call you that? Soldier?"

Kennedy nodded and smiled at her. She was probably eighteen or nineteen years old. Even at that, she was a breathtaking woman. Her hair was long and straight, held back by two small braids on either side of her forehead. A graceful, white flower was placed on the right side just above her ear. Playfully, she curled the bottom strands of her hair around her index finger, let it go and started again.

"What are you fighting for, Soldier?

"I don't know," Kennedy answered. She smiled at him and nodded her head. Bobby smiled. Dale turned suddenly to them both and passed the joint back. "Thirty seven, man. There's thirty seven," he stated, completely satisfied with his *scientific accomplishment.* "But you gotta hurry. That's the key, man. It all changes fast. Everything changes."

––––––––––

The light was beginning to fade outside. Kennedy opened his eyes. He was sitting, perfectly still, on the edge of her bed. The old diary was lying in his lap. A dream, a vision…he had never had an experience quite like that before. Crystal-clear. Real. He felt as if he had been in her physical presence. He knew her.

Calm and wide awake now, he looked up. A whispering ocean breeze moved the branches of an overgrown willow just outside the window, sending several long shadows, like fingers reaching through the window glass, onto the floor boards, making their way toward him. The sun still hung in the sky, but he knew, when you look out upon the ocean, the sun moves fast. When it hints at its final descent for the day, it wastes no time, sinking quickly into the ocean. It teases with a final display of oranges and vivid purples before disappearing entirely. Blackness waits impatiently, right behind it.

This diary, however, was more than compelling. He had a little time before the sun left him alone in the house. But he was no longer afraid. Not of her. He knew she had led him to the diary, and in that, felt a certain sense of security, albeit slight. He picked up the diary again and continued to read.

––––––––––

There was a heavy smell of gardenias wafting from the bushes up ahead of him. Not unpleasant, it was like the heavy perfume of an old woman. Kennedy found himself wandering through a park, grass-covered hills all around. He heard a guitar and people singing as he walked, not a care in the world. He smiled. The sun felt good on his face.

She was sitting on the grass in a group of people. They were all stoned, hanging out, singing. She was smiling, too, and motioned with her finger for Kennedy to come sit beside her.

"Hey, Soldier. Where'd you go?" Lydia asked as he plopped himself down beside her, crossing his legs. The others in the group welcomed him with smiles as they sang along with Bobby and his guitar. Kennedy thought he recognized pieces of the song they were singing. He did. But only in bits here and there. Afterall, it wasn't famous yet. Not like it would be.

"Just hanging out."

"I'm glad you're here. I wasn't sure if I'd see you again."

She turned her focus back to Bobby and the group and began to sing with them. Kennedy was struck by the sweetness of her voice. Innocent and beautiful. The more she sang, the more he wanted to hear. She was captivating, sitting there on the grass. Like before, she had flowers in her hair. Only more now. Almost like a crown. Another girl sat behind Lydia playing with her hair and adorning her with still more flowers. She would become famous, this girl. Nobody could resist her.

She turned her eyes suddenly at Kennedy. With an irresistible smile, she leaned into him and placed her mouth upon his. Her hand on the back of his neck, she pulled him tighter against her and bit his tongue tenderly. Just as quickly, she sat back and continued singing as the girl with the flowers leaned in to kiss him as well. Everybody was kissing everybody.

"Hey people," Lydia said, when Bobby had finished the song. "This here is Soldier. See," she said, pointing to the patches on his shirt, "he's the warrior of peace." Everyone nodded and said hello in one way or another. He was welcome.

"Soldier, you know Bobby and Dale. This is Katie, Mia, Tommy, Little Ben, June in the back there, and our very own Mr. Jack, the witch doctor."

Jack opened his coat and revealed several fat green baggies of weed. "Always open for business," he sang. "Goddamn the pusher man!" Kennedy smiled at Jack. He disliked him immediately. There was a different sort of energy about him than the others sitting in the circle. He wasn't there for the same reasons. Like a vampire, he was there to feed off them.

"Seriously, man, why the army getup?" asked Jack. "You for the war or something?"

Kennedy looked down at his shirt. "No. I don't believe in the war," he said. "I just like the shirt, man."

"Cool. That's cool. Why don't you come on down to the Avalon tonight," Jack said, changing the subject. "I'll see you have a good time. I lined up a good band, too… Purple Crow."

"Hey, Jack," Dale said. "You're in tight with Purple Crow, right?

Whaddya say you get Lydia a shot at a song with them? Girl can really sing, man."

"That's not a bad idea, little man. Not bad at all. You cool with that?" he asked, looking at Lydia.

"Very cool," she said, smiling and nodding her head.

"Let me see what I can swing," Jack said and stood, brushing the grass from his jeans. He pointed his finger at Kennedy and winked. "See you tonight, soldier man."

Lydia leaned against Kennedy as Bobby started strumming another song. She hummed quietly along with it, her eyes closed. Kennedy closed his too and smelled the flowers in her hair.

The sun began setting before the small group finally began to break up and go their ways for the evening. Some had houses to sleep in. Others wandered away to find a warm comfortable place to crash. Many of them would just huddle together, keeping each other warm, sleeping there on the grass under the oak trees up on the hill in the park. It was not an unusual sight, groups of kids, buried together under their blankets. Not in Haight-Ashbury. It was the norm.

Lydia lived down the street in the attic of a large Victorian with Bobby and Dale. It was converted into a two room apartment, had a small bathroom and a make-shift kitchen. They all slept together in one room. She nudged Kennedy on the shoulder.

"Hey, I gotta get going. Gotta shower. Will I see you tonight?"

"Yeah, I'll be there."

"Cool," she said, and kissed him on the forehead. "If you need a place to crash, Bobby and Dale are cool if you want to stay with us."

"Yeah, thanks," he said. Dale turned and looked at him and gave him a quick thumbs up. Lydia rose from where she had been sitting, took one of the wilted flowers from her hair and tossed at him. She smiled, waved, and walked down the hill, sort of dancing as she went.

"Nice, isn't she," Dale said to Kennedy. "You dig her, I can tell. It's cool, man. Don't be shy. We all do."

Bobby was snoring and curled up in a ball next to them. Kennedy rubbed his face and ran his fingers through his matted hair in an effort to comb it. It had gotten so long.

"Yeah, she's real," he said finally.

"Wait 'til you see her tonight, man. I'll bet she blows your mind. Outer space. Jack's gonna shit his pants. Just you wait."

They hung out together a little while longer, there in the park. Dale could not stop talking and telling jokes. Bobby woke up not long afterwards and joined seamlessly into the monologue. The two of them were like bookends. Not twins exactly, but they definitely belonged together. They would harass and make fun of each other, with unspoken permission of course. But ultimately, one could not finish a sentence without the other's input. A natural comedy team is what they were, and they had Kennedy laughing nonstop, in a way he could not remember. He sat there, gazing at the two of them, his stomach aching from laughing so hard, and thought, these guys are not real. They can't be. They're like Martians or something.

"I'm a caveman," Kennedy shouted. "I'm hungry. I need meat."

There was a sudden moment of unrehearsed silence. Only the bay breeze rattling through the branches overhead was audible. Then, almost on a count of three, each of them simultaneously burst into a riot of uncontrollable laughter. It went quickly from being funny, to being completely out of control. They fell over on the grass, tears poured down their faces, and for Dale, breathing actually became difficult. Bobby fell backward and rolled down the hill. Later, talking *about it over burgers, nobody knew why exactly, it had been so funny. But who cared? The duo was now a trio.*

Tonight, between the three of them, they had managed to scrape up enough money to eat something. Burgers. Big, fat and smothered in cheese. They had a large order of fries between them as well. Some nights were not as easy.

To all of these rambling gypsies, money was like firewood when you're camping. You never have enough of it. And for some reason, you don't even realize it until the sun falls on its face and suddenly, it's far too dark to go out and hunt for wood. It sort of sneaks up on you silently, like a lion hunting its prey and hits you from behind, and pulls you mercilessly down into the dirt.

Now and again, there was an issue with hunger. But for the most part, they ate. Tonight, they ate. Bobby had a certain secret he didn't like to talk about. But the secret always yielded a few extra dollars in his pocket and kept him and his brother fed. Lydia, too. Nobody needed to know how he got the money. Dale knew where and how he was getting it, but knew better than to press him for answers. It wasn't something Bobby was proud of. Nobody needed to know about that shit. And tonight, that secret had fed Kennedy as well.

Music was pouring out of The Avalon already as the three of them stumbled down the sidewalk. A line of people crowded in front of the old brick warehouse, waiting to get in. Purple Crow was a very impressive band, in an era where young musicians would find themselves banging away in their parent's garage one day, then suddenly spinning around the globe, jamming, partying and sleeping with such like-minded artists as Mick Jagger, Janis Joplin, and Jim Morrison... It was happening daily, as if they had grown up together. Along with the war, perhaps even due to it, a sudden shift in culture had dramatically changed everything. Now, in terms of music anyway, if fame and fortune knocked on your door, the door swung open instantly. Bands were forming and being signed by major recording labels almost on a daily basis. Everyone dreamed of it. And nowhere was it more possible than San Francisco.

Bobby, Dale and Kennedy made their way down the sidewalk, still giggling, as they had been for the last several hours. A massive black guy stood at the door with his bulging arms crossed defiantly over his chest, watching everyone as they obediently showed their ID's to another guy, far smaller with a greasy little mustache, sitting next to him on a wooden stool.

We're on the guest list," said Bobby. The black man turned his face toward them and blocked the doorway. "There ain't no guest list tonight," said the guy on the stool. "Three bucks. Each."

Luckily, Jack stepped up between them. "It's OK my friends. These guys are cool. Personal friends of Purple Crow and the soon to be famous...Lydia Carter. Please, stand aside my friend, for you are in the presence of royalty," he sang, as he pressed a small, paper tab of LSD into the bouncer's open palm.

"I told you I'd show you a good time," Jack said, as he wrapped his arm around Kennedy and ushered him past the bouncer and the crowded doorway. An immediate onslaught of bright blue and purple lights swirled across the darkened cavern inside. Kennedy stumbled slightly, finding it almost impossible to see where he was walking. He was forced to rely upon Jack, only holding a small amount of comfort in that Bobby and Dale were right behind him.

"I got her a spot," Jack yelled over the music. "She's back stage right now, getting ready to go on. You guys are just in time." Jack had also managed to secure a small booth situated just above the crowd. There was a small table and a row of padded seats with a perfect view of the stage. As they sat down, the thin smile slipped from Jack's face as he impatiently motioned for a waitress. It was as if he became another person for an instant and did so in such a way as to remind Kennedy of a southern plantation owner commanding his slaves. He ordered beers and shots of tequila for the three amigos.

Purple Crow had just ended a song and the crowd began applauding. Eddie, the lead guitarist, was struggling against the noise to tune his Stratocaster. A small, rail-thin guy dressed in black leather pants, he stepped up to the microphone. He probably weighed a hundred pounds. Ninety of it was hair. It was difficult to see his face and what was visible of it was covered in purple octagonal sunglasses.

"Thank you. Thank you very much," he said. "We're Purple Crow and we love your city. Thank you for having us. We might just stay a while." Again the crowd erupted in appreciation. Everyone was drunk and flying on something. Even though this was a small club show with a not-so-famous band, it was easy to get caught up in the moment and imagine this was the big time. People were excited and ready to party the night away.

"I have a very special guest I'd like to introduce to you," Eddie continued. "From the city of lost children…children who have found their way… One of your very own, will you please welcome… Sweet Lydia."

Again the house broke apart with a violent thunder of applause. It was deafening. Kennedy and the others rose to their feet and joined the throng. Lydia bounded onto the stage from behind and moved to the front. She looked like a completely different person, every bit the rock star Kennedy knew she was destined for. She wore the same tattered jeans she had from earlier that day but also a pair of suede leather, purple boots that came almost to her knees. A long flowing shirt, swirled in competing patterns, opened down to her stomach and revealed just enough to cause panic in those at her feet. A single strand of fake pearls fell around her graceful neck.

The band slammed immediately into a song as Lydia grabbed the microphone from its stand. This was not someone intimidated by crowds. This was not someone afraid of the stage. From the moment she stepped up, she owned everyone in the room. And when she opened her mouth the place went into full cardiac arrest. Kennedy was speechless.

Of course, he had heard her sing before, but he felt as though he was witnessing true divinity here tonight. He was smiling so heavily, that his cheeks began to hurt. Her voice was sweet and tender, yet forceful enough to command her audience. Kennedy, as well as everyone in the entire bar, was mesmerized.

Jack was seeing something entirely different in Lydia. He too had a smile plastered across his face, but his enthusiasm was based more on the fact that he considered the people's response as an obvious sign of success. His success. He suddenly saw Lydia as someone he had discovered and someone that might just take him to the top. He didn't know how right he was.

Noticing a face that he recognized, he rose from the table and screamed to Kennedy and the others as best he could over the music. "I'll be back! Order more beer." Then he melted into the crowd.

Kennedy barely noticed. He certainly didn't care. Lydia was all that he wanted right now. She owned him and he loved her for it. Bobby kicked him in the shin and grinned at him. He pointed his finger at Lydia and they both shook their heads in agreement. That was their girl up there and she was good. Better than good.

The song finished too soon as far as Kennedy was concerned. The crowd was screaming. Purple Crow stood up on stage, amazed as well, looking to each other as if they couldn't believe the response. Eddie stepped up to Lydia and threw his arm around her and whispered in her ear. She nodded her head and said something back to him. He gave a few instructions to his band mates and then shouted to the crowd. "Looks like you might want a little more!" Whereupon the music kicked in again and Lydia stepped forward.

This time it was a much softer melody. And it was an angel that was revealed, arms outstretched, blessing the crowd. She danced slowly, swaying as she sang and bent graciously to the people, now pressing themselves up against the stage. They were every bit in love with her. Kennedy closed his eyes and listened, her voice speaking only to him.

Jack saw none of this. He was too busy doing business with a guy he had met a couple of months earlier. Harold James. A record producer from Los Angeles. Jack had spoken to him earlier in the week and he had casually mentioned that he might be here tonight. Jack was counting on it, hoping to sign a deal for Purple Crow. He had not dreamed he would pull an ace from the deck in the form of Lydia.

Harold James was as impressed with her as everyone else in the place, and for someone who was trying to scratch out a career making records, Lydia was the answer to his prayers. The beginnings of a record deal were put on the table right then and Jack became Lydia's new, self-appointed manager. She would thank him later.

Lydia finished the song, again to a tremendous response from her new fans. "Thank you so much," she said. "Really, I had fun. I wonder," she continued, "if there is a soldier in the house." She placed her hands over her eyes, shielding them from the brightness of the stage lights, peering out into the darkness of the smoke-filled bar, searching for Kennedy. "Bobby, Dale, Soldier... I love you guys."

———

"Hello? Anyone here?"

Kennedy's eyes jerked open at the sound of someone shouting outside the house. He sat up, having fallen asleep there, and closed the diary. The room was ice cold and a shiver ran down his back. Confused, he was not sure how long he had been there, but it was bright daylight now, filtering through the dirty panes of glass. Evidently, he had slept through the night on her bed.

On the front step, detective Sam Blakey knocked on the open door. He was more than just a little on the heavy side. At fifty years old, his metabolism had not kept up with his passion for food and his bulging gut hung from below a well-worn tie. But despite his lack of physical charm, he was a pretty damn good cop. He had served on the force since his twenties and knew his job. He loved it.

"You live here?" Blakey joked, as Kennedy came down the staircase into the light from the doorway.

"No. Just visiting," Kennedy said. "What can I do for you?"

"I'm detective Sam Blakey, LAPD. I'm looking for a Ronald Stenton. You him?"

"No, I'm Father Shawn Kennedy. I couldn't find him either."

"He's been reported missing last couple of days. That's his car there out front."

An all-too familiar white light smashed instantly through Kennedy's mind like a bolt of hot lightening. It was a re-occurring "gift," providing strange glimpses of things he could otherwise not have possibly known. In quick flashes, he saw Stenton's face, eyes closed, his head surrounded by leaves. There was a cigarette too, still burning, lying on the ground. That was it. That's all he saw.

"Yeah, I know," Kennedy said, pushing back the throbbing in the side of his forehead. "But he's not here. I don't know where he is."

"What's your business here?" Blakey asked.

Kennedy scratched his head, preparing to give an agreeable answer, knowing full well there wasn't one. Another officer stood out beyond the gate, searching through Stenton's car. He looked up at waved at Blakey.

"Detective!" he yelled. "We got blood over here!"

Blakey eyed Kennedy suspiciously and asked his business again. No matter what Kennedy said, he knew it sounded really stupid. How do you tell a cop that you are trying to get rid of a ghost without sounding like a raving lunatic? You don't, and Kennedy didn't.

"I'm going to have to ask you to turn around," Blakey said, "and place your hands behind your back."

"Look, I really don't know where he is," Kennedy said.

"I'm believe you. Sorry, it's just procedure. Now please, just turn around." Kennedy shook his head and turned as Blakey snapped the rings of cold steel around his wrists and took the diary from his hands.

"What's this?" he asked.

"Just a book. A diary. I didn't kill anybody with it."

Blakey thumbed through it, unimpressed, closed it and with a firm hand on Kennedy's shoulder escorted him back toward the waiting unmarked squad car.

A spotless black Mercedes 530A sat down the street. The man inside held a well-used Nikon on his lap and waited patiently. The ocean breeze had picked up a bit, keeping the edge off the hot afternoon sun as he watched the two detectives put Kennedy into the back of their car and slammed the door shut, all of it captured in crisp frames of digital color.

CHAPTER NINE

As a reporter for the Times, there were worse beats than the Police Department. Tony Adams had long ago given in to the idea that his career in journalism probably wouldn't take him much further than this. At least he got to write about some juicy stuff once in a while. He even made the front page occasionally in a given year. Some people out there might even recognize his name.

He knew Detective Blakey, and waved at him as he trudged into the department following Kennedy in cuffs. "Be with you there in a second Tony," Blakey mumbled. Get some more coffee."

"No thanks. I'm too young to die."

"Aw come on, you pussy. There's no such thing as strong coffee. Just weak men."

"I like strong coffee," Tony said. "I just don't think that shit qualifies as coffee. It tastes like it came out of a horses ass."

"Actually, I think today we're serving 100% cow," Blakey said, as he sat Kennedy in a chair next to his desk and unlocked the cuffs. "Either that or moose. Not sure."

Kennedy sat patiently rubbing his wrists while Blakey sat down at his desk and opened some files on his computer screen. He put on a pair of battered glasses and looked over at Kennedy asking his name again and how to spell it.

"Am I under arrest?" asked Kennedy.

"Not just yet. What's your relationship with Stenton?

"None really. A friend of mine, Father Bernardo, was working with him."

"Father. Another priest?

"Yes, a priest. He's just died."

Blakey raised one eyebrow at Kennedy and began entering the information into the computer. Tony Adams just sat against the wall with his feet propped up, listening.

"How'd he die?"

"Heart attack it looks like. He was doing a bit of house cleaning, too, for Stenton."

Blakey swung his chair around and put his elbows on the desk and grinned at Kennedy. "House cleaning… meaning ghosts. Is that what you're telling me?"

Kennedy nodded his head and Blakey looked over at Tony, turned and shaking his head, entered it into the computer.

"Occupation?" Blakey asked, whacking away on the keys.

"Priest, like I said. Father Bernardo was a friend. When he died, I thought I would see what he'd been up to. That's how I know Stenton. But that's it."

"You have an address?"

"It depends. St. Augustine's just below Crescent City for the next six months or so. Unless I'm reassigned. But for the moment, I'm staying at the Waldorf downtown."

"Must be nice," Blakey smirked. He filled in a bunch of other information, saved the file and hit print. As the papers spit out from the printer, he grabbed them one at a time and placed them in a folder.

"Anything else, you'd care to add?" Blakey asked. Kennedy just shook his head. There wasn't really much more to say, again, without sounding like a mad man. Blakey placed Kennedy in a small holding cell by himself and promised it wouldn't take long to check out his story. As it turns out, it was about two hours before Blakey returned and opened the door, releasing him. He handed Kennedy the diary, his wallet and keys, and escorted him down a long corridor out into a dirty lobby filled mostly with disheveled women waiting for their drunken husbands to be released.

"I wouldn't go back to that house any time soon, there Father," Blakey said. The company that owns it has requested all your activity cease. And if you do leave town, drop me a line first, would ya? If we don't find this Stenton pretty soon I might want to come visit you again."

With that, he smiled again in a way that was starting to irritate Kennedy. It probably irritated everyone including his mother. Kennedy exited the department, stopped and looked around. He removed a piece of gum from his mouth and tossed it into the bushes, pulling a new piece from the dwindling pack in his pocket. He unwrapped it and systematically replaced the old one. Tony Adams was sitting on a bench with a paper cup half-filled with coffee, scribbling notes in a journal notebook jammed full of loose papers. He stood to greet him.

"Hey ya Father," he called out as he approached Kennedy. "What you said back in there, you're serious, aren't you."

"No, I'm a nutcase."

"Nice. Tony Adams. LA Times. Listen, if you're up for it, I'd like to know what you dig up, so to speak. You never know on things like this. I might be able to help. Besides, I like nutcases."

"You got a card?"

"Yeah, I got one here somewhere," he said, fishing around in his jacket pockets. He produced several damaged business cards and handed one to Kennedy. "But I'll do you one better. Give me twenty minutes. I'll buy you a cup of real coffee. I could use one after that crap in there."

"Coffee sounds good. Besides, I don't exactly seem to have a car anymore. Rental. Sort of left it behind when I got arrested."

"You live in the city?"

"No. Just…visiting. Staying at the Waldorf."

"Fancy. No worries. I'm happy to give you a lift if you need. Call the rental company…they'll pick it up."

"Thank you. I think I might just take you up on that."

"Coffee first? Tony motioned toward the beach. They shook hands and walked away from the police station. There was a hot dog street vendor an easy walk away and, despite his humble establishment, Tony knew he served some of the best coffee in LA.

They grabbed a couple of cups and Tony paid with several crumpled bills. It was the only money he had on him. No lunch today. He poured several spoonfuls of sugar into his coffee as Kennedy looked on. They retreated to a bench, the ocean lying flat and lazy in front of them.

"So, like ghost hunting, huh? Sorry, but I was sort of eavesdropping back at the station. It's what I do. You actually seen one…a ghost?"

"Many times. Twice this week." Kennedy said, pointing to the large, fresh scratch across his face as evidence. "The first time she wasn't too friendly.

"No shit. Oops…sorry, Father."

"Don't worry about it. I'm a priest, not a saint."

"Good. Saints make me nervous. So like, tell me about it."

"I'm not sure what there is to tell. Ghosts don't just hang around for no reason. If we have a man in jail who says he's innocent of killing her, there's a good possibility that's a reason. It's the only thing I've got, sort of."

"Sort of."

"Yeah. I found her diary," he said, holding it up for Tony to see. Tony took it and fanned the pages.

"No shit."

"No shit. Actually, she showed me where it was.

"And this ghost…Lydia Carter?"

"My guess, yeah."

OK, this is good."

"But that's where it stops," Kennedy said, a look of apology on his face. "I got nothing else to really go on. Truth is, I'm not even sure I want to try."

"What do you mean?"

"I don't know, but I have no idea how I get involved with this kind of crap…why I can't seem to just have a normal life."

"Nah, I don't buy that," Tony said, taking a gulp of his coffee. "I know people and I don't get that from you." He took another hit off his coffee and wiped his mouth with the back of his hand. "Listen, maybe I can help. Find some shit out. That's what I do. I could just dig around and see what's shakin."

"Maybe. Let me know. I'm staying at the Waldorf."

"So I heard. If I find anything, maybe I'll stop by and raid your mini-bar."

"Refreshment lounge. Be my guest, if there's anything left after I get back."

Tony liked Kennedy. The feeling was mutual. They both stood and shook hands, neither remotely aware that the man across the street shooting photos was not just another tourist.

The few that knew him, or knew of him, referred to him simply as Nash. He was a clean-up man, the kind of guy you call in to take care of messy situations before they get even messier. A seasoned professional, he could be trusted to do whatever it took to deal with the problems, keep everything clean and running smoothly.

It appeared an irritating Catholic priest, one Father Kennedy, was turning out to be one of those problems and it was Nash who was called in to set things straight. He placed the camera in a silver metal case on the passenger seat next to him and closed the lid. He had what he needed for the moment and decided to drive the short distance to a private little place he kept up in the canyon. He had an appointment with Hampton later in the day and had just enough time to go download the photos, make some prints and perhaps have a little fun with one of his special guests whom he had picked up the night before on the strip. She was waiting patiently for him to return and he didn't want to disappoint her.

He drove the distance in a matter of half an hour and pulled his Mercedes into an open carport beneath a row of overhanging eucalyptus trees. He checked his rear view mirror and scanned the property. It was quiet with the exception of the slight ticking noise from the engine as it cooled. He grabbed the camera case and stepped from the car, fumbling with the keys to several deadbolts on the door leading from the carport into his kitchen. Closing the door softly behind him, he redid the locks and took off his jacket, tossing it over the back of a long, red leather couch.

With a thin fire wire cable, he hooked the camera up to a computer sitting on a small desk in the living room. He clicked open the file containing his work that morning and began to download them into a folder on the hard drive. Reaching for a leather case on the desk, he removed a dark, slender cigar and slid it into his mouth, then selected several of the shots. An almost silent printer proceeded to spit out crisp digital prints of Kennedy and Tony Adams, laying neatly, one on top of the other in the tray. Nash picked up them up and thumbed through them quickly, admiring his work. Pleased, he lit the end of his cigar and slipped the photos into a large manila envelope.

Placing the envelope into the metal case, he rose from the desk and went over to stand in front of the living room window that looked down over the brown and yellow canyon below. First his shirt, then his pants, he removed his clothes, standing completely naked in the warm morning sunlight and stretched his six-foot chiseled frame. Dark blue and purple tattoos ran the length of his torso, cascading down his back, celebrating death, an ensemble of jawless skulls at the very center. He turned and walked into the bedroom and looked down at the pale, lifeless prostitute tied to the bed.

His large hands slowly crushing her throat, she had died the previous night. Her timing had been in perfect unison with his, taking her final breath just as he finished with her. He stood over the body, admiring his trophy. From a small drawer in the nightstand next to the bed, he removed a small, wooden box and opened the hinged lid. Inside was a jar of blue ink, several needles, rubbing alcohol and some antisceptic wipes. He held the box and sat at her cold feet, there on the edge of the bed.

The needle was sharp. He actually enjoyed the pain as he made a series of punctures, pushing the ink deep under his skin. She had no name, this hooker. In his twisted way of thinking, she had simply been born into this world for him, for his pleasure, and he marked the occasion on himself, recording it along with twenty-seven others, neatly lining the inside of his forearm.

He wiped the blood off with a clean antiseptic wipe and placed the wooden box back in the nightstand. She was actually quite beautiful as he gazed at her, lying there, eyes frozen open. Probably not yet twenty years old, nobody would ever miss her. They never did. Maybe a greasy pimp, but it was simply part of the business and he would just have to replace her and chalk up another loss.

Nash stroked her long blonde hair away from her face. Her skin was smooth and cold now as he leaned over and kissed her. She would be good for one more night. He lay down and placed his head on the pillow next to her, propping it up slightly on his hand, and gently began touching her.

CHAPTER TEN

Kennedy was back in his room and in way over his head. And he knew it. One minute he was enjoying the peace and solitude of a quiet monastery, the next he's a suspect for the murder of some real estate agent that had gone missing. He had innocently flown to Los Angeles to see Bernardo, a distant friend who needed him, and despite his current state of burnout and the need for escaping the cares of the world, he had come to his aid. He had never expected he would become embroiled in a full-on scandal. But above all, he had never imagined he would come to find Lydia.

He sat on the small hotel sofa and opened her diary, running his fingers over the flourishes of her delicate handwriting.

—— April 7, 1968 ——

People are calling us the Love Generation. I think that is very cool. Most of us are hip to it, but there's still a lot of shit going down around here. The Man sweeps the streets almost every day. The People are fighting it, but it's getting out of control. It isn't fair. We are not wanted here. They keep telling us to go home. But I am home.

———————

Growing patterns of blue and bright yellow swirled like melted electric butter in front of Kennedy's eyes. He reached out and stirred it slowly with his finger and smiled at the way he could control the flow of the colors, drawing it one way and then another, creating a symphony in the air.

Lydia sat watching him, perhaps seeing the same show. They were sitting together up on the top of Hippie Hill. There were kids everywhere. It looked like a traveling circus, everyone wearing the most outrageous clothes. Flowers adorned every head of wild, beautiful hair. A new generation of dreamers and artists, most of them looked as if they should still be in high school, but they were here now, from all parts of the country, following the streams and the rivers, drifting down the mountains, until they had all come together in the Haight. Dirty, hungry, and lost, at least now, they had each other.

There was a deeper love here, genuine acceptance, and this wonderful gift they called Orange Sunshine. Jack, the pusherman, had been spreading the stuff on the streets and at the music halls, getting everyone hooked. He was making a a good deal of money off of it, too, but nobody cared.

Lydia grooved to a song playing gently in her head. Small white daisies began to grow up, forming circles in the grass all around them. Lydia smiled. Couples held each other, enjoying distant trips of their own imagination. If only the other people in the world could understand, there was a better way.

Lydia took Kennedy's hand and began to trace her finger along the lines in his palm. She looked at her own palm and the lines began to connect, forming one intricate pattern of rivers that disappeared into their skin and flowed throughout their bodies and into their hearts. They were not two separate people. They were one. She looked up into his eyes and could see herself looking back. Perhaps they had switched bodies, flowing into and around each other and neither had been aware of it, until now.

"I want to see the ocean, Soldier," Lydia said. "I want you to make love to me in the ocean."

Kennedy smiled at her and, standing up, bowed gracefully, her majesty's ever-obedient servant. He began to dance around her in circles playing an invisible flute. He took her hand, helped her to stand and, still dancing, led her away down the hill.

Quite a hike to Ocean Beach, they strolled down Haight, headed toward Golden Gate Park as the people of the kingdom streamed passed them, greeting them with two fingers, beautiful smiles and an occasional kiss carried on the wind. Everyone knew who she was and they all loved her.

One girl with pink daisies painted on her cheeks, not a day over sixteen, stepped up to Lydia and handed her a show flyer announcing her own gig that evening.

"Will you sign this for me?" she asked.

"I don't have a pen," Lydia said, smiling. "But if you tell me your name, I will make sure they let you back stage tonight and I will sign it then. We can share some weed together."

"I'm Petal. Peace," she said and wandered away. They would never see her again. And they would never remember meeting.

On the corner of Ashbury, Dale and Bobby were sitting in the open attic window of their apartment passing a small ceramic pipe back and forth and releasing great puffs of smoke up into the air. They both smiled and waved down at them. Kennedy imagined the tall Victorian was a turret in a gigantic stone castle and that they were guards keeping watch over his city. Flowing red banners, trimmed in gold whipped in the wind above them. He waved back and bid them good day, granting them leave to resume their duties.

As they continued, passing the Free Medical Clinic on Clayton Street, Jack Hampton stepped out onto the sidewalk.

"Are you two flying?" he asked.

"We're birds. That's what we do," Lydia said.

"That's cool. Just make sure you're at the Matrix by 9:00 tonight. Back stage and ready to rock. I have more treats."

"Treats are a wonderful thing, Mr. Jack."

"And I'm the one who will always give them to you," he said, looking at her and then at Kennedy. "You too, Soldier boy."

Kennedy put his arm around Lydia's shoulder and pulled her away from Jack. "See you tonight, Mr. Jack," he said. "But for now, we must part, for the ocean is singing our names, calling us home, to live...and to love. Alas, we can not, we shall not... deny her."

Lydia laughed softly as Kennedy began to dance again, holding her hand there in the street and turning her in a circle. Jack studied them from the sidewalk as they wandered away. Kennedy turned and waved at him. He didn't wave back.

They walked on together, singing a song which they took turns making up, passed Cole, Shrader, and Stanyan Streets, then on into the big park. Freaks were everywhere and everyone was high. Couples made love in the open out on the grass. Others sat around examining the flowers, playing guitars, and generally just wandering around looking for a place to fall down.

They both knew the ocean was just north, beyond the park, and if they kept walking, they would eventually run into it. The police routinely raided the park, so it was not safe to stay there over night, although many kids had no choice. Many chose to harbor down by the ocean instead where it was easier to hide from the cops.

Coming finally to the end of the long stretch of the park, there was a well-worn, dirt path curving down the side of a hill that led out onto the open sand. A group of kids had a large bonfire going and were gathered around roasting a bag of marshmallows, licking them from their fingertips. They greeted Kennedy and Lydia as they approached and urged them to sit down. Kennedy became mesmerized by the long orange flames leaping up, desperately trying to escape. Someone started singing a Stones song and they all joined in.

A young woman they called Naomi, maybe in her early twenties, stood, crossed her arms at the waist, and pulled her long dress up over her head. She stood completely naked there in front of the fire and immediately started dancing, moving gracefully, the flames her partner, reaching up into the air. She wore her dark brown hair pulled back into a thick braid, forming a crown around her head and had inserted a sprig of green leaves and daises along each side. Her hair was so long, it fell almost to the back of her knees and, as she spun in slow circles there around the fire, the braid swung outward in an arc. Everyone watched in wonder as pychadelic trails followed behind it, trying desperately to keep up as it passed them by.

Then another girl, moved by this display of freedom, joined her, casting her dress to the sand and began to dance beside her. The men were not going to miss out on any of this and, in mere moments, everyone was laughing and helping each other out of their clothes. One fool threw his pants into the fire, chanting over them, an offering to the gods, never imagining that he might actually need them later.

Lydia too, stood and unbuttoned her dress, letting it fall to the sand at her feet. She stepped out of it and turned to face Kennedy. He reached up to touch her, but when she turned toward him, laughing, teasing him, she ran away, full speed out toward the ocean.

Kennedy pursued her, but could not reach her before she plunged into the surf. He yanked at his shirt and threw it behind him as he ran. He kicked off his sandals and stopped short of the tide, jumping up and down on one leg at a time as he struggled to remove his pants and under shorts. Lydia was bouncing up and down, up to her stomach in the waves, watching and laughing hysterically as Kennedy attacked her,

144

splashing as he ran forward and throwing himself into the water next to her like a dive-bomber.

He came up from beneath the swirling foam, his hair dripping and slicked back against his head. He grabbed Lydia in his arms and lifted her up into the air and plunged her back down beneath the cold green waves. She came up screaming as Kennedy took her again, firmly in his arms and kissed her mouth. She yielded instantly, her tongue tasting the salt. He wrapped his strong arms around her and lifted her, gently this time, and carried her to the edge of the water where he laid her down in the soft, wet sand. The fire blazed across the beach, and everyone was still dancing.

"I love you, Soldier," she said.

Kennedy smiled at her and touched her sweet face, pushing the wet hair back away from her mouth. He placed his fingers on her lips and she closed her eyes as he gently kissed them. The waves crashed softly behind them, rhythmically, rolling over their bodies, carressing them, as they lay there at the edge of the world.

He wrapped himself around her, and together, slowly, they began to match the rhythm of the sea, moving in time, one against the other, the intensity building like the waves beyond them. Lydia sat straight up as she felt the sudden rush of ecstasy, a violent series of intense convulsions shaking her body, followed almost immediately by those of her lover.

The water pushed up and circled around them, then slipped silently back again. Lying there afterwards, they held each other for a long time as the sun began to fall away, never wanting the moment to end. But eventually, the chill of the cold sand convinced them to pull themselves apart and retreat to the dry beach. They stood, still touching each other, kissing tenderly, and walked hand-in-hand, back toward the warmth of the fire.

They wrapped themselves in a blanket that somebody offered them and sat down in front of the delicious burning driftwood. The effects of the acid had long since waned and, together, they were pleasantly floating down. The hypnotic flames and crackling of the logs lulled them into a feeling of complete satisfaction and peaceful heaviness as Lydia pulled the blanket tight, leaned against Kennedy and drifted off to sleep. Kennedy too, closed his eyes, listening to the sounds of the fire and two girls humming softly. The flames were hot against his face as he held Lydia's soft, naked body tightly against his beneath the wool blanket.

Time was patient and the sun took its time for once before finally deciding to end the day. A ragged, dirty seagull waddled around them and flew away when Lydia finally opened those astonishing, blue eyes and rolled over. She looked up at Kennedy through astonishing eyes and with a raw innocence that caused him to melt inside. He remembered their love amidst the waves as vivid pictures flashed through his mind. There was never a time like this. And he wanted to be with her forever.

"We should probably be headed back," she said, stroking his smooth black hair away from his forehead. "Jack will explode if I am two minutes late."

She was scheduled to go on stage at the Matrix at 9:30. Jack had lined up all sorts of important record people to come out to the gig tonight. Tonight was, in fact, what they had all been working so hard for.

The band had formed, or reformed, the night Lydia had first stepped onto the stage at the Avalon. What started as a simple guest appearance, immediately became an offer to be

146

part of the band, due largely in part to Jack's timely footwork. There was nothing to consider, really. Everything they wanted was sitting on the table in front of them. Together, they were all looking at becoming seriously famous. Nobody passes up a deal like that. In the course of two songs, Jack had signed a record deal and everyone was in full favor of Lydia becoming part of Purple Crow.

They had played together for several months now and just the last two months in the studio. Tonight was the night they were going to make the charts and celebrate the release of Tin Roof, their first album.

"Where are our clothes?" Kennedy asked.

Lydia started laughing, their situation suddenly dawning on her. It had not seemed important to keep track of them. Kennedy began laughing as well, as he realized they were both naked under the blanket and if the ocean had moved in, taking their clothes away, they might have to bare it all to the world, through the entire Golden Gate Park, on their way back up to the house. It wouldn't be the first time someone had done that. Hopefully no cops would be around to intervene.

"Let's go hunting," he said, tossing the blanket aside and standing to his feet. Lydia rolled over on her back and closed her eyes. "I can't walk," she said. "Carry me, Soldier."

Kennedy laughed at her and turned around, obediently kneeling in the sand. Lydia quickly seized the opportunity and sat up, wrapping her arms around the back of his neck. He dropped the blanket and lifting her easily, stood and carried her on his back, down the long stretch of beach in search of their lost clothes. There were others, too, still on the beach, mostly like them. It was not out of the ordinary to see naked hippies on the beach. Nobody cared. Lydia certainly didn't. She thought it was beautiful. And it was.

Retrieving their clothes was not difficult. Only a little time consuming, as pants and shoes were found, dotting the shoreline every so often. It was evident they had come off in pieces as they made their way down the beach. Unfortunately they never were able to find one of Kennedy's shoes and he decided to cast the other one into the waves to join it, forced to walk home barefoot.

Holding their clothes in their arms, they decided they had found everything they needed and started to get dressed. As Lydia slipped her legs into her dress, however, pulling it up around her waste, Kennedy stepped up behind her and yanked it back down again around her ankles. Lydia screamed and ran after him trying to pull at his pants. He finally allowed her to catch him and grabbed her by the arms. She looked up at him as he gently leaned into her and kissed her.

Her soul melted. Her knees buckled willingly as he laid her down once more in the sand.

If she was late tonight, tonight of all nights, it would still be worth it all. After so many years of emptiness and pain, only this strange man, her Soldier, had been able to uncover her heart. She closed her eyes tightly as the waves built, climbing like moving walls, growing higher and higher inside her until she could not hold them back any longer. She dug her fingers deep into Kennedy's back and pulled at him, exploding like the waves themselves.

Jack Hampton sat in the tall weeds at the edge of the beach, watching them, biting his lower lip, high up on the edge of a rocky cliff several hundred yards to the south. The sun was plunging quickly into the ocean now, performing in its daily *talent show of colors. He did not take any particular notice, blind to beauty, not even remotely interested in it.*

———

By 8:00, Lydia and Kennedy had returned to her apartment and managed a shower, rinsing the sand and salt from their afternoon in the sea. They would have spent longer in the shower perhaps, but the clock had refused them that pleasure. Along with Bobby and Dale, they had eaten whatever they could find in the refrigerator, some bologna and old cheese, scrambled it with some eggs and dined on their last poor man's meal.

Sitting back stage now, with the other members of Purple Crow, she and Kennedy had made it with fifteen minutes to spare. The air was thick with excitement. Even though they were going to debut their album, they were still the opening band for Sopwith Camel, a much more significant band, but Lydia didn't care. She loved Sopwith Camel and was proud to share a show with them. Not everyone from Sopwith had arrived yet and it was getting to be time to get on stage. If they had any idea who Lydia was about to become, they would have regretted not being there tonight. She was about to change the course of history.

Jack was up on stage now, thanking the impressive crowd for coming out and told them they were great. He was talking about their money, but they didn't know it and responded with great applause. Jack greedily soaked it in. He loved it.

Lydia stood and kissed Kennedy on the forehead. She smiled at him and waited for Jack to finish his bullshit so she could take her rightful place beneath the lights. To a packed room of thundering appreciation, she and Purple Crow stepped out onto the stage. Standing room only, the house lined to the walls.

"Wow, you're all so beautiful," she said into the microphone. "Are you as high as me?" Again the mass of people erupted in staggering applause, screaming as loud as they could. Eddie slammed his guitar in gear, the lights came up full and bright and Purple Crow was off and running. Lydia began to dance as the drums filled in and the people went crazy. Many of them had seen Lydia perform before, but it was different tonight. Everyone seemed to understand they were witnessing the rise of a new star.

Jack's plan was working. It was easy to see Lydia was a money-making machine and that the song they were playing was an obvious chart-buster. "All of Me" was a song she had written with Eddie earlier in the month and tonight was the perfect night to introduce it. The record executives in the house were digging it even more than the crowd. They smelled exactly what Jack was hoping they would. The fun part would be after the show, when they would fight once again for Jack's signature. This time with a much more structured, multi-album deal. He was a powerful man tonight and it felt better than any drug to him. This was his definition of rock and roll.

Then, Lydia began to sing and his fate was sealed. The record executives had exactly what they were always searching for. She was everything they wanted. The way she sang. The way she moved. And unbelievably beautiful.

Standing next to Jack, Kennedy watched from behind the amplifiers on the side of the stage. Two guys stepped up and tapped Jack on the shoulder, shoving their hands at him as he turned. They didn't want to wait until the end of the show *to make their offer. Jack winked at Kennedy and stepped into the shadows behind the stage with the two cool cats in an effort to see how much blood he could drink.*

The second song, "Rambling" was a balad Lydia had written on her journey to San Francisco two years ago. Purple Crow had put their own mark on it, but it was pretty much the same as when she had written it and the people soaked it up. It became immediately apparent that she had a second hit and the other executives in the back began to search for Jack.

Kennedy watched Lydia beneath the lights, taking control of the stage. It was hard to imagine he knew this person. Intimately. She had seemed so much the lost little girl in the light of day, but here, this was another world, her world, and she ruled it. Kennedy could not stop smiling and thought about her that afternoon on the beach. This incredible girl singing her heart out to all these people, was his girl. He wanted to be with her, not just now, tonight, but forever. He was caught up in the energy of the moment, and the music seduced him. This was his world, too and he had never been happier.

The lights began to flicker and dim and the people just beyond the stage disappeared. The sound of their applause dipped. Lydia too, drifted slowly into the darkness and faded away. Kennedy struggled to see her, but she was gone now.

———

The lights flashed, glowing, becoming suddenly bright, flooding his vision. His eyes squinted, fighting against the onslaught, trying to adjust. Kennedy was sitting alone, on the couch in his hotel room, the diary spread open on his lap in front of him.

CHAPTER ELEVEN

Hidden behind dark, gold-rimmed sunglasses, J.W. Hampton sat in a padded, white iron chair in front of a ridiculously large, shimmering blue pool. It had been appropriately designed in the shape of a guitar. He wore a large, cotton robe that he allowed to fall open, exposing his already tanned skin to the sun. Behind him stretched a palatial mansion, secured somehow into the cliffs overhanging the ocean. It looked more like a castle made of glass. Everywhere, graceful palms, strategically placed in sets of three, bent in unison, as if slow dancing together, in the gentle morning breeze.

He sat here, next to the pool almost daily, making calls and checking his stocks on a thin silver laptop. His money was everything and he never felt comfortable if it was too far away from him. As far as he was concerned, the more access he had to it, the more he could make.

He watched passively as a young blonde girl, whose name he'd forgotten, swam naked, diving to the bottom in the deep end of the pool. Another, also blonde, and also naked, lay on the side of the pool, smearing oil over her shoulders, bronzing in the sun. Her name was Julie, or at least that was one of their names. She waved at Hampton, wiggled her breasts at him and smiled, unable to tell if he was looking at her or not. He ignored her, pretending not to see and sipped a rum and coke, swirling the ice in the glass.

Both girls not only looked like something off the pages of a magazine, they in fact were. One of his magazines. He owned three. He also owned a film production company, porno, and a handful of other smaller entertainment and distribution companies, including a majority share in AMI Records. All said and done, he was a king in his own right. Self-made, too, he would tell you. But it was AMI that had made him rich. The rest were just for fun and a convenient way to launder everything.

Nash approached from house, slowly descending a series of stone stairs leading from the upper terrace down to the pool. He carried a small leather brief case in his left hand and raised his right in silent greeting. Jack motioned for him to sit next to him. Neither spoke.

Hampton examined his closely cropped bleached hair. His jaw was razor sharp and he looked as if he could snap you in two with his hands if he wanted to. Nash set the briefcase on top of a small table next to them and peopped the locks open, lifting the lid. He removed a manila envelope and handed it to Hampton.

"He's a priest," Nash said as Hampton slid several 8X10 glossies of Kennedy out of the envelope.

"I'm aware of that," he said as he thumbed through them.

"The other guy there is a reporter. Tony Adams. Los Angeles Times. Nobody."

"Godammnit!" Hampton said. He spit as he shouted and used the back of his hand to remove the residue from his chin. "That's all I need now is a fucking reporter getting into this thing. And a priest… Why's a priest snooping around in my trash cans?" he asked.

"Trust me, I'll find out," Nash said. "And when I do?"

"I don't fucking know. Be nice. I don't have time for any more shit right now. Just make the son of a bitch go away."

The briefcase was snapped shut again and Nash sat patiently, waiting for any last instructions. But Hampton was done with him and his attention had drifted back again towards the girls by the pool. They were together now, kissing and Nash followed his gaze.

"Nice pair," he said, stood and walked back up the stairs.

———

Tony Adams sat at his small desk at The Times in a sea of bustling reporters. Everyone was wired from non-stop coffee and the undying hope of a breaking story. To the casual observer, they resembled a colony of ants, continually bumping into each other, sidestepping to the right or left, carrying on, driven to complete their important tasks. It was a chattering madhouse of one-sided conversations, ringing telephones, and the continual clicking of keyboards.

Tony had loved the energy from day one. It was as addictive as the coffee. He often felt as though he were situated in the middle of history as it was happening and being recorded each day. He loved being a reporter, even if he never would become famous or win the Pulitzer. It was a great job.

The police beat was rather trying at times, sometimes boring, yielding the same old stories about the same kind of criminals. But it really wasn't all that bad. As a side benefit, he had come to know everything that was going on in the city, underneath, where most people would never want to look. It would scare the daylights out of them. But to Tony, it gave a certain sense of comfort, just knowing the truth. It made him feel more awake that way. More in control. He had taken an immediate liking to Kennedy, perhaps for that very reason.

Kennedy, with his crazy little story, seemed a man interested only in pursuing the truth, simply because it was the truth. Plus, if he was right about Lydia, that there was more to her murder, just think of the story it would make. He rubbed at his unshaven chin, grabbed the coffee cup from the corner of his desk and stared up at the ceiling looking for some sort of direction.

"Something cooking?" Alice Watson asked, rapping a long yellow pencil against the arm of her chair.

Alice was a serious '60's throwback who sat at the desk just opposite Tony. She was more than a few years older than him, but he still found her rather attractive and never minded if she butt into his thoughts. In fact, he quite welcomed it. She wore faded jeans regularly and refused to dye her shoulder-length hair. Tony thought it made her all that much more interesting. Behind her librarian black-rimmed glasses, Tony knew there was an incredibly intelligent woman. But that's not what he saw when he looked at her. It was far from what he imagined.

"Yeah, I got something weird," he said.

"Weird's good."

"This is big time weird. What do you know about Lydia Carter?"

"Oh, I lover her! Huge fan. Why?"

"I found a guy, a priest...thinks maybe there was foul play in regards to her murder."

"Uh, I think that's sort of the meaning of foul play."

"Whatever. It gets weirder. He says he's seen her. Like you know..."

"Her ghost?"

"Serious. He's a priest. Why would he lie?"

"Priests do all kinds of things they aren't supposed to do from what I hear. I don't know. Maybe he's not all there. I mean, a guy would have to be half crazy to go off and be a priest in the first place if you ask me. What else did he say?"

"There's this guy in prison, for killing her..."

"Perkins. Howard Perkins."

"Exactly. He says he didn't do it. It's been almost forty years, man. He's already in for life, I mean, what's the point? He might as well just admit it, unless he really is innocent."

"I remember him," Alice said, placing the pencil neatly behind her ear and leaning towards Tony. He liked it when she did that. It reminded him of a schoolteacher or something. He found himself examining her delicate mouth.

"I was in my early twenty's, twenty two or three," she said. "I can't remember... but this guy was plastered all over the news, Life Magazine, everywhere. He was a total freak."

"Yeah, but what if he was an innocent freak?"

"There's your story. Write it. Even if it's not true, it might lead somewhere fun. Start digging the grave up and see who pops out." She took the pencil from behind her ear and returned to her work, scribbling something down, immediately erasing it and blowing the pink residue onto the floor.

"You've got a way with words," Tony laughed.

Thanks," she said, with a quick wink. "Let me know if you find anything."

Tony's coffee was cold. His coffee was always cold and he hated it. He put the cup down onto the desk, shoved it aside and logged onto the internet. He typed in the name Lydia Carter and hit enter, immediately rocketing him to hundreds of fan sites dedicated to her music and her memory. Tony was impressed. He knew quite a bit about Lydia just by being alive, but she had been before his time and he had never realized her significant popularity and how it had survived even to this day. Nostalgia is a strange thing, and evidently, when it came to Lydia, a lot of people refused to let it go. Based on the overwhelming number of sites he found, it would appear Lydia was more famous now than when she was alive.

Tony sat back for a second and laughed. His mind was racing. Forty or so years after she was dead, she was still famous. Now that's a rock star. He did a quick search on current record sales and discovered that she had steadily sold an amazing amount of records despite her death. In fact, sales had increased, often outselling the new stuff.

"This is pretty good," Tony thought. "The obvious question… who's getting the richest from all this? Just follow the money."

———

Kennedy walked the streets of the business district. It was still and gray in the few hours remaining in the day. People were stirring and the traffic had already begun thickening hours before.

He hadn't been able to get Lydia out of his head. It was a stupid dream. Just another one of his uncontrollable visions. He knew that. in reality, he had done nothing to forsake his vows…but her skin. Her touch. The taste of her mouth. The intensity of their shared pleasure. No, it had not really happened. He had done nothing wrong. Yet, even in his struggle to justify himself, it posed certain questions that seered a hole directly through his heart. Something had happened to him there in that house. And he could think of nothing else.

But now, walking in the cooler evening hours, holding Lydia's diary, he felt an increasing sense of calm. His mind was still racing, but he had returned only to help her. His intention was one of setting her free. His emotional or sexual feelings for her were not relevant and certainly not based on any level of reality. Normally he would have turned to Bernardo in a situation like this.

Bernardo was the kind of man that, whether he knew how to handle a difficult situation or not, somehow made concrete decisions all along the way, leaving you with a sense of confidence that he had traveled that road a thousand times and that he knew exactly what he was doing. It was that confidence that Kennedy needed right now. None of this made any sense. What had really happened to Lydia and why was she still hanging around? And the better question, who the hell did he think he was and could he really do anything at all to help her?

A towering Gothic Cathedral spire with a cross on top appeared up ahead of him, peering down from between two glass skyscrapers. The juxtaposition was odd, yet Kennedy found it beautiful. Two worlds colliding. Existing side-by-side in spite of their differences. Perhaps because of them or perhaps, when it came right down to it, business and religion were not all that different. Even so, the Gothic architecture drew him closer and he walked down the sidewalk and turned the corner until he came upon the church, St. John's, with its columns and balustrades, gargoyles and angels, standing there alone in a sea of modern angular boxes stretched into the sky.

He felt the inside of the pocket in his blazer where he used to keep the black beads. Old habit. He hadn't prayed in several years. The last time he had confession was with Bernardo and that must have been five years ago. It all seemed so futile. Painful if nothing else. Why go through it? God never answered. He never spoke. It was a one-sided conversation at best. It certainly wasn't the relationship he had been promised and it left him feeling somehow cheated. The only conclusion that had developed, deep down in his gut where he kept it hidden, was that God did not really exist at all. Despite any signs of His existence, it was almost easier to believe He wasn't really there, rather than that He had simply chosen to ignore Kennedy.

He found himself ascending the steps toward the massive arched front doors. They opened quietly and the familiar smell of incense floated out to greet him. He stepped inside the entry allowing the door to swing just as quietly closed behind him, plunging him into an eerie darkness. It was not uncomfortable to him. His eyes adjusted to the flickering candlelight as though he had been born in it. This was his world, familiar and safe. And despite the blackness of the main sanctuary, he could see straight across and up to the altar.

An older woman knelt by herself towards the front of the church, praying silently, her eyes fixed upon the gruesome crucifix hanging over the altar. The thorns piercing His head and the nails jutting violently from his palms, the blood pouring from His wounds… it was all crafted and painted with such great detail, that it appeared real. Whoever had been given the task obviously enjoyed it. Plaster saints lined the walkway on either side of the sanctuary, looking down sadly upon Kennedy as he took a seat in the shadows toward the back.

He laid the diary down on the padded seat next to a small toy dinosaur some child had left behind. Kennedy picked it up and turned it over in his hand, mindlessly feeling the bumpy plastic scales. He too stared up at his supposed Savior. He had died so long ago. It was foolishness to hope that he might ever come back. But not to the wrinkled gray woman ahead of him. Not to the millions just like her sprinkled on altars throughout the world. It was the hope that kept many of them breathing.

Kennedy sighed and placed the toy back down. He pulled the kneeler down into position and leaned forward with his hands resting on the worn wooden pew in front of him. The candles throughout cast a dancing show of dim shadows as he placed his forehead softly on top of his folded hands. His thoughts were now empty. There was nothing to say.

"Press on," he heard Bernardo whisper. "Seek and I promise, you will find."

"But I don't want to," Kennedy muttered aloud. "I am tired of all of this. The answers… they never come."

Outside a group of faithful pigeons gathered on the steps. Perhaps the old woman inside fed them each day. If so, to them, she was God. Kennedy pushed the great doors open and squinted at the brightness. The morning sun bounced blindingly off each building, happily repeated again and again like an unwelcome reflection from a hundred mirrors. It was getting late now, he should probably eat something and his stomach told him so. But as he made his way back toward the hotel, all he really wanted was to sleep again, to be with her.

CHAPTER TWELVE

The hotel elevator bank opened onto the corridor just several doors down from his room. As Kennedy stepped out into the long hallway, he withdrew the plastic coded key from his pocket and began to place it into the lock, before noticing that his door was slightly ajar. Housekeeping was cleaning his room, he assumed, and pushed the door aside.

It certainly wasn't housekeeping, unless they had done an extremely poor job. His suitcase had been turned upside down on the bed and all the drawers had been gone through and remained open.

As he moved deeper into the room, still not quite sure what to make of it, a hard metal barrel was placed gently against the back of his head.

"Nice and easy there, Father. No need for violence," Nash said in a deep, quiet voice behind him. "I just want you to listen very carefully, because how you decide to play the game means whether or not you get to live. Goes for your friend Mr. Adams as well. You start digging in other people's back yards and you start playing around with things maybe they don't want you playing with. It's none of your business, Father. I'm going to tell you this once. Pack your rosary and go home."

"What about Lydia? Does she get to go home?" Kennedy asked.

"You don't listen very well. I said go home, Padre."

Nash raised the gun quickly and brought it down hard across the back of Kennedy's skull with a crack. He pitched forward, out cold, hitting the floor by the side of the bed, the diary still clutched in his hand beneath him.

She was with him immediately, stroking his hair as he lay, head in her lap. He looked up at her, the sun forming a bright halo behind her head. She smiled.

"Hello Soldier. You've been asleep."

Kennedy sat up and rubbed his eyes. They were sitting comfortably in the back of a large tour bus rumbling down a highway with tall fields of corn growing thick and green on either side. Other members of her band sat around in different parts of the bus smoking and playing guitars. A few dozed.

Toward the front of the bus was Eddie, picking gently on an old battered acoustic twelve string. Edward Tuttle, Jr., born the first son of a shoe salesman from Fresno, California. Lydia referred to him lovingly as Mr. Turtle. He never seemed to mind and referred to her as Little Sister.

Eddie was the lead guitarist of Purple Crow and had a way about him, a style of playing, where his fingers never seemed to do what you thought they were going to do. Unexpected, always beautiful, his playing always led you off on some quick, magical journey, then safely deposited you right back into the melody of the song before sweeping you away once again. It was his style and Lydia's voice that had launched the band so quickly onto the national scene. That and Jack Hampton's shrewd sense of the deal.

Tommy Curtis, self-named "the Bone King," was the drummer of the band. He had a zest for life that showed up in his love for anything illegal, especially drugs. Heroine was his true love, but he often fooled around on her with whomever was in the room, so to speak. He was sitting directly across the isle from Eddie, eyes closed, keeping time with his hands against his knees, the sound of a full band roaring somewhere in the concert halls of his head.

Stretched out on a long red velvet couch was Tinsel... Jeremy Farrow... bass, keyboards and back-up vocals. He wasn't much for talking but the boy could sing. Truth is, he was much more of an accomplished musician than any of the others. He could actually read music while the others just sort of played by ear. They called it grooving.

Tinsel was sound asleep with his mouth wide open, snoring softly. Lying next to him, also sound asleep, was a young girl he'd found out in the cold in Minnesota after a show one night. Her name was Feather and that's all anybody really ever knew about her. She was as thin as a razor blade and looked like she was not much older than sixteen. One thing for sure, she was madly in love with Tinsel.

There were a few key roadies, Mac and Will, and Johnny their ever-faithful driver, sharing a joint by an open window up front. The other roadies were in the trucks behind them hauling all their gear. They would pick up additional crew in each town as needed, to unload and set up, break down and reload. Plus, you could always depend on a little help from the other band's crews, if you treated them right. Usually, everybody playing a gig acted like one big family and there was so much drugs and booze… it wasn't hard to treat them right. Jack was always the answer man. He could get anybody to do anything, because within reason, he could get them whatever they wanted. Liquid. Solid. Smokable. Shootable. Male or Female.

Jack was there, too, sitting just ahead of Lydia and Kennedy, his head propped against the window, trying to sleep. He wore a large brown felt hat pulled down over his eyes shielding them from the sun outside. With a full beard now, it clashed against the bright swirls of orange and purple velvet on his shirt.

On either side of him were a couple of long-time groupies, two sisters who would swallow anything he fed them. Both of them had red hair and looked like a pair of freakish bookends. The one on his right, Blaze, was strung out on something and had been flying around the bus earlier that morning singing and removing her clothes one piece at a time, giving each piece an exotic fairytale name before tossing them out the window at the passing cars. It might have been mildly erotic if she hadn't been so damn ugly. Her hair was made out of fiberglass and her skin looked like it had given up years before, pale, stretched thin, covered with an odd collection of freckles and one very disturbing mole on her hip. She was long gone now and probably would sleep right through tonight's show, waking alone later, in the cold bus, wondering what had happened to her clothes.

Rose, the other sister, was another story. It was never actually verified, but everyone assumed they were sisters. She had a mass of red hair as well, but preferred to play the quieter side of life, often lost in her own world, singing to herself and smiling all the time. It lent a sweet sense about her and nobody really understood why she was with Jack. Maybe she wasn't. Maybe she was just into Blaze and Jack was in the middle. He was pretty mean to her most of the time, but it never seemed to bother her. She just kept smiling, which seemed to bug the shit out of Jack all the more.

Now and then the bus would hit the bumps in the highway and shake like it was going to rattle the bolts loose. It gave you the feeling that it had seen better days and might not make it through the tour. Outside, lonely farms passed by the windows. Tractors and a sprawling museum of odd, rusted farm machinery sat out in the fields, waiting for tomorrow to begin, yet again, before the sun rose. Everywhere along the way, tall grain elevators stood lifeless like space ships. Ancient rotting barns, some edged right up against the road, others a mere dot on the horizon, waited painfully to finally give up and fall down.

"Where are we?" Kennedy asked finally.

"Almost there, I think. Not exactly sure. I've never played in Des Moines before. Don't think anyone has," Lydia scoffed. "All I can see is corn cobs forever."

Kennedy laughed with her. She had the most incredible laugh. It almost lit the bus on fire.

"I think Hendrix played there once," Kennedy said. "But the audience kept mooing."

They both bust up laughing and Lydia reached over with her toes and jabbed them into Kennedy's armpit. He grabbed her foot with both hands and began biting her toes, causing her to writhe and squeal like a little girl. He loved the impish look in her eyes and jumped on her, pinning her down against the mattress, tickling her mercilessly. Both of them roared in laughter.

"People are trying to fucking sleep!" Jack barked from beneath the brim of his hat. Lydia rolled her eyes and held her middle finger up for him as a peace offering.

"Some people forgot how to be happy," she said loudly, smiling at Kennedy and reaching up to kiss him on the mouth. Jack raised the brim of his hat slightly with his index finger and peered coldly at Lydia as if to silence her with his stare. She bugged her eyes back at him and puckered her lips. He glanced at Kennedy momentarily, a quiet challenge perhaps, then allowed the hat brim to slip back down over his bloodshot eyes.

Johnny pulled the bus off the interstate and headed south. This was the last leg of Purple Crow's first album tour and it had taken its toll on everyone. Jack mostly. His once charming veneer had rubbed thin and although the tour had proved immensely successful, it became obvious to everyone in the band that Jack didn't really enjoy their company any more. He no longer hung around with them after the shows and was always off doing his deals or fucking some young hopeful with stars in her eyes and magic in her veins. Lydia didn't mind. That's just what Jack did and all the band *members knew their success was due largely to his efforts. But the fact remained, Lydia was the real reason. There were a million Jacks out there. There was only one Lydia.*

The people had fallen completely in love with her. If ever there was an overnight success, it was Lydia. Purple Crow had started the tour as a warm-up band at smaller shows in the Southern states. Now they were still warming shows up, but to much larger crowds than before, often packing entire stadiums along with other bands like Jimi Hendrix, Grateful Dead, Janis, Big Brother and the Holding Company, all the big ones. The coolest thing was that now, people were actually buying tickets and pouring into the shows…to see her.

Jack had another album deal already in the works. It would be less than a year before they were on the road again, and this time, if things went according to Jack, Lydia and Purple Crow would be the headliner.

The whole thing spelled guaranteed fame and fortune for everyone that could hang on. Lydia was on top of the world. She couldn't understand Jack's darkness. The more success they tasted together, the deeper he sank and the further he pulled away from everyone. For Lydia, however, the days of pain were over. She was alive and refused to let him ruin her party.

The cornfields eventually gave way, revealing the skyline of Des Moines perched ahead on the horizon. It wasn't much to look at, but at least appeared an attempt at civilization and brought renewed vigor throughout the length of the bus after all those miles of corn.

Everyone began to stir and talk amongst themselves as the city grew larger and the traffic increased around them. Des Moines was a real city after all. They were playing a place called the KRNT Theatre. It was right downtown as they exited the highway and fairly easy to find. 8th and Pleasant. It was a pretty impressive building and Lydia fell in love with it as they drove up to it. With a huge arch cut into the face, filled with a series of smaller arched windows and a row of several arched doors below, it resembled an old haunted church. But this was a popular stop on the concert circuit and evidently, Des Moines, kissin' cousins aside, had developed a taste for good rock and roll.

Tonight they opened for the Turtles, which Lydia thought was hilarious because that's what she always called Eddie. He thought it was funny, too, and told her he was entertaining the idea of switching bands just to shut her up. Tonight was going to be a great show. Because tomorrow, after long hard months on the road, they were headed back towards San Francisco.

Kennedy sat up and watched Lydia, gazing out the window like a little girl as the bus circled around to the back of the hall, looking for the loading dock. She was lying on her side in front of him, giddy and filled with energy. She was buzzing. With a quick, cat-like turn of her head, she winked at Kennedy suggestively. It was all too much. Unable to resist her any longer, he moved in to kiss her.

The bus turned abruptly into a narrow gravel alley and hit a massive pothole going too fast, practically tearing the frame from the wheels. Lydia screamed as Kennedy fell on top of her and smashed his head hard, back against the window frame.

———————

Kennedy groaned and rolled over on the floor of his hotel room. The early morning sunlight boldly penetrated through a crack in the heavy hotel curtains, creating a narrow yellow spotlight upon the carpet. His head was pounding as he sat up and reached back, feeling his hair, wet and matted with blood. The diary was still cradled in left his hand.

He managed to stand up and decided quickly to sit on the edge of the bed. His head was spinning as he suddenly rushed for the bathroom, vomiting on the tile floor before he could find the toilet. Kneeling on the cold floor, his head burned as he continued to cough and heave, the thick yellow fluid gushing from his throat and nose.

As the churning subsided, he moaned, wishing the blow had been fatal. He reached over the edge of the tub and yanked angrily at the faucet dial, producing an immediate cascade of water from above. Although still freezing cold, the sound alone brought a sense that he would survive.

He fought against his clothes, yanking at them and then, giving up, pulled himself half-clothed into the tub behind the plastic translucent curtain. He lay down, exhausted, on his back in the tub and closed his eyes, allowing the jets of water to beat down over his face and head as it slowly warmed. He managed, with great difficulty, to remove the rest of his clothes as a thin river of red found its way quietly across the floor of the tub and disappeared down the drain.

———

CHAPTER THIRTEEN

"Here, check this out," said Alice Watson as Tony plopped himself down at his desk. "You're gonna love it." She handed him a stack of papers she had printed out after doing a little of her own research on Purple Crow.

"What is it?" Tony asked.

"I don't know. You got me all excited the other day when you were talking about Lydia. So I just sort of started noodling around and found this. It's the rest of the band. They're all dead."

"Really," Tony said, looking up from the sheets of paper. "How'd they die?"

"Read. It's interesting to say the least. Fits in with your priest and his story. But I have to jam. I have an interview, so enjoy."

"Hey, thanks Alice," he said as she stood, putting on a small lime green corduroy blazer. She winked at him, grabbed her purse and headed out of the thick, swarming editorial department. Tony pretended not to watch her, but Roberta, an eternally depressed, heavyset reporter sitting three desks away, busted him good as he checked Alice out as she passed by. Roberta stared at Tony, closed her eyes and shook her head in disgust before resuming her work. Embarrassed, Tony swung his chair around and began to read the articles Alice had printed out.

Eddie McCallister, better known as just Eddie, lead guitarist for the popular band Purple crow, was found dead on August 7, 1973 from a massive overdose of heroine and a smorgasbord of barbiturates. His body was found naked, draped over a bed in his Los Angeles mansion at 2 O-clock in the afternoon by his housekeeper. Friends said that they had been with Eddie the night before and that he had seemed fine. He had been drinking substantially, but that was not uncommon for Eddie.

The article said that Eddie had found fame and fortune at the early age of 23 along with equally famous band mate Lydia Carter who proceeded him in a grisly shooting death two years before at the hands of a drug-crazed fan. Eddie had no remaining family, the article went on to explain, but would be missed by the millions who adored him. Funeral services were a private affair, attended only by close friends and key associates.

There was a color photograph of Eddie, live in concert, playing like a madman directly next to a screaming Lydia.

Tony set the article aside and continued with the next. It contained several photographs, one of Purple Crow drummer, Tommy Curtis. The other photo was an aerial shot of an accident scene on a lonely stretch of curved mountain highway where Tommy, evidently, high on amphetamines, had driven his motorcycle off a sheer embankment and into a deep ravine below. He had not been wearing a helmet and died instantly.

The article also mentioned Lydia's murder, as well as a brief synopsis of their rise to fame together in the late 60's amidst the new free world of peace, sex and drugs. He was just 29. There was more than a slight sarcastic tone to the story, jealously suggesting perhaps, that Tommy was obviously a spoiled drug addict who had enjoyed his success briefly, but had inevitably gotten what was coming to him. Let the reader beware sort of thing.

The next story was about Tinsel. Jeremy Farrow. Committed suicide by hanging himself with a sheet in a Los Angeles hotel room. He had been reported severely depressed by his manager, Jack Hampton and was drinking heavily the night before his body was found. It was also reported by Hampton that he had started several fights in a local nightclub leading to his being ejected from the club by security.

Prior to his death, Tinsel had destroyed the hotel room, smashing tables and lamps as well as leaving several large holes in the walls. At least three hotel guest disturbances had been reported in the early hours of the morning, prior to finding his body hanging from a sheet wedged into the door jam of the bathroom door. Jeremy Farrow was 32 years of age, single and left no family.

Again the relationship to Lydia was mentioned as well as a nice suggestion that her death was even more brutal and that both of them paid the price of rock and roll fame.

Tony put the story on top of the others and sat back in his chair. Within three years of each other, the entire band Purple Crow, one of the most popular bands of the decade, had met their deaths. How ironic. Evidently, the only one originally associated with Purple Crow who hadn't died a miserable death was this guy, Jack Hampton, their manager. At least somebody got out alive.

The thing Tony suddenly noticed was that it didn't really even seem to faze him, whether they were alive or dead. It was like suggesting that several people had been shot and killed during a war. Some live. Some die. It wasn't just that he was a jaded reporter, more than likely everyone felt that way. It was sort of expected.

The same held true for Purple Crow. All the rock stars were dying back then. They still do. That's what rock stars do. They go and they go and they go until they burst into a ball of flames. Rock and roll and self-destruction were one in the same. Everyone knows that. Some guy hangs himself or runs his motorcycle off a cliff… so what? People were waiting for it to happen. Even the die-hard fans, who would cry, holding candles and photographs in the rain, praying and mourning, all secretly loved it. It validated their worship and gave them an opportunity to have their loyalty publicly recognized.

Nobody missed Purple Crow. Nobody mourned for Lydia. They were gone. Together, they had blasted into stardom, then left the stage just as quickly, no encore, but leaving behind an impressive pile of hit records that would keep fans satisfied for generations. It was not an uncommon story.

Tony logged on to *Google* and typed in Jack Hampton's name and clicked return. Immediately, volumes of information came back, yielding page after page of stories, news and information about the man. Tony began to dig. The more he read, the more pieces fit nicely together like a jigsaw puzzle. Hampton's humble beginnings started with the band Purple Crow. He had, according to the articles, discovered them back in the '60s and rocketed them into stardom. He had capitalized on his success, used it to start several other bands and eventually launched his mega successful recording label; AMI Records. And the silver bullet, *Purple Crow*. Even after all these years, Lydia was still one of AMI's hottest selling artists. How's that for good fortune?

Tony looked at his watch and swore under his breath. He looked nervously up at Roberta, to make sure she had not heard him. In a jaded Los Angeles Newsroom, she was one of the few who claimed to maintain Fundamentalist Christian values and when you swore, she'd give you a fat chunk of scripture across the forehead.

He had scheduled a breakfast with Detective Blakey and was already late. It was probably, OK. Blakey would start eating without him, but still, it wasn't polite and Tony hated keeping anyone. He shut down his computer, grabbed his sport coat from the back of his chair and hustled out of the newsroom.

It had developed into a perfect Southern California morning outside. The smog had forgotten to wake up and left the sky an unfamiliar shade of blue as Tony grabbed a newspaper from the vending machine on the corner. He had been so engrossed earlier, that he'd never gotten around to reading it at the office.

He quickly tore through the pages in an effort to see how a small piece of his on a recent string of burglaries had printed. He found it buried on the bottom of page 23, smiled, folded it neatly and tossed the remains of the paper into an overflowing trash can. He popped his cell phone from his pocket and dialed Kennedy's room as he continued down the sidewalk toward Thurber's Café where he would meet Blakey. He wanted to talk to Kennedy first, though, in case there was anything new that he could run by Blakey.

"Hey ya, Father," Tony said as Kennedy picked up the line. "Thought I'd check in, see if you found anything new."

"Um, well...I was bludgeoned pretty good," Kennedy said.

Tony listened in astonishment as Kennedy quickly sketched out what had taken place. He stopped on the corner in front the café and placed a finger against his other ear. It was difficult to hear Kennedy's quiet voice over the rising sound of cars rushing by and the crowds of people hustling passed on their way to work.

"You OK?" Tony asked.

"I've been better."

"Listen, I did a little homework," Tony said. "Just a thought, but does the name J.W. Hampton mean anything to you."

"Not particularly. Should it?"

"Don't know. But he's the one that, as far as I can tell, has made the most money off of Lydia."

"Wait, I do know him. Um, Jessica Burton's boss. The big wig from AMI records," Kennedy said.

"Bingo. I'm not sure if it's anything, but after Lydia was killed, she became even more famous. Like a lot more."

"What does that mean?"

"Like she's still famous, Father. Hugely. In fact, it's weird. There's a whole new generation of kids out there now that are into her. It's like a retro craze or something. Old is cool. Her records never stopped selling. Ever. And they're selling more now than ever. So I figured, if there's any kind of foul play… you just find out who's getting rich off it."

"J.W. Hampton."

"He's the guy. He built AMI Records from the ground up. Guess who was his first artist?"

"Lydia."

"She built him an empire, man."

"Shit," Kennedy said. "The J. It stands for Jack, doesn't it.

"I don't know, yeah, I think so. You know something about him?"

"Yeah, I know something about him. Jack was Lydia's self-proclaimed manager, agent or something. In the beginning. Before she was big. He's involved with this somehow."

"You're sure."

"Dead sure. I just got whacked on the head and told to go home. It looks like I'm making someone very nervous just being in town. I know this guy. Sort of, anyway. Trust me, I know things about him. He's got his greasy fingerprints all over this."

"I found something else out, too," Tony continued as he turned to head into the café. Detective Blakey was seated at a table already and waved at Tony through a large plate glass window. Tony smiled and held up his hand signaling that he would only be a few more minutes.

"I wasn't sure if it meant anything," he said, "but I thought it was a bit weird." Kennedy listened quietly. "Well, it's just… Lydia wasn't the only one. All of them, the members of Purple Crow, Lydia's band… they all died within a couple years of each other. One OD'd. Another was in a motorcycle crash. And one guy hung himself. Weird, huh?"

"Very," Kennedy said. "See what else you can find out about this J.W. Jack guy."

"You got it, Father," Tony said. "Anything else?"

"Yeah. Don't call me Father," Kennedy said. "I hate that."

———

Sergeant Blakey loved ham and eggs. Actually any breakfast was a good breakfast, as long as there were eggs involved. But ham and eggs were the shit. Add sausage and coffee and you had yourself a little party. The only thing that made it better was that Tony Adams was buying.

Tony had called him the night before and wanted to see if he could check out a few details for him regarding Lydia's death. The trail had long since gone cold, as they say, and the files were probably non-existent. But maybe Blakey could find something. As it turns out, Blakey had already done a little digging and suggested they meet for breakfast at Thurber's Diner. It was Blakey's favorite spot, for breakfast anyway. After hours, it was Hooters or any number of the strip joints as long as they served cold beer.

Thurber's was bright and cheery. The waitresses weren't as friendly as the girls in the strip clubs and they wouldn't hesitate to pour a pot of boiling coffee in your lap if you tried to shove a dollar bill up their skirt, but the food was good and they gave you a ton of it.

"So, you said you might have something for me," Tony said, stirring the clumps of coagulated cream floating in a circle on top of his coffee.

"Well, yeah, maybe," Blakey said, his mouth crammed with eggs. "Something you should be aware of anyway.

Like I said, I did a little digging myself, on this priest of ours."

"Whaddya mean?"

"Turns out he's a whacko," Blakey continued. His fork never stopped working as he talked, swishing back and forth across his plate. Even as he stopped eating to make a certain point, he used it like a wand in the air, emphasizing certain key facts, before thrusting it back down into his pile of country potatoes.

"Most people lose it, they get sent to an asylum or something, right? A priest cracks up, and the Catholic church… they quietly send you away somewhere quiet. Like St. Augustine's. Ring a bell?"

"I don't get it. Like a crazy place?"

"Well, they don't call it that, exactly, but yeah."

"He doesn't seem crazy."

"Wait. It gets better. This guy, he's a full-on demon chaser. He goes around you know, like the Exorcist and shit. That's his friggin' job. I thought mine was bad. Anyway, so like he can't deal with it anymore, snaps or something, and they tuck him away, hush, hush, in this place way up north with a bunch of gay Nazi monks. Know what I'm sayin'? The guy's cuckoo."

"I don't know. He seems depressed maybe. But not like a psycho or anything."

"Just be careful, that's all I'm saying. Psychos don't always wear a sign around their neck. Him and the old guy, Father Bernardo Schmernardo whatever, they're the only guys in California that do this stuff, for the church, right? And we both know, the old guy turns up dead… and hallelujah, thank you Jesus, guess who shows up in town?"

"Well, they probably knew each other if they both, you know, do that stuff. Demons and whatever. How'd the old guy die again?"

"Kennedy claims it was a heart attack. But one of the guys at the office checked it out, routine shit, says he looked like a friggin' boxer or something. All beat to shit. Scars. The guy's fucking left eye was missing."

"Shit. I never knew being a priest was a contact sport. Father Kennedy had a nice little scrape across his cheek, too, come to think of it."

"Betchya he's got a couple of slash marks across his wrists, if you know what I mean."

The waitress brought more coffee and filled both their cups. She spilled some over the edge of Tony's and onto the table, but it didn't seem to bother her much. She just moved on to the next table and endured life until her shift ended. Blakey continued to shovel. He acted as if she might come back and take his plate away before he was finished.

"Serious, you think this guy's a nut job," Tony said. He instinctively wanted to tell Blakey about the conversation he had had with Kennedy moments before, about the attack in his hotel room, but something stopped him. For some reason, he wasn't sure he wanted Blakey to know everything just yet.

"That's not the only thing," Blakey said, shoving a piece of toast in his mouth and washing it down with his coffee. "Looks like this Stenton guy, the missing real estate agent… we did a phone record search and who comes up?"

"You're shittin."

"Last guy he ever talks to. And, according to his nosey secretary, it wasn't a pretty conversation."

"How the hell do you find all this crap out so fast?"

"Oooh, wouldn't you like to know. I'm a cop. I got connections. People in places, know what I'm sayin? The secret is, breakfast," Blakey snorted, slicing a chunk off his ham and shoving it in his mouth. "Keep buying me breakfast and I'll tell you things that'll make a reporter famous."

After they finished eating, Tony said good-by and headed back over to the Times to start his day all over again. He was a good reporter and had been trained on the art of due diligence and tying up loose ends. Blakey's opinion of Kennedy had the wheels turning and he realized his homework would not have been complete without a thorough check on him as well. He had liked Kennedy from the beginning, but Blakey's comments disturbed him. So did the new information he so quickly uncovered.

Another Google search yielded Kennedy's name attached to an article in the *San Francisco Chronicle* a little more than a year earlier. Mia Perlioni, a young twelve year-old girl from Fremont, California had died. The headline claimed, "Demon Possession Ends in Youth's Suicide." Kennedy had been interviewed, saying very little, but the article made it apparent he had been involved in a situation he described as having evidence of demonic possession and that he had attempted to free the little girl from a spirit that had been increasingly attacking her for several years.

The article painted a fairly clear picture of a situation in which proper medical attention had been ignored in favor of a much more antiquated approach and of a radical priest who, only increasing the child's psychological torment, had driven her to throw herself through a glass bedroom window of a two-story apartment building. She had hemorrhaged in the parking lot and bled to death. Charges against him by the State of California were pending.

So Detective Blakey had been correct in his assumption. Kennedy was a little loose upstairs and it had gotten him in trouble in the past. Tony did a search on St. Augustine's, the monastery where Kennedy had been staying. There was not a whole lot of information available, but from what he could find, it sounded more like copy stolen from a travel brochure, referring to it as "a sanctuary of peace and solitude nestled in the pines above the rugged northern California coast where spiritually-minded men could escape the rigors of the world in their quest for a deeper more meaningful relationship with God."

It was a psycho ward for religious nuts, Tony thought. That's what Kennedy was doing there. He knew Kennedy wasn't looking for a "deeper relationship with God." It sounded like a little girl had died because of him and he had either been running away, hiding, or had embarrassed the Church so badly that they had put him away there until he got his shit together.

So now this same priest had escaped or something, shown up in LA and was seeing ghosts again. Two people were already dead, another assumed dead, was still missing. And Tony had made friends with him. Nice work Sherlock. There were safer stories out there and certainly better ways to spend his time than chasing wild ghosts invented by some crazy priest.

He grabbed his empty coffee cup and hiked over to the coffee machine buried between stacks of old newspapers against the wall.

"How's the old music career coming along?" Alice asked as she came up behind him.

"Hey Alice. Not so good," Tony said. "Not sure. Wild goose chase, maybe."

"Don't look so sad," she said, pinching his cheek. "That's what we do around here, little boy. We chase geese."

She used her finger to draw her mouth up into a smile, encouraging Tony to do the same. He smiled back at her. She was irresistible and if she wanted him to smile for her, he couldn't help himself.

"Maybe set it on the shelf for a day, then take another look," she said. "Then decide."

"I know, but I'm on deadline all the time," he said. "I've wasted a lot of time on this and I'm gonna get my butt chewed if I don't start producing. Alice glanced down at his backside.

"Not much to chew on."

Tony laughed and poured the pot of dark black coffee, filling his cup. Alice held hers out and he filled it as well. They toasted each other and walked back to their desks. She winked at him and went quietly about her own business.

———

CHAPTER FOURTEEN

The phone rang on Jessica Burton's desk, yanking her into reality from a depressed daydream. She realized she had been sitting there, doing nothing but looking out the window. Something she never allowed herself to do.

"Jessica," the receptionist said. "There's a Father Kennedy holding for you."

"Thanks, I'll take it," she said. Kennedy's name brought a sense of sudden dread to her. She didn't really want to talk to him and wished he had never bothered her in the first place. But, something had been eating at her since she had met with him. The things he said. The worms he was digging up. The way J.W. Hampton had responded when she told him about Kennedy's visit. Everything reinforced a silly suspicion she had been harboring for years. A suspicion she had never allowed herself to pursue.

"Hi, Father. This is Jessica." She said in her most polished voice. "What can I do for you?"

Well, I had a visitor," Kennedy said into the phone. "Directly after our visit the other day. In my hotel room."

There was a moment of silence in which Kennedy allowed the words to sink in, hoping Jessica might seize the opportunity to confess something. But she was clueless and did not know what he was getting at.

"I was beat up pretty good, Jessica. And told to get out of town. Any idea who might want me to get lost?"

"I certainly don't, Father. That's terrible."

"So, I can't imagine, you hiring a thug to come whack me. It doesn't fit you. But did you by any chance tell anyone about our conversation?"

"Absolutely not," she lied. "Why would I do that?"

"I don't know. But not that many people even know I'm in town, or why I'm here and I thought you'd be a good place to start. So you didn't say a word to your Mr. J. W. Hampton?"

Jessica swallowed uncomfortably, not knowing how to respond. Each second of silence gave her away a little more. She had achieved an incredible level of success for someone her age and for her sex, and was always afraid that at any time, it might all just as easily slip away, like water through her fingers. It had happened to countless others in the company, men and women. Blow it somehow, get on the wrong side of Jack Hampton, and before the sun went down, you were living on the street.

Jessica knew all too well that her success and power were paper-thin and had always let that keep her from drawing certain conclusions. About the company. About Jack

Hampton. And about Lydia. But Kennedy had stirred something in her.

She had been raised Catholic but hadn't actually been to church in a hundred years. Even so, being in the same room as a priest sort of made her feel dirty inside, like all her sins were completely visible to him. And the fact that he was so good looking hadn't helped either. His quiet honesty was what she kept coming back to, though. She had treated him like any good corporate woman should, with a firm handshake, a cold smile and giving him nothing, then using him as a way of brown-nosing Hampton. Kennedy in return, had been real. And it made her feel dirtier than ever. As a result, he had been beaten up and she knew damn well it was Jack Hampton behind it. But now, she was afraid and didn't know how to respond.

"I'm really sorry for you, Father. Really, it sounds just horrible. But I'm afraid there's nothing I can tell you."

"I understand," Kennedy said. " I just thought you might have told someone about our conversation."

"No, I'm sorry." she said. It didn't get any more comfortable as she said good-by and hung up the phone. She felt miserable. In an effort to further her career, she bowed at the feet of Jack Hampton one more time and in the process, betrayed a priest. Judas.

An idea, a foolish one, flashed through her mind. She knew it was completely stupid, but found herself rising from her desk and walking down the corridor towards Mr. Hampton's office suite. Everyone on this floor knew, J.W. Hampton never came in to the office before noon these days, if he came in at all. For some time now, she had wanted to take a look into some old files that were really none of her business. She just wanted to know certain things. She preferred to think of it as innocent snooping.

She stood next to a series of filing cabinets in the hallway and waited for the perfect moment when Hampton's secretary was occupied on a phone call. With her back turned away, Jessica quietly slipped into his office and shut the large double doors behind her, careful not to let the latch click. She knew that, innocent or not, being in his office like this, alone, would be grounds for immediate dismissal. It made her feel like a spy. And actually, that's exactly what she was.

Hampton's office was disgusting. It looked like he had purchased all the furniture and trappings straight out of a mail order catalog for wanna-be rich playboys that a man his age should have long outgrown. He probably even had a king-size bed hidden within one of the walls. There was a full bar sunk into the wall, why not a bed? The proverbial "casting couch" was written all over the room. On the opposite side of the office, dark oak filing cabinets stood tall behind a massive polished teak desk. There was not an ounce of dust on it.

She scanned the rest of the room. There were no photographs of Lydia either, as she had suggested to Kennedy, and she found that odd. Hampton had discovered Lydia, or at least that's what she recollected. She was his big star. He had photographs of other mega stars on his walls. But not Lydia.

Jessica made for the filing cabinets and quickly rifled through the drawers until she landed on the right one. In an instant she had lifted Lydia's surprisingly thin file. She cradled the file and glanced over her shoulder at the closed door. Paranoia was thumping wildly through her veins and she could hear her own pulse warning her to run. Intuition told her she needed to get out of there immediately. Closing the file drawer, she slid the file up underneath her blouse and tucked it into her skirt. Taking a deep breath, she almost ran across the length of the office and grabbed the brass doorknob at the same time as Jack Hampton.

He opened his door and stood face-to-face with Jessica. Awkward is a term used when you say something stupid or embarrassing in an important Board meeting. This was worlds beyond awkward. This was sheer terror and Jessica felt a wave of paralysis rushing up from her feet and washing over her. Like a disturbing dream where everything grinds into slow motion, the clock thundering one loud explosive click at a time, it felt like an hour had passed as Hampton stood there, eyes of ice, not saying a word, but demanding an immediate explanation as to why she was there.

"Oh, Mr. Hampton!" she laughed. "You scared me. I'm so glad you're here. I have good news on the old estate in the Palisades."

"Is that so," Hampton said. He moved forward causing Jessica to step aside as he entered his office and looked around. He turned and faced her, placing his left hand firmly on the open door as if to shut it and her outside.

"Well? Give it to me."

"Oh, um…well, it looks like we may have a buyer.

"Seriously? That's refreshing. A serious buyer?"

"Absolutely. I just spoke with the real estate agent and he seemed very enthusiastic. I just wanted to keep you posted. Cross your fingers."

She smiled and excused herself with a silly wave of the hand that she knew made her look like a sophomoric schoolgirl. She had not spoken to Stenton in days and he had, in fact, not returned several of her calls. It was time to replace him. Especially now. She quickly glanced back over her shoulder as she headed for the elevators. The secretary looked up at her in surprise, then over to Hampton as he stood emotionless in his doorway, his cheeks hanging loose, watching Jessica.

The elevator doors opened and she stepped inside. She jammed the button to her floor and leaned her head against the rear wall as the doors safely closed her inside. She was stupid for trying such a stunt. She didn't even know what she had hoped to accomplish. Hampton never was in his office this early. Why today of all days? This was corporate suicide.

She felt the file beneath her blouse and pulled her jacket tight around it to conceal it even more. It felt like a massive wart on her nose and she was certain that anyone getting onto the elevator would notice it bulging out of her the second the doors opened. She was suddenly grateful that it wasn't any thicker.

Back in the safety of her own office, she closed her door, twisted the blinds shut and removed the file. Placing it on the desk as though it were poison, she stared at it and carefully sat down, opening it.

A large black and white photograph of Lydia stared back at her. Here was another woman, Jessica thought, who had suffered from too much ambition. She was beautiful, too. Jessica flipped the photo over and thumbed through a small stack of papers and a few other old notes about concert dates and personal requests. There was another photo of Hampton, much younger and sporting a beastly set of ham-hocks, his arm around Lydia, standing in the middle of the band *Purple Crow*. They were all smiling and holding up a copy of *Blind Heat*, their first gold record.

Her original contract was underneath the photo, a simple two-page, type-written document bearing her signature and Jack Hampton's, scribbled in faded blue ink. It was probably the worst contract she had ever read, and she had read quite a few. The wording sounded like it had come from the pen of a first-grader pretending to be a sophisticated lawyer. There were even colorful old English words, like "begat" and "unto thee" that made it sound as if it had been written by a drunken monk transcribing the King James Bible. It was a joke. But it was legal. And after struggling through it, it clearly stated that AMI owned everything. Lydia had been nothing more than a well-paid employee. The entire estate, song rights, the house in the Palisades, everything belonged to AMI. And AMI was Jack Hampton.

———

At his desk, Hampton played with a pen and pencil set, moving it back and forth as he thought about Jessica. Something was not right and it was making him angry. She had been nervous coming out of his office, which was very unlike her. She had always been so aggressive, eager to kiss his butt and prove that she was a doer. But never nervous.

This fucking estate up in the Palisades was killing him, too. It was worth a fortune and to this day, he couldn't unload it. He had made it a priority for Jessica to deal with it once and for all. He hated that property and everything it stood for. The sooner it went away forever, the sooner he could let old friends go. Why was Jessica in his office? He mindlessly pushed the pen in and out of its holder when a disastrous thought hit him.

Placing the pen down, he rose from his desk and practically ran for the filing cabinets. He could see it immediately. One of the drawers was slightly open as opposed to the others, closed tightly, the way he liked it. He yanked the file drawer open and searched frantically for Lydia's file, but knew damn well it was not there. His blood began to boil, his cheeks turning red, as he looked deeper into the files, not willing to believe that Jessica had really taken it.

She had met with that son of a bitch priest. He must have said something to her. He had to of. Something to get her to do this. Hampton had promoted her three times in the last two years. Why the fuck would she betray him like this? It didn't matter now. Jessica was out on her ass.

Hampton tried to calm himself. Everything was fine. He slammed the file cabinet closed but it popped back open, causing him to swear and push it closed again. He walked over to the bar, poured a glass of bourbon from a crystal decanter, guzzled the burning medicine, then poured himself another.

There was nothing in that file anyway that could harm him. He knew the contract was a piece of shit and that it pointed a finger directly at him, but so what? Nobody cared. It would take millions of taxpayer dollars to bring him down now and nobody was even remotely interested. He would laugh if the priest or Jessica even dreamed of bringing charges against him.

Why was this happening? Why now, damn it? After all these years. Jessica, he would be deal with immediately. The priest hopefully would just go away. But he wanted that goddamn file back.

CHAPTER FIFTEEN

When J. W. Hampton threw a party, it was an event like no other. Nobody wanted to miss it. You couldn't. If you were fortunate enough to be named on the list of the chosen, you showed up or you would never be allowed the opportunity again. Parties like this made careers. Deals were made over too much wine and piles of cocaine. Partnerships were forged during cigars. And a few lucky kids became stars, shooting high into the sky overnight.

One of those kids, Briana, a seventeen-year old Wisconsin cheerleader from Mackinac High, was bent forward over the arm of a leather couch behind the locked doors of the library, her new fake designer dress pulled rudely up past her waist. Jack, pants and boxers on the floor around his ankles, pounded her hatefully from behind.

The fact that he was hurting her made it that much more satisfying for him, ignoring her quiet tears. It was all part of the game. He knew it. And he had easily convinced her of it as well. The pain and eventual humiliation would pass soon enough and serve, she imagined, as the key to unlock the door to a dream she had kept hidden from her parents until the day she left home. Jack knew this. It was the same stupid dream they all had and he didn't have the slightest intention of opening any doors for her, unless however, there was a buck to be made by it. There wasn't. He was simply her teacher at the beginning of a very long and empty education.

He finished rapidly and without a lot of effort. Not exactly romance, passion, or sweat like she had seen on the big screen back home. He yanked up his trousers, zipped them shut and smacked her on the ass. He smiled compassionately down at her as she turned her face to him, bravely smiling back, a river of mascara destroying her cheeks. She wondered how her deal would take form next as Jack turned and walked toward the library doors and left her alone to figure it out.

He walked out into a swirling pool of sequins and tuxedos, taking hold of the hands that reached out to greet him. Everyone loved Jack. Tonight anyway. He would feed them lobster and fresh tuna. He would uncork hundreds of bottles of ridiculously expensive wine. They would all be plastered, screw somebody they hated and wake up the next day not remembering any of it. People laughed hysterically, hugging each other and telling bad jokes. Circles of conversation moved like amoebas splitting off from each other, then melting together with another, forming a new one. Richly dressed bodies spilled out onto the terrace and down the stairway and flowed around the pool. The pool itself was calm for the moment, sprinkled with tiny floating candles. But before the end of the evening, class, sophistication and clothing would be tossed aside yielding happily to the alcohol as it numbed inhibitions and ignited certain suppressed and darker desires.

Polyester Mood, a new band that had just signed a three-album deal with Jack, was putting on a fairly decent show from a stage underneath a tent erected on the side yard. More than a few drunken people were dancing on the freshly mowed grass, a few falling down, staining white silk with green ink.

Hidden in shadow, dressed in a black shirt and a equally dark Armani suit, Nash stood alone in the corner on an upper deck, smoking a Cuban and watching, amused at the spectacle around him. He cradled a fine woody scotch and gently tapped the bottom of the glass against the stone railing in time with the music. He was in no hurry and waited for Jack to find him.

Assuming he was someone of quiet importance, not a star, but better yet, a producer, two young hopefuls noticed him from below and agreed to do their best to take him down. He eyed them, blonde and brunette, barely clothed and bouncing intentionally as they ascended the steps toward him. He sipped the Scotch.

"Hello there, lonely guy. I'm Miranda, the brunette said in a silky voice. "This is my extremely close friend, Nonnie."

Hi," Nonnie said. I'm Norwegian. Or my mother was." Her voice was not quite as erotic as Miranda's. Nash thought she sounded more like a cartoon character trying to sound sexy. But she was frighteningly beautiful and chiseled out of stone. And by the way she looked at him, completely ignoring the laws of personal space, Nash decided it might be worth the effort to put up with them both. The two girls parted and stood touching him on either side. "Seriously, why all alone?" Miranda said, watching the party below with him.

Nash just stood there and looked down at her. He took a small puff from his cigar and blew it politely up in the air away from her. "I don't like people," he said, smiling. "They irritate me."

"Me, too!" Nonnie squeaked, as if she had found the little nugget they had in common. Miranda gave her a look that told her to shut up and let her handle this mysterious hunk of a zombie.

"Would you like us to leave?" Miranda asked.

"Are you interested in what I like?" Nash said, sipping his scotch. "Because if you are, I would very much like you to stick around. Both of you. But, you should know... I can be difficult."

"Can you? I love a challenge."

"Very difficult. People around me often end up dead."

Miranda looked at Nash, trying to figure out if he was being sarcastic or what. She could not tell. He turned his head and smiled at her. All the warning lights were blinking and Miranda knew she had made a mistake. He was definitely an interesting man, but he just gave her the creeps. He was too cold behind the smile. Nonnie didn't seem to care about anything. She was drunk and all she wanted was to get Nash out of his clothes.

Hampton had spotted Nash from below and proceeded to lift his heavy frame up the steps one at a time. "Ladies, you are absolutely beautiful this evening," he said, as he managed the final stair. "I wonder if I might have a moment with our friend, Mr. Nash here."

"Come on Nonnie," Miranda said, slipping away from Nash and taking Nonnie by the hand. "Let's let the boys play business. Nice meeting you Mr. Nash. Jack…"

Jack smiled and lifted his glass to both of them as they walked across the deck and down the stairs. Nonnie glanced over her shoulder and winked at Nash, wetting her lips with her tongue.

The two men watched the women descending the stairs. Neither spoke. The fabric on both their dresses was so sheer, it left little to the imagination. Both Hampton and Nash waited patiently. It was almost an unspoken macho obligation to watch that sort of thing.

"Thank you for coming, Nash," Jack said, pulling a cigar from his inner pocket and joining Nash for a smoke. He snipped the end from the cigar and popped it in his mouth, lighting it with a small blow torch. "I seem to have another slight problem that needs immediate attention."

"Tell me what you need."

"Jessica Burton, a young woman employed by me. She lifted a file from my office. I want that file."

"And the woman?" Nash asked.

Jack pondered the question for a moment, even though he knew damn well what his answer was. He had been drinking heavily throughout the evening, but booze no longer seemed to have the normal affect on him. He just became more dark and angry.

"I cannot abide by insubordination. I want her dealt with."

"Done."

The two men stood there above the swarms below and listened as the band jumped into another song, sending a new flow of people onto the lawn to dance. Jack sucked on his cigar and quickly waved the thick white smoke away from his face like chalk on a chalkboard.

"Any word on the priest?" he asked.

"Just a warning, as you suggested. I don't think he will bother you again."

"Good. I have always appreciated working with you, Nash," Jack said. "It gives me great pleasure to have people I can count on."

"You pay well."

Jack laughed for the first time and lifted his glass into the air. "That I do," he said. "That I do."

"If you will excuse me," Nash said, extending his hand. "I have a date with a mindless body that I must attend to." Jack shook his hand firmly and occupied the upper deck alone with his cigar as Nash descended and melted into the crowd, hunting for poor Nonnie.

***

Kennedy was drinking in his hotel room. He could no longer feel the pain in his head, although he should have. The bourbon had done its job.

The city was alive with light. Blinking and streaming passed in every direction, millions of people trying to get somewhere. It was all so empty, Kennedy thought. All of this was just plain stupid.

"So, what would you do, O great teacher?" he said out loud to Bernardo. "Why should I even care about all this horse shit? And look where it got you."

His bags were packed and sitting on the end of the bed. He had decided to check out and head back to St. Augustine's. A quick shot of bourbon had seemed like a good idea, but he was on his sixth and still had not checked out. He emptied his glass and through blurry eyes, stared over at the diary lying in the center of the bed next to his suitcase. He did not want to pick it up again. He was not built for this. Bernardo was, but not him.

When he was younger, he had seen strange things with Bernardo. Things that he imagined should have strengthened his faith. Instead it had shattered it. A young Mexican girl in a farm community just outside of Fresno had started speaking in different languages in the middle of the night shortly after her First Communion. Or the old man who kept seeing his dead wife in the mirror, only she would turn into a hideous creature when he spoke to her. Kennedy had stories. People heard things moving in their attics, lights would turn on at three in the morning and it had somehow become his job to fix it. And now Lydia. He hated it. He was supposed to be done with all this crap.

St. Augustine's had been his escape. His refuge. And Bernardo, like always, had pulled him back into it again. And this time, it was messy. His life had been threatened and he was looking into the jaws of a monster that he had no skill in fighting. A stupid priest does not challenge an empire and expect it to bow before him.

He grabbed another small bottle of bourbon and poured it over the ice in his glass and took another drink. He knew he shouldn't be doing this, but it was too late now. He would check it out in the morning. Maybe drive up along the coast on his way back to the monastery. He thought about stopping in at Haight-Ashbury for a moment, then looked over at the diary. It was calling to him but he refused to answer.

His head had begun to bleed again and trickled lightly down, staining the collar of his white shirt. Lydia was dead. Bernardo was dead. Everyone was dead. Why was he still here? All those people out there, rumbling around in the dark, they didn't give a shit whether he stayed or not. The Church certainly didn't care, in fact, was embarrassed he even existed.

Kennedy's mind was turning back and forth in on itself, twisting into a knot. He leaned his forehead against the cold window glass and closed his eyes.

"Damn you, Bernardo," he whispered.

He turned, went over to the bed and picked up the diary. He drained his glass, set it down on the nightstand, and sat on the small sofa in front of the window to read.

— June 16, 1967 —

"I thought the Human Be-in was a trip, but this is completely wild. We are back stage waiting to go on at a huge festival gig in Monterey, California. I think there's something like 30 or more bands lined up. We all agreed to play for free, a charity thing, which totally killed Jack, but he agreed finally because it put us right in the middle of all these other great bands. Everyone is here. The Who, Janis, The Byrds. Mamas and the Papas… Jimi Hendrix lit his guitar on fire this morning. It was so crazy. I've never seen anyone play like him before."

Kennedy sat on top of a wooden picnic table behind the stage area eating a hamburger. There were thousands of people everywhere, shoulder-to-shoulder out in front of the stage listening to the Paul Butterfield Blues Band. Lydia sat next to him and he offered her a bite of his burger.

With her mouth full, she just sat there chewing slowly, enjoying the scenery. The smell of food cooking mixed together with a heavy scented cloud of marijuana. The concert was a complete madhouse, in front of the stage and behind, and she loved it. Lydia loved it.

Her eyes were painted a thick dusty blue and a fresh crown of pink camellias circled her head, her hair long and loose, flowing down her back. She wore a dark blue velvet choker around her slender neck with a delicate gold heart in the center that glistened in the hot afternoon Monterey sun. Kennedy could not take his eyes off her.

It was 1967 and Lydia had skyrocketed. Her name had become a household word. In fact, the band was now legally named Lydia Carter and Purple Crow. It was Jack's idea. They had busted three albums out, one right after the other, and each one had sold millions. She was wealthy beyond her dreams, but you would never know it by looking at her. She still looked the part of a young girl sitting there in her swirling neon paisley dress. A little weary perhaps, but wearing that constant smile, it deceived you.

The Paul Butterfield Band had finished and the roadies were clearing the stage, removing one row of equipment and replacing it with another. The crowd used the break to laugh with each other, eat something, or just lie back on the grass and nod off.

Purple Crow was on next and Lydia was getting a little on the jumpy side. She always did. It was sort of like getting butterflies in her stomach, but not entirely. It was more like a nervous energy that she had learned to use, letting it swell, holding it back so that she could tap into it, fueling her through the show. Eddie and Tinsel joined them and sat on the edge of the table next to Kennedy. Both were dressed casually, as far as rock stars go, old jeans and boots. Eddie had on a cool psychedelic purple shirt with a stiff Nehru collar, but other than that, they looked like a couple of ordinary college kids. Tommy was nowhere to be seen, off somewhere in the crowd, back stage getting loaded. Tommy was always loaded, a self-proclaimed stoner par excellence.

As gear replaced gear up on the stage, the crowd began to get restless, shouting. It developed into a series of dull roars that echoed and died before starting again. People everywhere were rolling their joints and passing them in friendly circles and on down the line. Girls had removed their shirts, uninhibited by somebody else's prescribed laws of decency, happy to experience their new-claimed freedom. Some people even chose to forgo clothing of any kind and danced naked as the people around them watched, happily accepting it as another groovy part of the scene. Couples huddled here and there, somewhat discreetly beneath blankets, making love to each other while others passed by. Everyone was high on something. LSD, STP, heroine, hash or dope, if you didn't bring any of your own, there was more than plenty available from the person standing next to you. A helicopter hovered overhead, grabbing footage and reporting live. It was a complete and total renaissance freak-fest.

There were uniformed police officers positioned around for security reasons, but they were powerless and knew it. Many of them were actually frightened by this strange crowd of human beings who had seemingly blossomed out of nowhere and challenged their world. The real security force

204

came in the form of a large group of Hell's Angels who had been persuaded by the lure of violence, being allowed the freedom to pummel anyone who looked sideways at them and a fat paycheck consisting of their favorite drugs.

Lydia kissed Kennedy quickly as she and the band were signaled that it was time to go. He followed them up to a certain point behind the equipment, and then remained there to watch from a privileged viewpoint. A deafening roar exploded from the crowd as Lydia strolled out onto the stage, lifting her hands above her head, greeting the crowd. She stood there for a moment, hands held high, grinning at everyone, as they threw flowers up into the air, a shower of red, pink and yellow blossoms, landing at her feet. The volume level flowing from the sea of people only increased as more and more realized who it was standing before them and that the show was about to begin again. It was the first time many of them had seen Lydia live and the fever was intoxicating.

She grabbed her microphone stand and pulled it toward her mouth and shouted out above the mayhem. "I love you!" She would cause a riot. The place went into an uncontrolled frenzy. "I love you!" she screamed again, walking now from one side of the stage to the next, reaching down and touching the outstretched hands of her worshipers. The floor of the stage was now covered in flowers as she bent, scooped up a handful and tossed them up into the air above her head. Kennedy just laughed. She was having a good time out there.

Tommy had appeared out of nowhere and had made himself comfortable behind his ruby red Ludwig kit. He started the show with a strong, steady beat, working the crowd and getting them to clap along with him. Eddie leaned in, throwing his head down, sliding his pick across the length of his guitar neck, a jet engine, blasting the band into space. Lydia was on top of her game as she joined the fray, dancing up next to Eddie and swinging her hair. The music stopped abruptly, as she cried into the microphone, and they burst into their number one hit, "My Girl." Insanity followed. Purple Crow had lit the house on fire.

Jack came up behind Kennedy and stood next to him, leaning against a stack of amplifiers that were not being used. He gave Kennedy a plastic smile. It was one of those things that he did. Kennedy knew it was meaningless. Jack had become cold. Not just to Kennedy, but to everyone. But especially Kennedy. Maybe he saw Kennedy as a threat to his plans, with the possibility of stealing Lydia away. Kennedy provided a strength she did not possess alone against Jack. He couldn't push her around as much when he was in the room. Kennedy knew he wouldn't stick around long. This was his gratuitous appearance. He didn't really like her music and the less he had to endure it, the better.

Purple Crow rocked the audience for over an hour, pumping the crowd into near fever before bringing it over the top to a final climax. Nobody had ever seen them quite like this. The music stopped and Lydia ran to the front of the stage, her hands raised high above her head, both waving the sign of peace.

"Thank you, brothers and sisters! Thank you, Monterey! I love you!" The crowd was absolutely insane, screaming and yelling her name. She took the flowers from her hair and threw them out into the sea of outstretched hands. "Love each other!" she shouted. "Don't forget to love each other. No more hatred. No more! Just love." She spread her arms wide, embracing the people who adored her, turned and left the stage. The audience erupted, stamping their feet and

206

yelling until voices became hoarse. Hands burned with pain as they were clapped together with increasing intensity.

John Phillips, the leader of the Mamas and Papas, and joint promoter of the show, stood back stage next to Lydia, grinning like a madman and watching the crowd. He turned to Lydia and shook his head.

"You took their hearts, Lydia," he said. "I think you better go give them something back."

She laughed and grabbed her old Gibson acoustic and strutted back upon the stage, waving her arms at the screaming hoard. She laughed into the microphone and slung the strap over her head.

"Thank you! I really mean it. You guys are incredible, man! This here, is for all the soldiers away from home. The one's who want peace, but have to fight. Our brothers."

The audience quieted slightly as she began to strum. It was not often that she played the guitar on stage anymore and everyone present knew this was a unique moment that they were experiencing. No one had ever seen her without Purple Crow behind her. And the moment was beautiful. It was tender. Just her and her people. Kennedy watched in amazement as the crowd swayed, eyes closed and like honey, the words poured from her mouth.

"Where are you?
Oh, oh. Where are you?

All this time, all these lovers.
All my heart, to all my brothers.
I really gotta know, I got to understand…
There is no meaning. There is no place to stand.

Oh, oh… Where are you?
Say, say…Where are you?

And fighting now, against your wishes.
Against your own, the ones just like you…
Say soldier, man, say can you tell me now…
when you coming home?

When will you come to me?
When will I see you?
When will we talk again?
When will you hold me tight?

Oh, oh. Oh, oh, oh.
Soldier, man.
Where are you?"

The volume of the crowd rose to an all-time high. Lydia removed her guitar and allowed it to fall at her side. She looked over at Kennedy, standing there watching her and smiled. The audience was in tears as she turned, bowed humbly before them and kissed them all goodbye.

She never wanted to leave the stage. She would have stayed all day, but the other bands were waiting their turn. She bowed one more time and walked backward, waving at the roaring crowd. They did not want her to go either, but quieted unwillingly as she stepped down the back stairs and disappeared. They had witnessed history and were quite satisfied even though the full weight of it would not sink in until many years later.

Kennedy greeted Lydia as she pressed through the wall of promoters and agents, musicians and lovers back stage. Everyone was reaching out to touch her, to take her by the hand, hug her and tell her that they loved her. She grinned her schoolgirl grin and thanked them all. But when she saw Kennedy, standing there waiting for her, she ran and jumped up into his arms. He caught her and spun her around in a circle as those who looked on laughed in appreciation of the moment. She kissed him hard on the mouth and then all over his face.

"Was that out of sight? Was that completely out of sight?" she said. "I didn't ever want it to stop."

"You were incredible, Lydia," Kennedy said. "Everyone's going crazy. But be careful. Jack's looking for you."

"What the hell does he want?"

"Promotion. He wants a photo session. Some new label thing he's got cooking. He told me to tell you to meet him up at the tent."

"I got a better idea," she laughed. "Let's get the hell out of here."

"I thought you wanted to see the rest of the show."

"Not anymore!"

She grabbed Kennedy by the hand and proceeded to push passed all the people. A group of leather-clad Hell's Angels guarded the back fence around the stage, but when they recognized Lydia, there was nothing but smiles and peace signs. They parted like the Red Sea and allowed her and Kennedy to pass through like royalty. One big grizzly bear patted Kennedy on the back as he passed by. Outside, on the fence line behind the show, Lydia's limousine was parked next to a tightly packed line of equipment trucks and other Limos. Johnny, her driver was waiting obediently, sitting on the hood smoking something, biding his well-paid time. When he saw Lydia approaching, he slid off the car and went into full driver mode, reaching the back door before them in an effort to open it.

"Just you two, Ms. Carter?"

"If you call me Ms. Carter again, I'm gonna bop you good, Johnny," she laughed. "Yeah, just us two. Get us out of here!"

They jumped into the back of the long, black limousine and Johnny slammed the door with a smile.

Inside, Lydia was all over Kennedy, kissing him and tickling his ribs. Johnny sat behind the wheel and looked in the rear view mirror for instructions.

"Pardon me, Lydia. Not to interrupt... any particular destination?"

"Anywhere," she said. "Just open space. I need someplace to breathe!"

Johnny started the engine and began to back the long car up. He stopped, seeing Jack Hampton running through the gates behind them waving his arms over his head.

"Um, looks like Mr. Hampton is wanting a word with you, Ms. Lydia," Johnny said, pointing up into the rear view mirror. Lydia jerked her head around and looked out the small back window at Jack running up to the car.

"Shit," she screamed. "Go Johnny, go!"

Jack had just reached the car as Johnny shoved the accelerator down producing a terrific brown cloud of dirt. As the limo lurched forward, spinning to the left and then right, the swirling dust storm cleared enough to reveal Jack bent at the waist, coughing and spitting. He stood up straight and swore at Lydia, picked up a stone from the dirt and threw it as hard as he could. But the limo was now beyond reach and the stone bounced harmlessly on the road and off into the weeds. Lydia and Kennedy waved at him from the safety of the back window.

Inside, even Johnny was laughing. Lydia could not contain herself.

"He's gonna kill me!" she screamed.

"What are you talking about?" Kennedy said. "You just made him a millionaire. He loves you!"

"True. He loves being a millionaire. He hates me, though," she laughed. Johnny nodded to them both and proceeded to roll up a dark window between them, a professional gesture, granting complete privacy of which, on cue, Lydia took full advantage.

They drove for about half an hour from the concert area. It didn't take long in that part of the country to find what she was after. Everywhere you looked, on either side of the car, seemed ripped from the pages of a travel brochure. They rolled the windows down allowing the wind to whip through the car, filling the entire back with a miniature hurricane.

Lydia noticed a lonely field off to the east in the distance. It was surrounded by an ancient wood and barbed-wire fence, untended and falling down in most places. A small forgotten road, consisting only of two packed dirt tracks opened in the fence ahead and she pounded on the window and yelled for Johnny to stop.

He obeyed immediately, pulling over to the side of the road and rolled down the electric window to ask if anything was wrong.

"Can you take us down that road, there?" she said with her incredible irresistible smile, pointing toward the fence ahead. He looked out the windshield at the small dirt path, pot holes deep and great tufts of grass running up the center.

"Down there?" he asked.

"Yeah. You can do it," she promised. "Let's see where this ship will take us." Both she and Kennedy laughed as Johnny shrugged, obeyed as usual, and pulled forward, narrowly slipping through the makeshift gate and navigated the long battleship down the path. They bumped up and down inside, hitting their heads on the roof and laughing. Lydia slid the sun-roof open and yanked Kennedy by the arm to join her as they stood up into the breeze and blue sky. The road twisted around an old gnarly oak tree and gradually lifted them up over a small green hill and down into an open valley on the other side. Smaller oak trees, coupled together here and there, dotted the lush velvet panorama on either side of the dusty road as it disappeared into the distance.

"This is it!" she cried down to Johnny. "Pull over here."

The car stopped on command and Lydia climbed out through the roof. She stood up on top of the car and screamed as loud as she could. Kennedy followed her as she jumped off the car and landed in the tall grass, running down the hill. Johnny shook his head, watching them wading waist-high in the grass, turned off the engine and waited patiently for their return.

There were small blue flowers growing everywhere. It thrilled Lydia as she spun through the flowing grass. She fell down and began swinging her arms and legs, flattening the tall blades of grass around her like snow angels. Kennedy ran up behind her, breathing hard and dropped down next to her.

She sat up and pulled a crumpled joint from her pocket.

"Lookee what I got," she laughed. She produced a square metal lighter and placed the joint in her mouth, flicking at the flint. She sucked hard at the tip as it sputtered and spit, glowing bright red with a thin white tail of smoke rising up above the grass. She held her breath, savoring the delicious smoke, and handed the joint to Kennedy. He sat up next to her, took it from her, and before he could take his turn, she leaned forward and kissed him, placing her mouth over his and releasing the contents of her lungs into his.

They lay back down in the grass, using their arms as pillows and made up stories about the clouds drifting lazily by overhead. They smoked the rest of the joint while laughing about the things that they could see. One cloud in particular had made them lose control entirely, when Lydia suggested it looked like Jack when he was throwing one of his fits. She almost wet her pants.

They quieted after awhile and just lay there next to each other, dreaming about life.

"That was some show back there," Kennedy said finally.

"You liked it, huh?" she said.

"No, actually you were horrible."

Lydia pinched him and stuck her finger in his ribs. He tried to swat her away like a gnat.

"Really, I think you became famous, today," Kennedy said. "I'm not kidding."

"Jack would love to hear you say that," she said. "With him, it's all record sales. Sometimes I don't even know why I'm doing this."

"What do you mean?"

"It's like the bigger we get, the less freedom we have. We need bigger and better equipment. Nicer restaurants and faster cars. We want to travel by plane, so we can do more shows so we can sell more records so we can make more money. It's like this circle of greed or something."

"You're a rock star."

"But that's not who I am. That's not what I believe."

"What do you believe?"

"In us. In me. In you. In love… This is real, sitting here right now. With each other. This is real. Everything else is just a show."

She paused, allowing the moment to hang in the air, her thoughts racing back in time. "Remember when we met?" she said. "You, me….Dale and Bobby. That was real. When we sat in the park all day and just made music. We were free then. Now I'm in prison most of the time, trying to be someone I don't think I was meant to be."

"No Lydia, you have a gift. You need to share it. That's what you do."

"I know, Soldier. I know. But, I mean the machine. The record making machine that Jack has built out of me. I belong to it. I mean the money is wonderful. I'm rich. Everyone wants to be rich, right? But it makes me feel dirty when I see all those kids out there. They can't even afford to buy a sandwich and yet they'll pay to come see me sing. Half of them are shipped off to a war they never believed in and get their heads blown off. And for what? So some guy like Jack can make even more money? I don't like money. I don't like what it does to people. What it does to me."

But the show you just did, that was for charity. It was free."

"No it wasn't. Not really. It was the only way around getting the permits and crap. Jack wasn't going to have anything to do with it at first. Until he saw how it would work towards selling more records. There was nothing free about that show. It's all about selling records."

"Money makes the world go 'round."

"It destroys you. I mean, look at Jack. Something happened to him along the way. You can't even talk to the guy anymore. He's not really there. Maybe, somewhere, buried inside himself. But he's ruled by this demon."

"Quit," Kennedy said. "You don't have to do this."

"Jack would kill me. He would, too. Besides, I can't. I owe the guys everything. It's not just my life any more. It's everyone in the band. It's the fans. People look to me. I give them something they need. I just wish it didn't have to be so money driven all the time, that's all. It's like religion, you know?"

"How so?"

"It starts out so beautiful. So pure. Unconditional love. Giving yourself to others. Then someone like Jack comes along and realizes, hey, you can make a buck off this shit and before you know it, he's got it all organized, the people are pouring in, the money starts rolling in, rules and regulations pop up and all of a sudden, you're a prisoner to your own religion. Pretty soon, you don't believe in anything, you're just following everybody else and doing things because you're supposed to… not because that's what you really believe in your heart. You move through life, wondering what it's all about, people pushing you here and there, telling you who you are and what you believe. And you obey. You obey because you don't know the truth. And you're afraid."

"*Afraid?*"

"*Yeah. Afraid. Afraid they know something you don't know and it's terrifying to try to live without knowing things for sure. Uncertainty is terrifying. But it's also the foundation of real freedom. It's in exploring the uncertainty, making the mistakes, falling on our face, that we find the truth. Then you can really grab it, hold on to it and really, really believe it. Not because someone told you, you should believe it, but because you found it yourself. It belongs to you. Am I just stoned, or what?*"

"*No, Lydia. No, you're right. I never saw it like that before. It's true. Religion has become a business and we all follow the rules because that's what we're supposed to do. Traditions, rules, everything…it's designed to keep the machine running. Just like the music industry. It's not about music anymore, truth or love. It's about keeping the money coming in no matter what.*"

"*That's it! That's what I'm talking about! It's not real anymore. So, it's not like I need to quit. It's just like I need to change it or something. Bring it back to what it's supposed to be.*"

"*What about Jack?*"

"*Yeah, that's a problem. If I do anything that interrupts his precious cash flow, he will go insane. I think he really is possessed by some sort of demon.*"

"*I don't doubt that for a second.*"

"*Will you be there, Soldier?*" she asked. "*When I need you?*"

"*You know I will, Lydia,*" he said. "*You know I will.*"

Kennedy closed his eyes and allowed the sun to soak into his face. The bright light felt good against his eyelids. Lydia was right. He had pursued the truth, but followed based on fear. Not love. He had always been afraid. And here was this beautiful young woman, lying here in the grass next to him, loving him and she knew everything about him. She had exposed his soul. And he loved her for it.

He smiled and opened his eyes. The only sound was the whisper of the wind licking the tall grass. Lydia was no longer lying next to him. He sat up and looked around, but she was nowhere. He stood and looked off toward the limo, but it too was no longer there. The entire field in which he stood had changed as well. No longer was it green, but a light golden valley of wind splayed wheat. He stood alone, up to his waist, turning in a slow circle, searching for her, there in the center of the field, the graceful strands of wheat shuddering, bending in unison as the breeze rippled though, twisting left, right, and back again for miles in every direction.

———

CHAPTER SIXTEEN

Jessica Burton stood in line at the *Starbucks* around the corner from her apartment, waiting for her non-fat triple caramel macchiato. She wasn't going to go to work today, making it the first weekday in almost two years that she had not gone into the office. She felt a quick stab of guilt but knew she needed time to think and clear her mind. She wished she had some way of contacting Kennedy and giving him the file. Then she would be done with it. As it was, the stupid file only served to complicate her already complicated life. The truth was, she had a fairly boring life. Beyond the faux glamour of the record business, a thin vaneer that had grown increasingly distasteful to her, this was not the kind of excitement she would have chosen. Corporate espionage was not her sort of thing.

Ronald Stenton was a confusing issue as well. She had finally spoken to a girl in his office and was told that nobody knew where he was. Bizarre, to say the least. He just disappeared. They had reported him missing. Whatever. Jessica despised the man, completely. Like most men. But damn it, he could have put her in touch with this Father Kennedy.

She grabbed her drink and headed out onto the sidewalk, sipping it carefully for the first time. It was too hot, so she popped the lid off and blew into the cup, cooling it down. Nash stepped up out of nowhere, like a hawk upon a rabbit, placed his arm inside of hers, and pulled her down the sidewalk, away from all the people.

"Take a quick walk with me, Jessica," he demanded. "This will only take a moment." The fact that he knew her by name caught her calculatingly off guard. She didn't imagine she should resist.

"You have a file that belongs to someone else," he said. "Trust me, I am not going to hurt you. I just need you to give it to me. Now. Do you understand?"

"I… I don't know what you're…"

"Jessica… Please. I really do not have time for bullshit. Tell me you understand that. Give me the goddamn file. Really. That's all I want."

"I don't have it. Not anymore," she cried. "I mailed it."

Nash gripped her arm hard, digging his fingers deep into her flesh. She began to cry and tremble as Nash forcefully directed her toward a black Mercedes sitting at the curb.

"Who did you mail it to?" he demanded, opening the passenger door and nodding with his head for her to get in. "Don't worry, I'm not going to hurt you, Jessica. I just want the file."

Two off-duty Sheriff's deputies who had stopped in to the *Starbucks*, had just walked out, cups in-hand, laughing at some inside joke. Nash saw them and gripped Jessica's arm even tighter, quietly forcing her into the car. She instinctively resisted, panicked, and pushed back hard against a massive wall of unforgiving muscle. Best of luck.

Slurping their morning brew, laughing, just shy of twenty minutes into their morning shift, the two cops were completely unaware of events taking place directly in front of their faces. In a matter of two seconds they would be comfortably back in their car, on the streets, drinking their franchised coffee and looking for dangerous criminals.

"Pervert!" Jessica screamed, throwing her cup of coffee up into Nash's face. He screamed, dropped her arm, and backed away. Taking advantage of her escape, Jessica immediately began walking toward the cops, who by now, had given the situation their full and immediate attention.

"That man over there," she said pointing at Nash, purposefully appalled and appropriately furious, "he just tried to proposition me!" The two deputies watched as Jessica stormed off in righteous indignation. She was pissed. And they, well, they were supposed to be the community knights in shining armor. So, they decided to pay Nash a little visit. On behalf of the little lady, it was the only respectable thing they could think of. And it worked, keeping Nash occupied for the moment, while Jessica stole away.

Her victory, however, didn't last all that long. Once back at her apartment, sheer panic suddenly gripped her and tried to tear her head from her neck. She had been such a stupid, stupid fool and she suddenly realized it. By heading in the wrong direction, away from her apartment, in an effort to prevent Nash from knowing where she lived, she had taken far too long getting here. Of course he knew where she lived! He was probably right behind her, coming up the stairs. She was not thinking things through. She was merely reacting to the seriousness of her situation as it bore down more heavily upon her.

Frantically, she grabbed a stack of clothes from her dresser and smashed them into a small suitcase as well as a few selected essentials yanked from the bathroom cabinet. She thought briefly about calling her mother, just in case, but there just wasn't time. Not now.

The Lydia Carter file was sitting on her kitchen counter. Taking a business card from her purse, Jessica tossed it inside the folder, found an envelope among the mess of papers in one of the drawers, licked it and safely sealed it all together inside. With a thick, black felt pen, she quickly scribbled the letters "LAPD" across the front, slung the suitcase over her shoulder and unconsciously, locked the apartment door behind her.

The cement steps echoed too loudly as she raced down the stairs, her hard soled shoes rapping against them. Stopping at a row of mail boxes in the lobby, she quickly dumped the envelope into the outgoing mail slot, scanned the parking lot for Nash and ran out the door toward her little red Saab. She yanked open the door and threw the hastily packed suitcase into the back seat, jumped in and cranked the engine over. The street was quiet in front of her apartment as she put it in gear and rolled out as unsuspectingly as possible onto the boulevard.

She was running and she hated herself for it. She had never backed down to a man before. Not for doing something she knew was right. But this was different and she was terrified. If she returned the file as Hampton had demanded, there was no telling what he would do. Her job was gone. Probably even her career. She might even face criminal charges. But there was something more at stake here and she could feel it in her bones. By mailing the file, she had felt it somehow ensured her safety. For a little while anyway. It put her on the offensive and that's the game she had always played best. So again, she asked herself why she was running. Nash was why. She had not thought of that aspect.

She never imagined the file was really all that important. If Father Kennedy had stumbled onto something, and if everything running through her mind was true, then the information in the file could do Jack Hampton some pretty serious damage.

Her mother owned a small beach house along the coast, just north of Mission Viejo. The school season was back in high gear now and the beaches would be empty, offering solitude and the ability to see anyone approaching. Nobody knew about the house, not even her friends, who these days had become increasingly sparse. She had wanted to reach Kennedy, to show him the file, but had no way of knowing where he was. Stenton had been their only connection and now she thought she might know why he had never called back.

She swung onto Interstate 5 and headed toward the coast, paying close attention to her rear view mirror. It was about an hour or more drive, maybe a bit longer depending on traffic, but the further she got from downtown, the safer she felt.

She could feel her heart in her chest. She became suddenly angry that she was so terrified and that Jack Hampton was behind it. She had never admitted it to anyone, but she hated him. The truth is, as it echoed in her head, was that she hated herself. She had wanted the position at AMI to such a degree that she had agreed to his loathsome proposition. She had tried to pretend that it was a surefire way to break the proverbial glass ceiling, that women did it all the time, that it was actually a form of power women held over men... but it had been humiliating and left scars so deep they would never heal.

There had been other times, too, after she had been awarded the job, in which Jack had felt entitled to additional pleasures, often behind the closed doors of his office. They were never part of her initial agreement, but she had nothing to fall back on. There was nowhere and no one to turn to. It wasn't something she could discuss. It devastated her. The way they all looked at her, the stifled laughter... everyone knew.

Her heart began to ache as she tasted her humiliation. How could she have tried so hard, all through college and a promising career, only to turn around and do something so disgusting? She had always been a harsh judge of the sleazy prostitutes she saw lurking on the sidewalks each night as even sleazier men poured out of their posh office high-rises on their way to the bars. Those were women who had given up. They were shallow and worthless. She hated them. Because, in a sense, she was one of them.

Not only did she wish she had never met Jack Hampton, but now it had all backfired in her face. She was running away and could never go back. She thought of all the personal items in her office that she would never see again. Photographs and mementos, books and other items, most of which might otherwise have seemed worthless, meant the world to her. And of course, her damn degree. She was proud of it and thought that it had looked so great hanging there on the wall next to her big, stupid glass desk.

And who was that freak of a man who had tried to shove her in his car, anyway? She shivered at the thought of what he had intended to do. Maybe he was just a thug or somebody that was supposed to pick her up and take her to be confronted by Jack. But something inside her told her it was a little more serious than that. That was not the kind of man you ever wanted to meet.

In her blind spot, an older white Corvette jammed on its horn, causing her to swerve instinctively to her right. She had not been paying attention and had begun drifting into his lane. She felt increasingly stupid as an older man with a goatee, passed by in the fast lane, giving her his rigid middle finger.

Jessica began to cry, wiping at her nose with the sleeve of her sweater. She looked at herself in the rear view mirror, an even mixture of fear, self-pity and tears filling her eyes. She was falling apart and then suddenly, her fear turned inward once again, yielding anger and a deeper self-loathing. She was so stupid. Only an idiot would have screwed things up this badly.

All she had ever really wanted was to do something important. To be someone. To make her mom sit up and take notice for once. To say nice things about her to her friends. And now this.

She pressed the accelerator down a little further. The freeway behind her was packed with a thousand cars. Anyone could be back there and she would never know. But she was just being paranoid and she knew it. Even so, the more room she put between her and downtown, the better. She would spend as much time away as she wanted. The apartment would be fine. The rent was paid. She could visit in a month, at night or something, claim the things she needed, then have a moving company take care of the rest. She could handle this. If she could handle the vile things Jack Hampton had done to her, the pain she had buried, she could deal with this as well. It would just take a little time and her brand of determination.

It took a little over two hours to reach the beach house. Neatly tucked between the dunes and the sea, it sat alone at the end of a row of other tiny vacation homes just like it. She smiled when she saw it, pulling off the road and parking in the sand. It had been almost two years since she had last been here and she wondered why. Most people worked their lives away for a place like this. She had one and, for some reason, chose to work anyway.

It was cold and musty inside and looked as though it had been a hundred years since anyone had been there. Her mother was in a rest home now and would never see the place again. She had a brother somewhere, but nobody had heard from him in over five years. They used to rent the place out during the summer months years ago, but it took too much work to stay on top of it. So the house just sat there, like her, getting older.

Lifting the bamboo blinds, she let the sun pour into the front room. She opened several windows and immediately the house began to fill with new energy as the thick salty air poured in. To the right of the kitchen sink, a thin cupboard hid a small water heater. Her brother had taught her how to light the pilot when she was a teenager, and even though she had done it many times, it always brought a sense of trepidation. It had to be done, though, and like always, she ignored the irritating fear and pushed herself to complete the task.

Her reward was a cup of hot lemon tea. She filled an old chrome pot with ice-cold water from the tap and set it on the stove, lighting it with another match. Outside the window, the beach was a blistered white, stretching out from the house about a hundred yards into the Pacific and off in either direction for miles. There were some people, a couple it looked like, much further down the beach, little dots on the sand, walking aimlessly, stopping now and then to pick up shells. An old man stood ankle deep in the tide, wasting time, casting a line out into the surf. Other than that, the beach was empty.

When the teapot finally began to make itself heard, she poured the steaming water into a favorite ceramic mug she kept above the refrigerator. She would never have a cup like that in the city. It was not her style. It belonged at the beach house and here it was perfect. She placed a bag of tea in the cup and retreated to the rocking chair in front of a large glass window looking out onto the beach. "Everything is going to be all right," she told herself. "Perhaps, this was actually an opportunity, a way to find myself again." She had been on a long journey and now it was finally at a close. She was grateful. It might even be time for her to pick up where things left off with her mother. As painful as it sounded, she missed her and knew it was the right thing to do. Even if her mother wouldn't recognize her, she would know she'd done the right thing. And that was weighing heavy on her right now; doing the right thing.

She sipped her tea and thought about all those wonderful summers spent out there on the beach. From little girl with a sand pail and shovel, digging for buried treasure, to the teenage years, drinking with friends and telling ghost stories around the fire late at night while her mother thought she was asleep in her room. This place was a symbol of her life and the fact that she had not been here in so long, suddenly proved to her that she had abandoned herself as well somewhere along the way.

Her tea finished, she was feeling much better now. She grabbed her suitcase, walked into the bedroom and tossed it onto the bed. She clicked the latches open, lifted the lid and removed her toothbrush, toothpaste and a few other personal items and stepped into the bathroom. She opened the mirror and set her things on the narrow glass shelf. The toothbrush, she placed in a small glass on the sink and stood back, pleased. She knew it was sort of stupid, but little things made her comfortable and the sight of the brush on the sink made her feel a little more at home.

She reached behind the tub curtain and turned on the water. A thin, brown grime belched from the faucet, choking and spitting as it forced the rust from the pipes, then suddenly became clear. She plunged her hand beneath it, feeling it warm, pulled the little lever on the faucet and brought the shower to life.

One by one, she undid the buttons on her blouse and wiggled out of it, hanging it neatly from a small hook on the back of the bathroom door. She watched herself in the steaming mirror as she undid her bra, tossing it in the corner behind the door. Several years past thirty, she had not lost as much form as some of her friends had. The ocean air must have been having a positive affect. She was beginning to feel better about herself.

As her reflection faded into the steamy fog, she climbed out of her jeans, depositing them in the corner as well, stripped completely down and stepped into the warm world inside the tub. The jets of water welcomed her and at last, she felt she was home.

228

Funny how her career, her need to succeed, had driven her further and further away from some of the more simple things that meant so much to her. Like the beach house. She loved this place. As a little girl she had spent entire summers here, even weeks in the winter during Christmas break. She had lost her virginity to a kid named Ian when she was fifteen, just down the beach in Randi's Cove.

But there were a lot of things she had ignored in an effort to concentrate on getting somewhere else. A lot of people, too. Jessica had systematically pushed the people she cared about most, at a safe distance, out of her life. They had served as constant interruptions in the world that she thought she wanted. Now she was all alone and it felt that way.

She turned the knob and shut off the water and slid the glass door aside. The brisk ocean air hit her hard as she stood there dripping in the tub. But it was nice and she enjoyed it for a moment, letting her body experience the sensation before reaching for a large yellow towel on a rack above the toilet that had been patiently waiting for her for the last two years.

There was a fat, little savings account she had faithfully built and it would serve to hold her steady, even if she decided to hole up here for a while. Maybe even as much as a year. It would allow her the freedom to rethink some things, examine her heart and who knows, maybe even find out who she really was. The music business was ruthless. In fact, she laughed at the irony of the two words together, music and business. It had nothing to do with one and it was all about the other.

She rubbed the steam from the mirror and wrapped the towel around her. She was still young. There was plenty of time, she told herself with confidence, to do the things that were meaningful. She was done with AMI records. She was done with her stupid career. And maybe it was the freshness of the ocean penetrating her soul, but she was happy about it and felt a new sense of freedom growing inside her. She shook the water from her hair and stepped out onto the rough hard wood floor in the bedroom.

In an instant it all changed. Everything shattered. Confusion and terror swirled through her mind and the last thought she had was of her mother and who would tell her… as someone gripped her hard from behind and placed a soft cotton gauze over her mouth and nose. The sickening sweet smell of ether overpowered her as she fell limp and closed her eyes.

Nash caught her in his arms, lifted her effortlessly and placed her gently on the bed. He stood back for a moment, pondering his calculated steps and looked at Jessica sprawled on the mattress. He had not expected she would be quite so attractive. He grabbed her towel and pulled it away, leaving her exposed upon the bed. The urge to take her like that was powerful and he was more than poised to do so. But he wasn't stupid. With his gloved hands, he removed a syringe from his coat pocket, and placing a rubber strap around her left arm, he sank the needle into her vein and pumped her full of heroin.

He placed her fingers gently around the empty syringe and pressed the tips into the plastic, then tossed it onto the bed next to her. He removed the strap from her arm and placed another clean syringe in her purse and set it on the table across the room.

Turning, Nash stood and looked at her again, naked and dying. He sat on the edge of the bed next to her, gently stroked her thigh and removed the small wooden box from his inside coat pocket. The familiar sting of the needle felt delicious and almost as satisfying as having Jessica might have been. As the ink penetrated below his skin and the tiny beads of red blood emerged, Nash closed his eyes in pleasure.

He looked at her one last time and examined the fresh mark on his arm. Number twenty-eight. Jack Hampton would probably be upset about this. He hadn't meant for Nash to kill her. But Nash only took orders as he saw fit. Jessica should never have thrown coffee in his face. This was just punishment.

He wanted her badly now and could feel himself losing the ability to resist. If he took her now, the way she needed to be taken, it would leave too many signs. He pulled himself off the bed, replaced the wooden kit inside his jacket and left the room.

A moment later, the front door closed quietly and the house fell silent once again, the only sound, the song of the waves crashing outside, grinding the sand into a smooth gray sugar. Jessica lay alone, naked and still, remembering a beautiful time, not so long ago, with a boy she met one summer. Down on the beach. At the bonfire that amazing Friday night. There in Randi's Cove. He took her by the hand and stole her away into the shadows, lying down together between two massive black rocks, there beneath the overhanging cliffs. Away from the warmth of the flames. Away from everyone. She had wanted him so badly. She needed his hands to know her. Like no boy had ever known her.

But it just kept getting darker. Colder all the time. Then, he too was gone. She tried to call his name, but there were no words. She was standing now, alone on an empty beach, the icy wind blasting through her, as it got darker and darker. Black as ink. Alone. And so very, very cold.

———

Detective Blakey knocked on the door jam of Captain Allen Murch's office. He was on the phone, sitting behind and old beat-to-shit wooden desk, but he motioned for Blakey to come in and sit down. While he talked to someone on the other end about ignoring policy and procedure and getting the job done, he pushed a file across the desk to Blakey and indicated with his eyes that he should read it.

Blakey picked up the file and opened it looking at the photo of Lydia. The other pieces of paper in the file made little sense to him. Confused by the file's meaning, he waited as the Captain hung up the phone.

"What is this?" Blakey asked.

"I thought maybe you might know," the Captain said. "It came in the mail, addressed to LAPD. No return address, nothing. It has to do with that Lydia Carter rock star chick… I thought maybe that might be of interest to you."

"Oh, it's of interest. I just don't know what the fuck it means."

"Well you might want to start here," he said holding up Jessica Burton's business card.

"Thanks. I'll check it out," Blakey said. He stood and took the file, thumbing through the contents again as he walked out of the Captain's office.

Blakey set the file down on his desk and pulled his chair back, plopping his bulging frame into it. He picked up the phone and examining Jessica's card, dialed her number.

"Yeah, Detective Sam Blakey. Jessica Burton, please."

The woman on the other end of the line was quiet for a moment, then tried to piece her words carefully together.

"Well, this is very strange," she said. "We were just about to call the police. It seems Jessica is missing."

Normally, it would have taken a week or more before a missing person report reached Blakey's desk, if it ever did. Even then, he rarely took much more than a obligatory interest in them. Most were unimportant and involved unsolvable family matters, marital problems, people running away, that kind of thing.

But since this file folder indicated that this Jessica Burton was intimately involved with all this Lydia crap, and now she, like Stenton, was missing, it was more than of interest to him.

He got Jessica's home address from the girl at her office and decided to stop by before lunch and see if she was there. He knew she wasn't. But he had to cross his t's.

The apartment manager, William King, was a pasty crank addict and all too eager to assist Blakey in entering her apartment. He said he knew everything about everyone in the building and it seemed, Jessica in particular.

She had not been home in the last couple of days, which was not like her. She never went anywhere or did anything but work. Home by 7:30 every night, didn't date to his knowledge and hadn't for almost two years. In bed by 10:00. Up at 6:00 to run. Good tenant, no pets, always paid her rent at least two days in advance. You couldn't ask for a better renter. Cute too, although she did seem depressed quite a bit. William assumed she was probably on meds of some sort.

Blakey had simply wanted to take a look around her apartment. He never expected that it would come with a convenient personal tour guide. He eventually had to dismiss the overly enthusiastic manager, politely explaining that he needed no further assistance. William was apologetic, but again, willing to do whatever was helpful to the police; his sudden civic duty. Blakey could tell he had hurt his feelings. Whatever. Go watch a cop movie and get over it.

Jessica's apartment was what you'd expect a chick's apartment to be. Clean, tidy, well decorated. She had a little money, too. You could tell by her taste in furniture and all the shit around it. It looked like she was living in a *Pottery Barn* showroom.

There were several photographs, apparently of Jessica and probably her mother. Another series of photos on a book shelf, showed Jessica again, standing next to a mangy bunch of guys with more hair than skin. Evidently, she was a reader, too. Fiction. Romance. And tons of it. "How could anyone read so much?" Blakey thought. He hated reading. It was a total waste of time and always made him fall asleep anyway.

He wandered in to the kitchen and looked in the refrigerator. She ate well. Juice. Milk. Fresh vegetables. Lettuce. Pricey looking cheese. Yogurt. No meat... Figures. He laughed.

The freezer had three cartons of Chocolate Marble Fudge... Busted.

The bedroom was a little different. She had obviously packed some clothes and apparently in quite a hurry. Several drawers were left hanging open. A pair of purple underwear was hanging out of one of them, along with other bits and pieces of clothing thrown across the bed, evidently not making the cut. A maroon leather journal sat on the nightstand next to the bed. Blakey sat down, opened it up and thumbed through it.

Notes and more notes. Thoughts, ideas, new connections and meetings. She was one busy woman, this Jessica. All her notes and deadlines were scribbled everywhere all over the pages. Blakey turned the last several pages, slowly using his thumb, reading her entries and absolute must-do lists.

He stopped. "Fuck a duck!" he muttered out loud. Right there on the last page, in her own damn handwriting, was a direct connection to the missing real estate agent, Ronald Stenton. "Nail down Ronald Stenton today or fire his ass!!!" There it was. Just the sort of thing that makes a detective very hungry. Blakey thumbed back through the pages and Stenton's name or initials were everywhere. She had been working with him on something, a property, possibly the old house in the Palisades, certainly not her apartment. The manager had said she was the perfect "renter." First Stenton and now Jessica. Both connected. Both missing. And everything pointed to that damn lunatic of a priest.

CHAPTER SEVENTEEN

Kennedy was awake in his hotel room, drinking a five-dollar bottled water from the mini-bar. His eyes were bloodshot and his head was pounding. He had ordered breakfast, so it came as no surprise when there was a knock on his door. Expecting room service, he got Sam Blakey instead.

Kennedy stood in the doorway, staring at him, mind numbed, circles under his eyes and his hair a wad of tangles. He hadn't shaved in two days and looked like a war victim.

"Can I come in?" Blakey asked.

"I would really prefer that you didn't."

"I could take you with me, if you… prefer."

Kennedy swung the door open wide and motioned sarcastically with his arm that the entire room was at

Blakey's disposal. Kennedy followed him as he stepped in and looked around the room. There were little plastic bottles of bourbon here and there, with a small gathering of them clustered on the coffee table.

"Have a party?"

"Yeah. Sorry, I forgot to invite you," Kennedy said. "What can I do for you, detective?"

"What do you know about a Jessica Burton?" Blakey asked sitting himself down on the couch and making himself comfortable. It looked like he was ready to enjoy a nice, long conversation. Kennedy felt like he was going to throw up. The room spun and in a flash, he saw Jessica lying there on a bed.

Kennedy rubbed his eyes and tried to focus.

"You OK?" Blakey asked.

"Yeah. A little dizzy. She works at AMI Records. Executive. Why?"

"So you do know her?"

"Not really," Kennedy said sitting down on the edge of the bed. "I met her. Once."

"Recently?"

Again Kennedy's mind flashed and he saw Jessica lying there cold and still upon the bed.

"Yes, recently," he said, shaking his head. Blakey sat back and observed him, thinking the guy was more than a little strange.

"She was in charge of getting rid of the house," Kennedy continued. "The one where you and I met. I needed information about Lydia and that's how I met her. What's going on, anyway?"

"She's missing. Just like Stenton. The only one that's not missing, is you."

"Come on, Detective. I didn't do anything with either of them. You know that."

"Do I?"

"OK, fine. I'm a rogue priest who goes around killing people because the Church is so damn boring I don't have anything else better to do."

"I've seen worse. Why do you think Jessica would send me a file? Lydia's file."

"She sent you her file? Well, she was trying to tell you something, obviously."

"Obviously."

"I have no idea. Ask Jack Hampton. That's where you should be putting your energy."

"Who's he?"

"He's the man behind the curtain, pulling all the levers. He's the CEO and majority stockholder of AMI and filthy rich because of one Lydia Carter. Probably do anything to prevent losing it, too. You think I'm connected to Jessica and Stenton… try that son of a bitch."

"Sounds like a plan."

Room service knocked on the door and Kennedy rose to open it. A young kid in his twenties entered the room and very politely set the tray down on the table in front of Blakey. Kennedy signed the tab and thanked the kid, closing the door behind him. He turned to find Blakey had lifted the metal lid of his breakfast and had moved a piece of toast aside and was inspecting the eggs, smelling the delicious aroma as the waves of steam rose up to his nose.

"Do you mind?" Kennedy asked.

Blakey set the toast down, replaced the lid and stood up. "Enjoy your breakfast, Father. I'll be talking to you. And uh, take a shower. You're not looking so good."

"Yeah, thanks," Kennedy said.

Blakey made his way to the door and smiled back at Kennedy before leaving him alone to deal with his food. He had already had his breakfast this morning, but suddenly another one sounded like it just might just fit the bill. He closed the door behind him as Kennedy sat down on the couch and put his face in his hands. He wasn't hungry anymore.

Lydia was reaching out to him. She was trying to show him something. And he knew it was about Jack Hampton. Was she trying to tell him that Jack had killed her? It was really the only thing that made sense. Otherwise, what was all of this about? When he was with her, he loved her. Why was that part necessary? It made no sense. He never knew Lydia. She was dead. How could he love her? And it was impossible to believe that she might love him as well.

Who was he kidding? This was ridiculous. He was getting caught up in a childish fantasy that was going to drive him mad. He was having intense sexual desires for a woman that was dead. Priests don't normally do that. And now the police were barking at his door. He was getting beaten and having his life threatened. And for what? To right a wrong? To balance the scales? That would be so very heroic. Whatever he was doing, sitting here hung-over in a Los Angeles hotel room, it sure as hell didn't feel heroic.

He kept thinking about Jack Hampton and if he indeed had anything to do with her death, Kennedy wanted him to pay for it. So, was it simply revenge? Because that was ridiculous. Revenge required a deep, intense emotion. And that was what was driving him out of his mind. He was defending someone he loved. And he could not love her.

The diary sat next to him, slipped into the crack in the couch. He lifted it, peeled back the pages, and leaned back on the couch with a moan.

October 24, 1969

"We're in the studio again. This time with a producer cat named Hash Brown. We've been hitting it pretty hard, going on a month now. Jack won't let up. He wants another Gold. I keep trying to tell him we're not machines. That he's going to destroy the art. I think he's afraid we are going to dry up, so he's trying to get as much out of us as fast as he can. But it's the other way around, man. He's the one that's draining the well. But he is so blinded by the money, he can't see it. All those times back on the Haight. We all would hang around getting stoned, talking about the new way of life, telling the Man to fuck off. And all this time, Jack was the Man. He never saw the vision…not ours, anyway."

The control room was dark and smoky, lit by a hundred tiny blinking red and green lights and two small reading lamps aimed directly at the mixing console. Jack sat fighting with an empty pack of cigarettes, crumpled it and tossed it in a small beat up metal can in the dark corner. William Brown, or "Hash" Brown sat back in his chair and produced another pack from his pocket and handed them to Jack. Kennedy watched from a leather chair in the opposite corner.

Hash was a pretty cool guy, even by his own admission. The last time he cut his hair was back in 65 and even though it had started to recede just a bit, he had more hair than most women. He also had the advantage of growing a beard that, along with his ever-present torn jeans and plaid shirt, gave him the appearance of a wild hillbilly. But his overall demeanor was very laid back, always nodding and swinging his head lightly to the left, then the right, listening to some song inside that soundproof room in his head. Very cool. He only spoke when he needed to, or when he wanted to, which wasn't often. But when he did, you listened and everybody knew it. If you didn't, you'd never work with him again. Ever. If you did, you might just end up with gold, on your record and in your pocket. Hash Brown knew his way around a studio and worked a mixing board like he was making love to it. And the sound he produced. It had made him a star to the stars and he was sought after by the biggest. They all wanted him, a few even convinced that his fingers were magic and that their records would fail without him. It might have been true.

They had been in the studio for the past three weeks, putting down some of the stuff Lydia and Eddie had written in the hotel rooms from the tour. She had been able to take a week off in between, but Jack had the studio booked and was not about to attempt pushing anything back and risk losing it altogether.

The tour had been a raging success and clearly positioned Lydia right up there with the mega stars. Her last album, "Tin Roof," was selling through the roof and now she would have another one right on its heels. That's the way it needed to be done according to Jack, as if he had done it a million times now.

They had all traveled by plane, then by bus to cities across the country Lydia had never even heard of before. So many, she could't remember all their names. She had revisited a few that she really loved, too, including of all places…Tacoma. Much of it looked the same as when she was a kid, growing up there, but like her, it too had changed and would never be the same. "It's ok," she noted. "Nothing stays the same. It can't… Plus, by now, nobody here would really remember me anyway. Not the real me. Not the person I am down inside. Even if they did, nobody has said anything about it. Except Soldier…he is the only one. He knows me."

She and Kennedy stole away one morning after a show the night before. It was early and still dark out as they walked down the empty sidewalk on Belvedere Avenue, right where Parker's Music used to be. It had been turned into a diner of sorts at some point, but looked like it had probably been closed for at least a year or more.

Her eyes lit up and she became animated, like a little kid, as Lydia described all those wonderful polished pianos sitting there in the window. She actually jumped up and down, both hands covering her mouth, when recalling the arrival of the new electric guitars…all of them, so shiny and new, hanging there in a row all along the wall.

And of course Annie, the quintisential piano teacher, always instructing her on how to properly hold her fingers over the keys, sit up straight, breathe…her sweet mother… she would have died laughing if she knew where those lessons would take Lydia. Either that, or cried her heart out.

Being on tour was one of the most rigorous times. You couldn't stop to breath. Even on the bus or in the plane, you couldn't really unwind. Sleep came in small chunks and usually only when you passed out. City to city, it all became a blur. The overall excitement never died down, it was always exhilarating to see all those people, screaming your name. The lights, the music, everything, but it took a heavy toll. Add way too much booze and drugs and Lydia was cracking at the seams. They all were. By the time they had rolled into Los Angeles for their final show of the tour, they could barely climb up on stage. Jack had the answer with a handy dose of STP or some other amphetamine that pushed them through the show. But the crash afterwards had been brutal. There were three days in some expensive hotel that she would never remember.

"Let's do it again," Jack said to Hash, lighting up his cigarette. "She's not putting her heart into it."

"Maybe she needs a break, man," Kennedy said from the corner. "The chick is tired."

"Fuck that. We're all tired. You don't see me slowing us down. Of course she's tired. She drinks too much. Take her fucking whiskey away and maybe we'd have an album by now."

"Babe, let's do that last chorus, one more time," Hash Brown said into a microphone on the console. "Will you do that for me?" Lydia was sitting on a stool in a bright studio room on the other side of two thick sheets of glass wearing a pair of headphones that pinned her long hair to the sides of her head. She waved her hands upward and smiled at him as if to say she didn't really have a choice. But she loved Hash Brown. He was good to her and she knew if he was perfectly happy, he wouldn't let Jack push him around. She wanted to give him what he was searching for in her.

Another stool next to her served as a coffee table, holding a stuffed ashtray and a glass of Jack Daniels. The other band members had laid down some great tracks earlier in the week and were not scheduled to be in the studio today. The entire session belonged to Lydia and since the studio was booked by the day, not by the hour, Jack intended on getting as much out of Lydia as she had to give. This next album needed to get out by Christmas and they were already behind schedule. If anyone was exhausted, it was him. He was tired of having to push everyone and then taking the shit because he was so greedy. Fucking babies. You think anyone was the tiniest bit grateful for how far he had taken them in the last three years? Rags to riches? Fuck. These people didn't have a clue what it took.

"Here you go, Babe," Hash said. "Maybe try standing up for a bit. Get the blood flowing. We're needing a bit more of your heart. Especially in that part. And I know you got it. That's where you come alive, Babe."

"Yeah, OK. I got it," she said with a groan, standing to her feet and sliding the stool away from the mic. She picked up her glass and gave it a good tug and swallowed hard.

"Think of your people. Think of their pain."

"Yeah, that's good," Jack said.

"OK. We ready? And... rolling tape. Take five," Hash said as he punched a several buttons and the reels of tape on the wall clicked, spun quickly, then rolled slowly forward. Lydia closed her eyes and swayed to the music now pumping through her headphones. Jack, Hash Brown, and Kennedy watched her, waiting. And she didn't let them down.

She began to moan and her voice cracked slightly as she launched into the chorus. It sent shivers down Kennedy's spine. Hash looked over at Jack with a huge grin. Immediately they all knew they had heard something good. Take five was going to be pressed into plastic. It was going to make history. And she didn't let up, using as Hash had directed, the pain she had seen in all the kids on the Haight. The feeling of being lost. The misunderstanding. The emptiness. The confusion. She took it all and pulled it straight out of her soul, singing there in that little sound proof room on the other side of the glass. She was so close you could almost touch her.

"Come on, baby!" Come on, now!" she screamed. "You got to give me… got to, got to give me, give me…"

Lydia stopped and let the music continue without her.

"What the fuck is she doing?" Jack yelled.

The empty whiskey glass slipped from her fingers and bounced on the thick Persian carpet. Her head fell forward onto her chest and she staggered. They all watched through the glass as her knees buckled, sending her directly into the floor. Her boots smashed against the stool, turning it over and sending a spray of cigarette butts and ashes into the air.

Kennedy was out of his chair and through the doors into the next room followed by Hash Brown. Jack sat in the sound room with his head in his hands, cursing her. She opened her eyes as Kennedy and Hash Brown picked her up and laid her on a couch off in the corner of the room.

"Love me, baby. I'm so tired," she said as Kennedy stroked her hair. "Don't you ever leave me. Don't you…"

She closed her eyes again and smiled, touching Kennedy's hand with her own and kissing it. Hash Brown stood by waiting for direction from Kennedy. Jack was counting his losses, growing madder by the second. This was his money burning here, not Lydia's. She had no sense for money or respect for it. She would have played for free if Jack let her. Then Jack suddenly looked around the room and smiled. The tapes were still rolling. They had captured all of it. The whole stupid ordeal. It was better than perfect and he was

246

going to sell it. "Now, this is fucking art," he thought, laughing. Her fans would eat this shit up.

Hash had gone to get her some water as Kennedy sat on the couch next to her. He looked up to see Jack, grinning like the Cheshire Cat, alone back there in the dark, enjoying his cigarette.

"Let's call it a day," Kennedy said to Jack. Jack's smile disappeared. He grabbed the control room microphone and put his mouth up to it and glared back at Kennedy.

"I don't think so," he said.

"Come on, Jack, this is bull shit. You're killing her."

"She's killing herself. She'll be fine."

"I'm taking her home."

"The fuck you are!" Jack said and stood up. Kennedy began to lift Lydia from the couch as Jack pushed his way into the room, his authority challenged and looking for a fight. Kennedy held Lydia in his arms with his back to Jack and didn't see him coming as he shoved Kennedy forward causing him to fall on top of Lydia on the couch.

"Did you hear me? She's not going anywhere!" Jack yelled.

Kennedy calmly stood up and looked down at Lydia, making sure she was all right. Her eyes were half open but she had no idea what was happening. He looked at Jack and stepped forward.

"Do not ever touch me again," he said.

Jack puckered up his face like a five-year old bully and laughed. "Oh, fuck you…"

Kennedy's fist shot forward and caught Jack hard on the right side of his mouth, sending him crashing backward against the studio wall and down onto the floor. Hash Brown stood in the doorway holding a paper cup of water, with a smile. Jack sat up, protecting his pride, but could not stand.

"You just fucked yourself, asshole," he said. "Get the fuck out of here."

Kennedy turned and lifted Lydia once again. Hash Brown opened the back door onto the parking lot where Lydia's Rolls Royce was parked and the two of them walked out into a bright Los Angeles day.

Johnny Taylor, her driver, jumped out of the limo and opened the back door as Kennedy gently laid her on the back seat. She smiled at him and drifted off once again.

"She'll be all right," he said to Johnny. "Let's just get her home." Apologetic, he turned and looked at Hash Brown standing behind him.

"You ok, man?" Hash Brown asked.

"Yeah. But that asshole in there needs some serious help."

Hash Brown couldn't hold back a good laugh at Jack's expense. "This here animal just punched the shit out of Jack Hampton," he said to Johnny, placing his arm around Kennedy's shoulder.

"Good man, Soldier," Johnny said. "Glad somebody finally did. Freak has had that coming for years."

"You take care of her," Hash Brown continued, giving a gentle nod towards Lydia. He smiled and put out his hand for Kennedy to shake.

In the quiet and solitude of the back seat, Lydia slept, her head cradled in Kennedy's lap. They made their way out of the city with all its traffic and stress, Jack with his manic demands and headed west, eventually winding along Highway 1 up the blue coast of California toward the Palisades. Kennedy stared off onto the vast horizon as they twisted around sheer cliffs, crumbling slowly away.

He thought about Lydia, lying there, an amazingly talented person. She had always simply just followed that talent and unquestioningly pursued her passions. That's who she was. And it had lead to stardom. But he wondered if it all was really worth it. This is what everyone wants, isn't it? But does anybody know what it really costs? Does anybody know what it's like and what it can do to you? Everyone wants to be filthy rich. To be loved by millions. Their name known around the world. Nobody would ever realize how empty it can be, until it's too late. Like a rusty bear trap long hidden beneath the fallen leaves in the forest, it lunges forth, unforgiving, clamping onto your leg and refusing to let go, ripping skin from bone.

The limo slowed and turned right onto an almost invisible road directly off the highway and headed inland, away from the rolling blanket of blue water. They spiraled up the hill into the dark green and misty pine trees covering the cliffs. She slept, peaceful, as Johnny navigated his way up the hill like a steady corkscrew. The spires of her mansion could be seen between the trees as they straightened out at the top of the hill. In a moment, the trees cleared and revealed the massive house, sitting pristinely behind a great set of iron gates sunk into stone.

The car rolled into the courtyard as the gates opened gently and closed behind them. Kennedy lifted her head and stepped from the car in complete awe of the house. It was immaculate, with a fresh coat of bright white paint, the lawns and hedges manicured like a lady's fingernails. There were flowers, too, everywhere he looked, and the fountain in the center, it was alive, a jubilant spray of water shooting straight up, splashing down, dancing between the innocent granite cherubs.

Johnny led the way and opened the front door as Kennedy lifted Lydia from the car and carried her into the house. It too, was magnificent, decorated and filled with furniture fit for a Queen. Bright Persian carpets lined the polished marble floors, paintings and more flowers. Everywhere flowers. The windows were open and the coastal breeze filled the cavernous halls with a sweet scent of heaven. Kennedy knew where her room was and carried her up the stairs to lay her in bed.

"Don't leave me," she begged, opening her eyes.

"I'm right here, Lydia," he said, pulling the covers up around her. "Don't worry. Sleep now. I will be here when you wake up." She didn't hear him, but she understood. A soft smile graced her delicate face as she drifted off to sleep once more.

Kennedy stood in her room and looked around. Its peach wallpaper and striking freshness. The mirrors, the candles and the lace. This bed, with polished posters of cherry, crisp linens and silk. It was all so warm and familiar to him.

Lydia lay sleeping beneath him, like a child buried beneath the soft down pillows under tumbling waves of deep chocolate hair. Was it possible that she loved him? How could it be? Was this incredible creature actually his? Like her guardian angel, he stood there gazing upon her, his eyes heavy with moisture, then leaned silently towards her, gently kissing her soft lips.

He woke up, lying on the couch in his hotel room. The phone was ringing, but he did not answer it. His head still hurt as he sat up and looked out the window. It was not quite dark outside, but the day was gone. He was not even sure what day it was. He was not sure of anything and began to argue with himself in his head again, telling himself he was a fool. That he was making a mess out of things he knew nothing about. The man who hit him had told him, it was none of his business. Nobody dives head first into a deep pool of water without first knowing what lies beneath the surface.

Kennedy did not know what he was doing here. All he knew was that, with these bizarre visions, he was somehow acting as a witness. But his actual responsibility in it all, that was anything but clear to him. He did not have the foggiest idea what he was supposed to do next. Unfortunately, he knew all too well, however, how all this was going to end. He wasn't sure when, exactly, but he knew how. And he also knew, as much as he wanted to, he would never be able to stop it. That then, was his obligation, his task, to observe. Everything. Even her death. To sit there, powerless, and watch it happen. All of it.

He was still holding her diary, the outline of his left hand imprinted lightly on the leather cover from the sweat on his palms. He stood up, still gazing out the window. He had been unconscious through most of the day and shook his head. Some help. If you ever need a murder solved, just call on Father Kennedy. He's the one. He'll get drunk and sleep all day.

An idea suddenly crossed his mind and he turned from the window, went over to the desk, opened his lap top and punched the button, bringing it to life. He searched through a small stack of papers that was collecting on the desk there next to it and found Jessica Burton's business card that she had given him during his visit at her office. jburton@amirecords.com

On an educated hunch, he sat down and keyed in *jhampton@amirecords.com* instead, then proceeded to type a quick, personal note.

"Lydia says hello…"

Kennedy sat back and looked at his little message, rubbed his forehead and, before he could stop himself, pushed send. The arrow began to spin in the bottom corner of the screen and the e-mail was gone.

His breakfast from earlier that morning sat watching him from beneath the silver cover over on the coffee table. He pushed his chair back and went over to it, lifting the lid. Cold eggs and sausage. It suited him just fine as he sat down again and placed a sausage in his mouth.

Half way through his scrambled eggs, a familiar sound came from his computer indicating that he had mail. Still chewing, he walked over and saw a message from Jack Hampton. With a quick double-click on his mouse, Kennedy opened the file.

"Go fuck yourself, priest. I know who you are and if you have any brains at all, you would get as far away from me as possible."

Kennedy had acted on a hunch, figuring Jack was not a man whose massive ego would let him back down. He was dead right. But he never expected such a quick reaction. Jack must have been sitting at his computer at the same time. In fact, Kennedy had not really thought about what he would do with a response of any kind. Without a clear plan, he had flushed Jack Hampton out of the bushes and in to the open. Unfortunately, Jack wasn no small, timid creature. He was a viscious white shark, bloodthirsty, and Kennedy had jumped in the water. It was pretty stupid, perhaps, but he felt a certain satisfaction that, on a whim, he had hit such a major nerve.

CHAPTER EIGHTEEN

Ian Cornell, a security officer who patrolled the vacation homes lining the beach, drove up almost silently behind the expensive looking Saab parked outside the old Burton house. Most of the homes were empty at this time of year, but he knew this place in particular and knew damn well nobody had been here for quite some time. He prided himself on knowing the comings and goings up and down his stretch of the coastline. He would be the first to tell you he pretty much knew who was doing what, when and why… at any given time. He knew the Burtons, too… Jessica, her brother and her mother, or at least had at one time long ago. But didn't recognize Jessica's car and with not much else to do, he decided it was worth having a quick look just to make sure.

He cut his engine and lifting a small notebook, jotted down her license plate. What the hell. If nothing else, this would make a good time to have another cigarette. He stepped from the vehicle and slammed the door behind him, grinding the gravel beneath his dull black boots as he moved authoritatively toward the front door on the opposite side of the house facing the beach. The old wooden deck creaked painfully as he stepped up onto it, under his rather insubstantial weight. The beach house itself was dark.

Taking immediate notice that the blinds had been lifted, he knew someone was in residence and knocked politely on the door. It was locked as he wiggled the knob and knocked again.

Walking along the deck, he pulled a half empty pack of *Winstons* from his jacket pocket, slid one out and placed it to his lips. He fished into his pants pocket, retrieving a book of matches from Benny's Bar and Grill and lit it up, puffing furiously for a moment in an effort to get things going. The officer contemplated the possibilities, then turned instinctively, and placed his face against the dark glass of the bedroom window, seeing the naked form of a woman he had known many years before.

It took detective Blakey a good two hours to reach the beach house after receiving the call about Jessica. He wore his badge hanging from his pocket and the few uniformed officers standing around paid no attention to him as he walked from his car toward the house. He introduced himself to the detective in charge at the scene, shaking his hand roughly and described his involvement in regards to Jessica and Stenton.

"What do we got?" Blakey asked.

Stupid bitch OD'd," the detective snorted. "Looks like heroin. Who knows? Make yourself at home." With that the jaded detective had seen enough and decided to take the rest of the day off, allowing Blakey to have his turn snooping around.

Officer Cornell stood in the corner of the room, his back turned, looking out the window as a photographer snapped several pictures of the naked Jessica lying there, sprawled on the bed.

"She wasn't a stupid bitch," Cornell muttered to himself.

"Excuse me?" Blakey asked, looking over at Cornell.

Officer Cornell turned from his silent world at the window and studied Blakey for a moment. Blakey studied him right back. His eyes were slightly swollen and red. His jaw was clamped tight and he appeared ready for a fight, perhaps the self-proclaimed guardian of this dead woman between them.

"She was a good person," Cornell said.

"You knew her?"

Officer Cornell's hard exterior softened as he dropped his eyes toward Jessica and back out the window. He shoved his right hand in his pocket.

"A long time ago," he said. "We were just kids."

Blakey inspected the drug paraphernalia littered on the bed.

"A good person, huh? Don't meet many of those these days."

Cornell did not respond. He simply stared out the window at the small white caps decorating the distant blue waves as they rolled continually forward. He was thinking about a girl he knew, how beautiful and innocent she was. How much they had in common back then. How she had grown up and drifted away and how he had missed her. He turned to see Blakey pulling her toes apart and examining the bottoms of her feet.

"What the hell are you doing?" he demanded.

"Relax there, cowboy," Blakey said, continuing his examination of the cold body.

"Can't we cover her up now?" Cornell said, softening his tone slightly, remembering his rank and the required level of respect, but still wanting to protect and watch over her. This was his patrol and Jessica had died right within his reach. He had somehow failed her and was trying now, in vain, to make up for it.

"What are you looking at, anyway?" he said.

"Looks like she got a little carried away here," Blakey answered, standing up straight and staring down at her. "That much is fairly obvious. The thing I don't quite understand," he continued, "is why someone like her would get into something like this."

"What do you mean?" Cornell asked.

"You were right, Officer. She was a good person. Pretty, physically fit, had a nice career going... people like that don't generally just up and start shooting heroine one day."

"What makes you think she just started?"

"Needle marks," Blakey said. "There's not another needle mark on her entire body. She was either very unlucky her first time out or..."

"Or what?" Cornell said.

"I don't know. Or someone helped her."

———

Tony Adams stuck his head in the doorway of Robert Tanner's office and rapped gently. It had been a seriously

256

long day and Tony was tired. The last thing he wanted to do was have a little chat with Tanner. When he wanted to see you in his office, it couldn't mean anything good. Not lately anyway.

Tanner was the Chief Editor at the LA Times. You don't pull down a position like that in the land of hardened American journalists without years of getting beat up and beating others in return. He was damn good at it. Probably because he enjoyed it so much. People feared Robert Tanner. They respected him, his frightening intelligence and his years of consistent performance. The man knew what he was doing. But he could come across as a blistering asshole on a bad day. And most days, seemed to be the bad ones.

Today was no exception and Tony could tell by the furrowed brow and complete lack of warmth draped across Tanners jowls, that he might even be getting fired.

"Hey Bob. You wanted to see me?" Tony said.

Tanner motioned for him to enter the office and close the door while he finished listening to the messages on his phone. As he scribbled notes on a small pad of paper, Tony sat down and crossed his legs, waiting patiently and painfully for the man to finish.

His office was not what you would call neat. While his position could be referred to as that of a high ranking executive, Tanner didn't give a shit about corporate politics and the game most people felt it necessary to play. A tidy office took too much time away from the things that demanded his immediate attention. He was busy.

Stacks of newspapers, not just his own, but others from around the country, lay leaning haphazardly in seemingly random piles here and there, at the corners of his desk, possibly anchoring it to the floor. When he had the news around him, he felt in control. He was not a man who could deal well with not knowing what was going on in the world at any given moment. It made him uneasy. Anxious. Especially if it was taking place, right at his feet, in the domain of his own newsroom.

"What's up, Tony?" Tanner said, placing the phone back in to its cradle. He tapped his pencil repeatedly against the wood edge of his desk and looked at Tony as though he had more pressing issues to deal with.

"Um, Alice said you wanted to see me."

"Yeah, I did. What's up?" he said. "I'm not getting anything out of you these days. Is there a problem?"

"No, no problem. I just…"

"What are you working on?"

"Well, sort of a long shot piece. Lydia Carter."

Tanner stopped tapping his pencil and just looked at Tony with blank eyes. He knew how to rip a hole in a man's chest without the use of his hands. Tony already felt guilty for pursuing this stupid story and he wore the look of shame that Tanner despised.

"Yeah, I've heard," he said. "What the fuck is that, Tony?"

"Well, her murder. There's the hint of foul play.

"Foul play? That was a hundred years ago, Tony. That's not news. That's ancient history."

"I know, but it seemed like it might have merit. It's plausible."

"Tony, don't go there, OK? Don't do that. You report on crime. Current crime. I have a newspaper to put out. I don't have time for murder mysteries. So please, do me a favor. Stop with this shit and do your job. Come on. Help me here."

Tony nodded silently in agreement. Tanner was finished with him and there really wasn't much else to discuss so he got up to leave.

"You're a good reporter, Tony," Tanner offered. "You just need to focus."

"OK, Bob. Focus…"

Tony gave a slight wave of his hand and opened the door, leaving the office. He looked across the editorial pit where Alice sat waiting to see if he came out alive. She smiled, but Tony, embarrassed, just rolled his eyes, shoved his hands in his pockets and walked in the opposite direction.

He took the elevator into the basement and wandered in the increasingly loud direction of the presses. When he needed to think, being down here, in the belly of the newspaper, drowned by the roar of the towering presses, he felt comfortable and able to roll things around in his head. The velocity with which the continuous web of paper flew through the press overhead, would terrify most people who had never witnessed the gargantuan machinery, standing a full three stories high and so deafeningly loud it would compete easily with standing directly in front of a jet engine. But to Tony, it brought a sense of solitude and peace.

He leaned against the cold cement wall and watched as a crew of inky pressman scuttled about, watching and maintaining the ink flows and making sure the photographs did not drift out of registration. He wished he were one of them. They knew their jobs. They didn't struggle. They never wondered what was up ahead. What would happen next. Theirs was a world you could count on, day after day, always the same. Comfortably predictable.

Still, there was something about Father Kennedy that he could not shake. Tony's uncle, his mother's brother, had been a priest and this had given him an innate respect for the clergy. They were men who had given their entire being to God. Talk about unpredictable. But Tony understood it and respected it all the same. And Kennedy had this thing about him. You just trusted him, crazy or not.

Tony was a good reporter. He knew that. Maybe Tanner was wrong. Maybe he was just an asshole, like everyone said. Unfortunately, he was still the boss and Tony had to deliver something that would satisfy him. Something quickly. Even if it was the same old crap that people loved to read. Who was he kidding, anyway? Tony was no journalist. Not a real one. He was a salesman with a pen and it made him sick.

Alice stood quietly next to him and took his hand. Tony turned and looked at her, eyes full of sweetness and compassion. She smiled knowingly.

"You OK?" she asked.

Tony could not hear a word. The screaming presses made it impossible to communicate verbally. But, clear as day, he saw that look in her eyes. Nobody could hear the team of pressmen either, standing in a line by the roaring presses, momentarily turned away from the monotony of the rolling newspaper, all cheering as Tony took Alice's hand, pulled her to close to him, and kissed her the way she had always wanted him to.

———————

CHAPTER NINETEEN

Blakey decided to follow up on Kennedy's advice now and go have a word with this guy, Jack Hampton at IMA Records. The following morning, he had placed no less than five phone calls to the man. He had proved impossible to nail down, but Blakey was persistent, annoyed with the feeling that perhaps Hampton was avoiding him and decided to camp his butt outside Hampton's office and wait for him to come back after lunch.

Like a spider waiting for a fly, it worked. Hampton rolled into the office around 1:30, at least two solid martinis under his belt. The receptionist was appropriately apologetic as she introduced them, explaining the reason for the interruption. Hampton looked at Blakey for a moment, shrugged his shoulders and ushered him into his office, closing the door behind them. He had spent decades dealing with cops and this fat pig didn't ruffle his feathers in the slightest. Not outwardly anyway.

Not waiting for an invitation to sit down, Blakey dumped his body onto a soft gray leather sofa and, seeing that he meant to stay for a while, Hampton reluctantly joined him.

"So you have heard about Jessica Burton, I presume?" Blakey asked.

"Horrible, yes. We were all shocked."

"Did you know her well?"

"She worked for me, but no, I cannot say that I knew her well."

"Did you know she had a heroin problem?"

"No, but it doesn't surprise me."

"Really? Why is that?"

"A lot of people in this business have drug problems," Jack said with the wave of a hand, as though it was common knowledge and not really very important. Blakey looked at the skyline outside the window and scratched his forehead.

"How about Ronald Stenton?" he asked.

"I'm not sure I am familiar with that name."

"He's a real estate guy. Evidently, he was working with Jessica to sell that old creepy house up in the hills. I guess it belongs to you."

"Yes."

"Nobody's seen him. He just up and vanished."

"I had Jessica working on selling the place, but I didn't know him. You think there's a connection?"

"Didn't say that. Could be. Hard to say." Blakey chewed on his fingernails and examined the plasterwork on the ceiling. Hampton began to grow uncomfortable and edged up on his seat, subtly signaling that he had nothing helpful to offer and that the meeting was over.

"How about a priest?" Blakey asked. "A Father Kennedy. Does that name mean anything to you?"

Hampton had a gift for lying and slipped into it as if it were his first language, showing no trace of his internal reaction to Blakey. Inside, his guts twisted in a sudden surge of shock and adrenaline at the sound of Kennedy's name. Outwardly, he appeared thoughtful, pleasant and wanting to help, but struggling valiantly for any kind of recognition. Furrowing his brow in quick concentration, he shook his head slowly, looking down at the carpet.

"No, I'm afraid not. Should it?"

"He was involved with Jessica and Stenton just before they both disappeared. I guess Stenton actually hired him to bless that house or some crap like that."

"It could use a good blessing." Hampton laughed. "The place is falling to pieces."

"Speaking of, that place… it used to belong to Lydia Carter, is that correct?"

"Yes it did. Actually AMI owns it, but she did live there, yes. A long time ago."

I used to listen to her, way back then. Did you know her?"

"You could say that," Hampton said with a smug smile. "I discovered her."

"Is that right?" Blakey said, allowing Hampton to wallow in his own pride. He hated men like Jack, sitting there, believing he was far better than Blakey, honoring him with his precious time. They were men who rode through life on the backs of others, building a world that catered to drugs and every sort of crime. Guys like Hampton became kings while guys like him got paid minimum wage to wade through the sludge every single day trying to clean it up. People like Hampton had no idea the corruption and filth they left in their path. Not that they would care. Blakey looked at Hampton and came close to smacking the smile from his face.

"OK, well, I think that's all I need to ask you," he said standing. "Thank you for your valuable time, Mr. Hampton."

"Of course Detective. Anything I can do. Don't hesitate."

Blakey shook Hampton's hand and headed for the door. As he was about to leave he turned and raised his hand, as though remembering one last thing.

"Any idea why Jessica would send a file to me?"

The blood drained visibly from Jack's face. He studied Blakey for a moment, regained his composure as quickly as possible and shook his head.

"I just find it strange," Blakey continued, scratching his head. "A smart, young, successful woman feels it necessary to mail a file, Lydia Carter's file, to the LAPD. No explanation. Then that same smart, successful woman goes off and shoots herself up with enough heroine to kill an elephant. I don't get it."

Blakey stood there for a moment, leaving the observation hanging in the air, then shrugged his shoulders and waved goodbye, leaving Hampton to ponder it, sitting alone in his office.

Jack ground his teeth together and grabbed his cell phone from his coat pocket and dialed Nash.

———————

Blakey made the long drive up into the Palisades again. The last time he had been here, he had discovered this whack job, Father Kennedy, lurking about and taken him in for questioning. But it had produced little, only a growing distrust for the priest, but certainly not enough to lock him up. Not yet anyway.

Ronald Stenton's car had been there as well, along with a shirt covered in his blood. Other than that, no other sign of the realtor had shown up. Officers had combed the house and the property, found zip, and given up. Clearly, though, Stenton had been at that house and he sure as hell didn't drive away.

So, despite the fact that he was alone now and that the house gave him the full-on creeps, Blakey decided he should have one more look around.

It was getting late in the day when he pulled his Crown Victoria up in front of the gate. There was sufficient light left to check around, but it would be fading fast. He had laughed with the other officers, back at the precinct, about the ridiculous ghost stories, but out here now, he wasn't about to be caught alone when the sun went down.

Stenton's car had been towed away, but a small circle of Winston cigarette butts, clearly indicated where someone had patiently leaned against it for some time.

Blakey looked up at the dark house, feeling suddenly as if it were almost looking back at him. He swallowed the stupid thoughts and made his way into the courtyard beneath the trees.

A smaller iron gate toward the left of the house swung slowly in the breeze and groaned, clanging repeatedly against an old iron clasp set into a small wall of crumbling mossy bricks. Blakey decided to have a look, as he had not ventured back there before.

Through the little gate, he followed the overgrown pathway around the side of the house and down toward the back. The ivy had grown so thick in parts that it acted as a barrier, preventing him from entering. He bent low and pushed his way through, coming out into the light in the back area of the house. There was a large, curving stone staircase that led up to a set of white wooden doors, now blistered and falling apart. Behind them was nothing but black emptiness. If Ronald Stenton was somewhere, lying dead in that tomb, Blakey had no idea how he would go about finding him. He could be holed up behind some wall deep in the basement or shoved in an old trunk in the attic. If that were the case, Blakey suddenly could not find the courage to continue. The house was clearly telling him to stay out. He could not remember ever feeling this cowardly. He was acting like a frightened little boy and it made him angry.

He laughed nervously at himself, clenched his fist and defiantly made his way toward the steps leading up to the house. Covered in ivy and old leaves, he looked down, choosing his steps carefully and stopped suddenly, bending to pick up the remains of a half-smoked Winston lying in the debris.

Stenton had most definitely been back here, standing in this very spot. But he had not finished his cigarette. By the looks of all the discarded butts outside the front gate, Stenton had been a man that enjoyed every last ounce of tobacco in his cigarettes, sucking them straight down to the filter. But for some reason he had not done so with this one.

Blakey hesitated and took a couple of steps backward, looking up at the house again. His foot suddenly plunged off the edge of the pool hidden beneath the leaves,

266

sending him toppling backwards into the stinking swamp below. He thrashed wildly with his arms, pulling his head above the muck and spitting out a mouthful of thick oil. He choked and spit as the cesspool swirled in, closing around him, pulling him down. With his hands he searched frantically in a wide circle for the edge of the pool and caught Ronald Stenton's rotting corpse by the neck. He yanked it up out of the thick, black soup and greeted it face to face, eyes wide-open in terror, the mouth gaping, dripping with sludge.

Finally losing his war with fear, Blakey let out a scream. He gulped for air as the sewage poured into his mouth. With both arms thrashing madly, he found the stone edge, pulled himself out from the pool and lay there in the leaves, his chest heaving. He struggled for each new breath as Stenton's decayed body sunk slowly back into its oozing grave beneath the leaves.

Tony Adams had taken the warning from his boss to get to work and deliver some news. He had read between the lines and knew it meant his job would eventually be on the line if he didn't. The whole Lydia thing served as an irritating source of embarrassment. He was more than aware that the other reporters knew about it and figured they'd all had a good laugh at his expense. Yeah, like they'd never made a mistake.

They didn't have the affections of Alice like he did. There was that.

He had been sitting down at the precinct waiting for Blakey to show up, trying to dig up enough scoop for something good to write about. Anything. That's when the call came in. Blakey had found Stenton and Tony's story suddenly got legs again and started walking. If they pulled Kennedy in now, he would have a solid story, crazy or not. Eviedently, patience is a virtue. So is revenge. If Tony played his cards right, by mid morning the next day, he would have enough information to begin a whole series of articles. Definitely front page material.

As soon as he reached his apartment, he stripped off his tie and threw it over the back of the chair sitting by the front door. It was late now, almost midnight and he had been at it since six that morning. Even though he was exhausted, his mind was racing with the sense that something really big was breaking loose. He wanted desperately to call Kennedy, to tell him, to warn him perhaps, but he knew he couldn't.

The bedroom light clicked on. A moment later, Alice appeared in the hallway wearing only one of Tony's white work shirts. Her smooth legs shot up from the floor and disappeared somewhere beneath the shirttail. So absorbed in his mission, it caught Tony by surprise, even though he had given her his key and asked her to wait for him.

The two new lovers had spent the remainder of that first afternoon in bed together, telling each other all the little secrets that they'd kept from each other for the past couple of years. It had made what started as a bad day into one of the best days of Tony's life. You're not supposed too fall in love with a woman that fast, but he was in a swiftly moving river and he didn't care where it was taking him. He could swim.

He and Alice were supposed to have had dinner together that evening. Alice chided that he needed something home-cooked. As much as he was impressed with the fact that she could cook as well as make love, however, Tony had pleaded for a rain check, giving in to the pressures of the job. He had to produce a story and deadlines were eating him alive. Something only she could understand. And she had. She had simply grinned at him and told him, like the previous two years, she could wait.

"Wow. You're really beautiful," he said, the hallway light piercing the white shirt from behind and highlighting the contours of her body.

"And you're really late. Must be something good. I opened some wine earlier. Want a glass?"

"Need a glass," he said, slumping down backward onto the couch. Alice wandered over to the counter separating the living room from the kitchen. She lit a match and placed it against the wick of several candles on the counter, then grabbed a clean glass hanging in the rack above. She had removed the cork earlier from a nice bottle of Cabernet and used her teeth to yank it out again as she approached Tony on the couch. She wasn't trying to be sexy, it just came natural and Tony, like only a reporter can do, soaked in every single detail.

She sat down on the couch next to him and curled her legs up underneath her and poured him a glass large enough for two to share. She handed him the glass and as he took a sip, she caressed the back of his neck and ran her fingers through his hair.

"So tell me what's got you going. At work, I mean," she giggled, responding to the wide-eyed look Tony shot her. Tony sipped the wine, smiling. He knew what she meant, but the joke was too good to pass up.

"Well, you know Tanner ripped me a new one. Told me to get serious and stop wasting my time on the Lydia story, right? So I did. I went right back to the basics, hitting the streets, hanging out at the precinct, waiting for a bite…

when it comes in. Blakey found that realtor guy, Stenton. He was in the pool or something at the old mansion up in Palisades. Lydia Carter's mansion. Blakey's going after the priest."

"Wow. That's a nice piece, even for Tanner's tastes." Alice took the glass from Tony and swirled it gently and placed it to her lips. She filled her mouth with wine and swallowed, studying Tony. She had worked with him long enough to know the subtle expressions on his face. He was like a little boy and she found him fairly easy to read.

"How does that make you feel?" she asked.

"Like I'm betraying him."

"Father Kennedy?"

"Yeah. I know. Calling him would be interfering with the law. I could lose my job, everything, but somehow I feel like I should warn the man. Blakey says he's crazy. Now, he's got some pretty good evidence, but my gut… I'm just not sure."

"If he is innocent, Tony, there will be other ways for you to help him. Stepping in now, interfering as you say, would be a wrong use of your job as a reporter. You have privileged information. That's part of the deal as a reporter. You can't use that information to help people get away from the cops. Even people you like."

"I know. But it's not that I like the guy, it's just, I don't think he could kill anyone."

"That's not for you to decide," she said. " I know how you feel. But you have a responsibility to uphold the law, no matter how nice of a guy you are."

Tony took his turn with the wine and breathed in deeply, closing his eyes and relaxing into the soothing feeling of her fingers in his hair. She pulled herself closer to him and lay her head on his shoulder.

"Blakey's gonna eat him for lunch," Tony said.

"Shhhh," Alice whispered. "Let it go. You need sleep. Tomorrow will be different and then you can decide what to do."

Tony turned his head. Her mouth was right there and he kissed her gently. He took another sip of wine and winked at her.

"Would it be OK if I didn't go right to sleep?" he said.

Alice took the wine glass, set it on the coffee table and stood up. With an impish grin, she took Tony by the hand and pulled him from the couch.

"Such a naughty little reporter," she said. "Somebody is going to have to discipline you firmly." She turned on her heel and wandered off toward the bedroom.

CHAPTER TWENTY

Kennedy woke up in a sweat around 1:00 that morning. Something was wrong. Dead wrong. He had never gotten a good look at the man who had whacked him from behind, but knew instinctively it wouldn't be long before he would come face-to-face with him again. Maybe he had acted prematurely in pressing Hampton like that. That was the trouble with e-mail; you can do stupid things a lot faster than normal. It was decided there, in the dark hours of the early morning, that he should check out of the Waldorf once and for all and find something a little more under cover.

He clicked on the lamp on the table next to the bed and sat up. Grabbing the remote control, he checked out using the express services on the television, then got up and threw his belongings into a green canvass and leather bag sitting on the floor of the closet. He double-checked under the bed for socks or anything else he might have otherwise left behind. Lydia's diary was sitting on the nightstand. He unzipped his bag, placed it carefully inside, and re-zipped it, quickly leaving the room and any danger in which he may have ignorantly placed himself.

As he punched the elevator button, the doors opened on command. Nash stood alone in the opened elevator looking back at him. Kennedy did not know who he was, but his guts flipped over inside. The white light flashed blindingly through his skull and he saw Nash standing over Jessica Burton's naked body, lying on a bed. He saw clearly, the small blue marks etched into his forearm, one of them fresh, still bleeding.

It was one in the morning and the hotel hallways were deserted. Nash stood patiently in the elevator waiting for Kennedy to get on. But Kennedy just stood there, his mind clicking. The elevator had been coming up to this floor and yet this man was not getting off and was now waiting for Kennedy to get in, so he could go back down.

Kennedy smiled at Nash and backed away. "I forgot something in my room," he said. "Sorry."

Nash had a blade in his hand suddenly and lunged out at Kennedy, thrusting at his neck. Kennedy pulled back, ducking to the left and swung his heavy bag in a half circle, connecting with the side of Nash's head, sending him back into the elevator. The doors began to close, but Nash managed to stick his foot between them, causing them the stop and safely reopen. Kennedy had bolted toward the opposite end of the hallway and was through the stairwell doors before Nash stumbled out of the elevator and into the hallway. He was two seconds behind Kennedy and was not going to let him get away. Now it was personal and there was going to be a sufficient amount

274

of pain to go along with permanently shutting this stupid priest's trap.

Kennedy raced down the cement stairs. He could hear Nash as he entered the top of the stairwell in pursuit, a good two flights above him. He thought about exiting on one of the floors on the way down, but decided to try for the garage instead and continued spiraling down the stairs, skipping the last several and jumping from landing to landing.

The steel door to the garage swung open and smashed into the cement wall behind it as Kennedy burst into the dimly lit, iridescent underground cavern. He knew exactly where he had left his car and it gave him the extra edge he needed to keep his distance from Nash.

He raced between the parked cars, bending low so as not to be seen. The *Nissan* was parked along the wall just up ahead. He had his keys in his hand now and pressed the alarm unlocking the doors accompanied by two irritatingly loud beeps and the bright illuminating flash from the brake lights. If Nash didn't know which direction Kennedy had gone, he certainly did now.

But Kennedy was inside the car with the key in the ignition. He started the car and quickly jammed it in reverse. Nash stood only ten feet away and raised his revolver as Kennedy backed out of the tight space. The rear window exploded in a shower of glass as Nash pumped several bullets through the barrel. The Nissan stopped and Kennedy, visible through the gaping window, slumped forward against the steering wheel.

Nash lowered the gun to his side and quickly scanned the garage for security cameras. Even with a silencer fixed to the barrel, somebody was bound to have heard the commotion and breaking glass. He carefully approached the vehicle as Kennedy sat up and slammed the accelerator to the floor. Nash raised his gun and fired again, but Kennedy caught him hard with the rear of the car and pushed him violently up into the air, toppling him backwards over the trunk of a parked sedan and on to the oil-stained floor of the garage. Shoving the *Nissan* into gear, Kennedy pierced the garage with a long squeal as the tires spun in a whirl of white smoke, then smashed into another car in front of him, bouncing off and fishtailing sideways as he disappeared down the curving cement structure.

He removed a twenty-dollar bill from his wallet and stopped briefly to throw it at the old man sitting in the small yellow booth.

"On the run," Kennedy said. "No time to talk."

The old man looked suspiciously at his car, chunks of glass lying on the trunk and across the back seat. Kennedy was bleeding from his neck.

"You OK?" he asked and punched the button lifting the black and white striped fiberglass arm, opening the way for Kennedy to escape. Kennedy didn't reply and sped out into the empty street and drove away, careful not to attract any more attention than needed.

He wasn't quite sure where he was going, but knew that he had to keep driving. There were no headlights following him that he was aware of and he breathed slower. He suddenly became aware of a sharp pain in his neck and shoulder and accidentally slammed on the brakes, sliding sideways as he realized his shirt was covered in warm sticky blood. He regained control of the car and pulled it to the side of the road, turning on the interior light above the rear view mirror. There was a small gash across the side of his neck and, opening his coat, he discovered a hole about the size of his little finger in his upper left shoulder.

"Oh, Jesus," he said. "I'm dead. Help me."

He glanced in to the rear view mirror once again and pulled back onto the road. If he checked in to a hotel this time of night, looking like this, they would report it to the police. That would be a complication too difficult to explain. The only place he could think of, of all places, was the old house in the hills.

Nash had picked himself up and quietly left the scene in the parking garage, his forehead and ego bruised. This priest was starting to really annoy him, and the new respect that began to form in his mind, made him want to kill him all the more.

He sat in the dark in the front seat of his *Mercedes* and watched the tiny blinking red light of a tracking device he had placed underneath the bumper of Kennedy's *Nissan* two days before.

"Where the hell are you going, Father Dumbshit?" he said. Removing a pack of cigarettes from his inner pocket, he placed one in his mouth and lit it with the hot, glowing lighter from the dashboard. The little dot on the hand-held computer screen continued, blinking on and off, moving toward the coast.

Detective Blakey showed up in the lobby of the Waldorf around 1:30 in the morning with two uniformed cops sticking to him like bookends on either side. He had done his homework, scrounged up a quick search warrant and demanded the key to Kennedy's room. The clerk at the front desk told him he was too late. His computer showed that Kennedy had checked out half an hour earlier.

It wasn't exactly the kind of stuff that would hold up in court, but Blakey knew enough about the way criminals think. Kennedy was on the run and he wouldn't have to run if he wasn't guilty of something.

The desk phone rang as Blakey was still standing there and the desk clerk picked it up professionally. But his face told Blakey something was wrong. The clerk hung up and looked up at Blakey, standing there expectantly.

"Key? I still want to search his room," Blakey said.

"Um, certainly, detective. But that was the garage just now. They said some guy just left the garage in a hurry. Covered in blood."

Kennedy was sitting in the front seat of the Nissan parked at an angle just outside of Lydia's front gate. His body rebelled in a torrent of pain causing him to clench his teeth and bare down. He vaguely remembered driving here and was not quite sure how he had made it. The bleeding was stopped now, but he was dehydrated and covered in competing layers of wet and dried blood. He had lost a lot of it, too and felt as though he would pass out. He knew he needed to fight to stay awake, to keep going.

Fumbling for the door handle, he opened the latch and fell out onto his knees in the sand and gravel. Forcing himself to stand, he grabbed the side mirror and pulled himself up, pushing his legs toward the iron bars of the gate ahead. If God would not save him, perhaps Lydia could.

Help or not, she was waiting for him just beyond the gate. He pushed it aside with the groans bellowing from the uncooperative hinges and staggered into the courtyard.

"Lydia!" he yelled. "Lydia!"

He hoisted himself up, one stone step at a time and threw himself against the great door. He managed to open it without much effort and fell inside against the adjoining wall. The house was dark and moist as before. What was he doing here? He would probably die here, like Bernardo, unable to finish what he had started. He had been a fool getting involved in this mess, with powerful people he knew nothing about, trying to bring down an empire by throwing rocks at its windows. Like Martin Luther centuries before, who did he think he was attacking this great whore?

Her bedroom was at the top of the endless stairs. In the darkness of the dusty shadows, each step looked insurmountable and larger than the last as they rose upward into the blackness above.

Then from the top of the stairs, a warm light began to glow and spill out over the railings, filling the house below. Kennedy could smell the sweet scent of sandalwood incense. Respectfully, he entered the room, made his way to the bed and fell down. He laid his head against her diary, his eyes gently closing.

It was dark and Kennedy was not sure where he was. Standing alone in a long corridor, he thought perhaps underground, the only light was coming from directly ahead. He followed the corridor leading out to an open space behind a huge stage.

Hundreds of roadies, the guys responsible for hauling and setting up all the band equipment, were hustling back and forth in a frantic effort to put a show together, just like the one they had in another city the night before. Each one, focused, knew his job well and went about it with the determination of an ant in a long line of workers responsible for feeding the entire colony.

Shirts were cast aside and the sweat flowed down muscled arms. It was a mixture between a high-rise construction site and a traveling circus being erected. Ropes hung everywhere, lifting long steel frames with a row after row of colored lights attached. Miles of cables stretched everywhere as men connected them to microphones, amplifiers, and a mountainous wall of speakers, somehow able to tell which cable went to the correct place. Just passed the stage, out front, Kennedy caught a glimpse of the auditorium itself, empty seats, waiting, as it rose high into the air and pushed back from the stage into a great amphitheater.

"Hey, you're not supposed to be back here, man," a roadie said as he brushed passed Kennedy carrying an arm full of black sound cables.

"No, it's cool. I'm with Lydia," Kennedy said. "Have you seen her?"

"Not lately," he said. "We do a sound check in less than half an hour, so she's probably around somewhere. Check the dressing rooms."

"Dressing rooms?"

"Back down the corridor, there," he said, rather sharply, irritated with Kennedy for slowing him down.

"Thanks, man," Kennedy said and turned to walk back through the dark tunnel. It smelled like wet cement in the center and his eyes had difficulty adjusting to the lack of light. But towards the end, he could see several doors in the wall to the right. He knocked gently on the first one and

opened it, the door old and creaking slightly. Several of the band members from Purple Crow sat around smoking. The Bone King was stretched out on the couch with his feet up in the air slung over the back.

"Hey Soldier," he said. "Looking for your lady?"

"Yeah, anyone seen her?"

"Last I saw her, she was having a nice heart-to-heart with Jack. Pretty heated. Maybe check her room. It's the last one there, on the right."

"Hey, thanks Tommy," Kennedy said and waved at the rest of the guys in the room. He closed the door again and turned to the other two doors a little further down the hall. He could hear them arguing before he even reached the last door and stopped outside to listen, not wanting to interrupt anything that was not his business. But it didn't sound like an argument. Lydia began yelling, followed by the sound of furniture moving.

"You belong to me, you fucking whore!" Jack yelled as Kennedy tried to open the door. It was locked, but he opened it with a quick kick from his boot, slamming it hard against the wall behind. Light from the room instantly flooded into the hallway. Jack stood over Lydia, his pants undone. She lay on a couch beneath him crying, her shirt torn open.

"Get the fuck out!" Jack yelled, pointing his finger defiantly at Kennedy. "This is my fucking band and you have no business here!"

"Oh, I've got business," Kennedy said and moved into the room like a hurricane, blocking Jack's attempted swing with his left arm and catching Jack under the rib cage. He grabbed him with his right arm and violently threw him up against a row of shelves along the back wall. Everything came crashing down on top of him. He struggled quickly to get to his feet, but Kennedy was on top of him, pounding his jaw with a series of quick burst from his clenched fist. Blood began to spray from Jack's nose and mouth as Kennedy stood and yanked him to his feet, a rag doll losing consciousness. Again, Kennedy grabbed him by the shirt and hurled him to the floor through the open doorway.

Lydia, now curled in a ball, was crying on the couch. Kennedy looked at her then back at Jack, his jaw clenched shut like an iron bear trap.

"Big mistake," Jack said, spitting blood. His mouth was filled with red and his eyes were starting to swell. He tried to get up, but stumbled and fell back on the floor, thrashing in a furry.

"Goddamn you! She fucking belongs to me!" he screamed, finally managing to stand. He backed away from Kennedy, but kept jabbing his finger at him like a knife. "You fucked everything."

"Touch her again, Jack, and I will kill you. Do you understand?"

"You're already dead. Both of you. You're both already dead."

Jack turned and stumbled out of the room. Kennedy walked over and closed the door, turning to see Lydia crumpled on the couch, hiding from him.

"It's OK, Lydia. It's over now. It's OK, I'm here," he said softly, sitting beside her and stroking her hair. She cried for a few minutes and then placed her hand in his, looking up at him. He held her close and rocked her gently back and forth until she stopped crying and began breathing more regularly.

"What happened," he said.

"He said he loved me."

"He loves you?"

"Yes. He said he always has and that I was meant for him. I didn't know what to say. I didn't mean to, but I just started laughing. He went insane."

"Did he hurt you?"

"He hit me. He kept saying, over and over, that I was his, that I belonged to him and that he could do anything he wanted with me. He ripped my shirt and pushed me down."

She was crying hard now and the words became jumbled and difficult to understand. She struggled to breath and talk at the same time, becoming hysterical.

"He told me to…" she stopped altogether, breaking into tears, her body heaving, the sobs choking out every thing.

"It's ok…you don't have to say anything." Kennedy didn't need words, easily putting the pieces together. His fury and hatred for Jack swelled at the sight of what he had done to Lydia. "You hold all the cards, here," Kennedy said, holdig her in his arms. "Just fire him…"

"Fire him? I can't!" she yelled. He owns me!"

"No, he doesn't own you. Fire him, Lydia, or I'm going to end up killing the son of a bitch."

"He owns everything!"

"Not you. He doesn't own you. If we have to, we just start over. Do it all again. Dump the bastard or one of these times, I might not be there."

Kennedy listened to the sound of his words echo through his head. They had a meaning that sent a shiver down the center of his back. He hated that he had spoken them. Lydia sat up straighter now, still holding him, sniffling and wiping the tears from her eyes.

"Soldier," she said. "You're such a good man. You're so good to me." Kennedy shook his head but she stopped him.

"*No, please. You have. I don't deserve you. I love you. I always will. But I cannot stop this. You know I can't.*"

"*Yes, you...*"

"*Shhhhh.*" *She whispered. She was quiet for a moment, then looked up at him. "It's 1971, Soldier. October 6, 1971. My time has run out." She kissed him softly on the lips and the tears began to flow once more. Kennedy sat there in silence, her words now piercing his heart. He was confused. The year, the date, he did not understand. But something inside told him he would never see her again. She kissed him again and placed her head against his chest, sitting alone there, together on the couch.*

"*You have to go now,*" *she said suddenly without emotion.* "*There is someone in the house.*"

Kennedy awoke instantly. He sat up, realizing that he was on the old bed in her upstairs bedroom. It was just before daylight now, early in the morning, still gray outside and he was freezing. He stood, her words still echoing in his head.

"*There's someone in the house.*"

He went for the door and yanked it open. In an instant, he knew he was trapped. Nash stood in the hallway at the top of the stairs, his gun cradled loosely, smiling.

"Good morning, Padre. Sleep well?"

Nash raised his gun slowly, allowing Kennedy to imagine his fate. "I imagine you already said your prayers, a man of the Cloth and all, so no need for any final words." Behind him on the stairs below, Lydia stood watching. She looked up at Kennedy and he saw her there, her face sad and empty. Nash followed his gaze and stepped back, swinging his gun back and forth in sudden panic between Kennedy and Lydia. Her fiery eyes locked on Nash, she began to rise up the staircase, moving toward him, a wind shrieking through the house.

"What the fuck?" he stammered. Fear now covering his face, he looked to Kennedy for any explanation, but was provided nothing. He pumped two bullets, then another at her, but they disappeared into the wood paneling of the wall. He fired another, but it too, simply passed through her and sunk into the wall, spraying tiny splinters of wood.

Nash was not familiar with all the stories about this house, it's haunted past, but what he was seeing right now was all too apparent. This shocking realization caused him to lose his composure and, for the first time in his deadly career, he panicked. He turned the gun suddenly on Kennedy instead. Lydia stopped, almost hovering at the head of the stairs, ten feet away, her eyes burning a hole in Nash. The gun was shaking violently in his hands.

"Tell her to go away!" he yelled through clenched teeth.

"I don't think she will listen. This is her house," Kennedy said.

"Tell her to go the fuck away!" Nash yelled, now in utter terror.

Lydia turned her focus downstairs. In the dark recesses of the old, musty library room, still leaning against the fireplace where they had sat unused for so long, a set of iron fire tools rattled violently.

Kennedy stood frozen in the doorway of her bedroom, watching Nash, waiting for him to squeeze the trigger and end it all. The gun, however, dropped from his hands as his body shuddered, the front of his head exploding in a violent spray of blood, as the tip of a fireplace poker burst through.

He tried to speak, but could not. His eyes rolled backward, up into his skull, as he stumbled backward, flipped over the stair railing, instantly disappearing into the darkness below. In the short silence that followed, the sickening impact of his body could be heard, shattering upon the ground floor, rising up, bringing the years of dust billowing behind it.

Kennedy stood alone in the doorway, his heart pounding. Lydia was gone. On the marble landing three stories below, Nash lay twisted, his body broken, a small trail of blood staining the corner of his mouth. His eyes were still open in terror. Kennedy descended the stairs as quickly as he could and came upon Nash at the bottom. In the darkness of the early morning hour, he looked closer and realized there was an ornate iron fire poker piercing Nash's head, like a spear, from behind and out through his forehead. Kennedy nudged the body gently with his left foot and looked off in the direction of the fireplace on the back wall of the next room.

"Thank you," he said, looking around. He knew she was still here. Somewhere. He knew she saw and heard everything. Then, something outside, towards the back of the house caught his eye, like a yellow flag blowing in the wind. He turned, confused, and walked towards the living room windows and beheld a scene he could not quite understand. The entire back area, everywhere, was all cordoned off with strips of yellow and black police tape. It was a crime scene, just like the ones in every movie he had ever seen.

The whole house, it occurred to him, was off limits legally and he was standing here, smack in the middle of it, with a dead man, an iron firepoker through his head. He had to get out of the house and get out fast, but he knew immediately, even that was no good. He had been bleeding heavily. His blood and damning evidence would be all over this place. The police would take two seconds to figure it out.

But he couldn't stay here. Not now. He decided to continue to head for St. Augustine's, to lay as low as possible until he could get control of this ridiculous situation. He was not thinking clearly as he walked out the open front door, across the courtyard and to his car.

As he slipped through the gate, he saw Nash's *Mercedes* parked along side of the road, just passed the house and went to check it out. It was unlocked and he opened the door and sat down inside. The compartment between the seats yielded a leather wallet, identifying the man inside as Richard Nash. There was a cell phone as well. Kennedy flipped it open and instinctively pressed the send button, calling the last number that had been dialed.

"Hampton," a voice answered.

Kennedy was silent. He had placed a call from a dead man's phone. A man who had died, at the hands of Lydia, no less. A man who obviously was trying to kill him, and Jack Hampton had answered it. Kennedy hesitated for two beats, then spoke.

"Your man Nash…he's dead," he said. "I think you and I need to talk."

CHAPTER TWENTY-ONE

It was still early, around 8:30 in the morning, and the Times editorial department was buzzing with a renewed energy as they started all over again in their daily attempt to put a newspaper to bed. Tony's phone rang and he yanked it from the hook.

"Adams, LA Times."

"Hey, Tony. This is Father Kennedy."

"Father! You checked out of your hotel," Tony said. "Where the hell have you been?"

"I'm at the house. Lydia's house. Any idea what's up with all the police tape? It's all over the place."

Tony hesitated. It was do or die. He either trusted Kennedy or he didn't. Any information he gave out at this point could be considered aiding and abetting a fugitive. Not something a crime reporter wants to have on his resume. He knew in his gut what he wanted to do, but his head was holding him back.

"Look, Father, I shouldn't even be talking to you."

"Why not?"

"I can't really...I could lose my job, man. Maybe worse..."

"Tony, listen I need you to be straight with me here, ok? I really need your help."

"Do you have any idea what this all looks like?" Tony objected.

"Yes! I do!" Kennedy blurted out, his utter frustration reaching the boiling point. "I look like a crazy person! I know, Tony, I know! My whole life, I've looked like a whack-job, batshit-crazy person...but I can't help it! I can't help the things I see! The things that happen! I can't help it! None of it! None of it..."

There was silence on the phone. Kennedy breathed deeply. "I just need your help. Please, Tony..."

"OK, shit," Tony agreed. "Look, I'm not sure why I'm telling you this, but I am... Blakey is looking for you. Wherever you are, you gotta get out of there. He's gonna pull you in again and book you."

"Book me? For what? I'm the one getting the shit beat out of me."

"The real estate guy, Stenton... They found him."

"So?"

"At the bottom of her pool. Lydia's pool."

"What? And... and Blakey thinks I did it?"

"You were the only one there, man. There was blood, he had a massive head injury or something, and you...think about how it looks."

"Not good."

"Listen, Father... Blakey knows all about the little girl, too. The one in Fremont. The one that died. He thinks you're... he thinks you're psycho, OK?"

Kennedy was silent. There it was again. You give your life over to something, you try to help people, you give until it hurts…and it all just comes back to bite you in the ass over and over again. He didn't do anything but try to save that girl's life. And now his was on the line because of it.

"You there, Father" Tony asked.

"Yeah, I'm here. Listen, it gets worse, Tony," Kennedy said finally. "I've got another dead body up here. There's blood everywhere. Some of it's mine."

This time it was Tony who went quiet. He suddenly regretted having picked up his phone this morning. He should have gotten a number to call Kennedy back and then reported it to Blakey. As a reporter, he was way over the line. He knew he was in too deep. He looked over at Alice, sitting there at her desk watching him. She nodded her head, urging him to continue.

"What did you do, Father?" he asked.

"I didn't do anything, Tony! Some guy, I think he works for this Jack Hampton, cornered me at my hotel last night, takes a poke at me with a knife and starts shooting at me. I ran. What would you do? Then he finds me again, somehow, and I don't know… now he's dead."

"What do you mean you don't know, Father? You're not making any sense."

"I've been shot, Tony. My neck is cut open. The guy follows me here, and then I find him at the end of the staircase with a fireplace poker through his head, OK?"

"A poker? Holy shit. OK, look… take it easy. Maybe I should just have someone come pick you up. You need help."

"That would be the end of me, Tony. This AMI Records guy, Hampton, I'm telling you, he's dirty. He's probably even hooked up with the cops."

"What do you want me to do?"

"I don't know. Think of something. Keep Blakey away from me. I need time to think."

"Look, call me crazy, but you need a place to stay," said Tony. "I know someone, too, like a nurse. Well, she's not really a nurse, but she can take a look at you. Can you drive?"

"Yeah. I think. Are you sure about this, Tony?"

"Hell no," Tony said. "But I can't just let a priest bleed to death. That's like a sacrilege or something."

"I appreciate this, Tony."

"Don't thank me yet. We may both end up in jail."

Tony gave him detailed directions on how to reach his apartment in the city. They agreed to meet within two hours. Tony felt like he had done the right thing, but was suddenly very afraid he was really blowing it. He hung up the phone and looked sheepishly up at Alice as she sat patiently waiting, looking back at him.

"Now, that's what I call chasing a wild goose," she said. "So, now what, I'm a nurse?"

Kennedy sat in Nash's *Mercedes* and looked in the rear view mirror at the thrashed *Nissan* parked up the road behind him, its rear window blown out and the driver's side crushed in like an aluminum beer can. Nash's keys hung in the ignition. It would be suicide to try and drive the *Nissan* through downtown Los Angeles. The police would have a difficult time not noticing something like that. It was almost an advertisement saying, *"I'm a criminal. Pick me up.*" But in the City of Angels, crusing along in a polished, jet black, convertable *Mercedes*, he would blend right in.

He looked at himself in the mirror and was amazed that he was still alive. Blood was smeared across his unshaven cheek and covered his neck. The knife wound was about two inches wide, but not very deep. It would heal. It was his shoulder that was causing him the most concern. It hurt like hell.

He turned the ignition and the *Mercedes* roared to life. Bernardo was probably laughing at him somewhere, covered in blood and driving a car like this, running for his life. Yeah, it was real funny. He shoved it in gear and pulled a u-turn onto the road, looking at the totaled *Nissan* as he picked up speed passing by. The house behind the gates, stood watching, dark but not empty.

———————

The drive back into the city was a complete blur. Kennedy would remember nothing about it. Once there, Tony's apartment had been fairly easy to find, thankfully, but climbing from the front seat of the car had been an ordeal he was not prepared for. His body had become welded to the seat with his blood. He held Lydia's diary close, clutched to his chest, and stained now too, with the same blood. He tried to remain as inconspicuous as possible, but for those who had taken a closer look, Kennedy would have passed for a zombie straight out of a B-horror film. He even had the stagger down as, bright red, he stumbled across the sidewalk.

Tony and Alice had been watching for him out the window and raced out to help him. Tony threw his arm around him and helped him into the cement breezeway dividing the building in two.

"Shit, you weren't kidding. You're a mess," Tony said. "This is Alice. She's a friend."

"Good, I need a friend," Kennedy said, smiling at her.

She smiled back and joined Tony in his effort to support Kennedy as they made their way into the safety of the apartment complex. Most everyone who lived there was off at work, leaving the place deserted. As another small stroke of luck, Tony's apartment was on the bottom story. Kennedy didn't think he would have been able to make it up a flight of stairs. The front door was left open and together, they pulled Kennedy inside.

Once behind closed doors, they sat him down in a chair in the kitchen and peeled his coat off. He was wearing a light blue broadcloth shirt turned almost entirely red. The back of his shirt was a solid wall of blood. Alice undid the buttons and carefully pulled it back to reveal the wound, just below his left shoulder blade. She lifted the shirt and pulled it off, the fabric sticking to his skin. The bullet had gone straight through.

"I'm not much on bullet wounds," Alice said. "But I think this is a good thing. It looks like there are holes on either side. It went straight through, so I guess we don't have to go dig anything out."

"More good news," Kennedy said.

Tony had brought a washcloth and a metal bowl of warm water. Alice took the cloth and soaking it, dabbed gently at the wound, cleaning off the blood. It looked smaller than she expected it would, again, not that she knew anything about gunshot wounds. Kennedy just moaned slightly as she pressed the cloth against him, letting her do all the work. He was in good hands. Tony just sat in the chair next to him and watched. This was out of control and he was as grateful as Kennedy at the moment, that Alice had entered the picture. She seemed so calm and like she knew what needed to be done, taking it on bravely, one step at a time. Tony was now, respectfully, the assistant and sat by patiently awaiting any instructions.

The blood was more frightening in appearance than anything and cleaned off rather easily. It gave them all a sense of hope, mostly Kennedy, that he just might get through this.

"What's that?" Tony asked pointing to the diary now sitting next to Kennedy on the table.

"Her diary," Kennedy said.

"Really? Like Lydia Carter's diary?"

Kennedy nodded his head. "Her whole life, right there. In her own handwriting."

"Wow. That's pretty cool. Might have to clean it up a bit first," Alice said, nodding at the blood smeared on it. "But I'll bet you could get a chunk for that on e-bay."

Alice placed clean cotton gauze on both sides of his shoulder and wrapped it tightly. She suggested the couch and Tony helped her to lift Kennedy and walk him into the living room to lie down. Kennedy picked up the diary and they all waddled together towards the couch

Tony wanted to call Blakey. He knew he should. But with Alice here, he was managing to hold the panic back, sat himself calmly down in an oversized, stuffed green chair and started to think things through. Alice found a soft thin blanket, placed it over Kennedy and retreated to the kitchen.

"I'll make some sandwiches if you have stuff to make them with," she said to Tony.

"What happened to upholding the law?," Tony teased.

"Just because I'm older than you, doesn't mean I know everything," she said with a grin. "But you better be respectful or I'll send you to your room, little boy."

"Sorry," he laughed. "Yeah, there should be something in the fridge. Thanks."

Kennedy looked over at Tony and raised his eyebrows several times as Alice wandered off into the kitchen humming a happy melody. Tony dropped his head and grinned as Kennedy closed his hand tightly around the diary and shut his eyes, drifting into a distant dark place.

———

The flames leapt three times, jumping furiously from the barrel of the gun. Lydia, standing in the center of the stage, was knocked violently backwards, the holes desecrating the entire front of her chest.

Kennedy stood, impotent, unable to reach her, to help her, even to move, buried as if in a pit of quicksand, there in the mass of people below, watching it all.

The music stopped and people all around him began to scream, first one, then several, as the entire auditorium began to understand what had just taken place. Lydia lay dead on the stage. He turned and looked up at the tall man standing next to him holding the smoking gun. The man's hand was gloved in black leather as he reached out and grabbed a young kid in front of him by the collar, yanking him backwards, up close to him. He pushed the hot gun down the back of his jeans and shoved him forward again onto his knees into the crowd. The kid immediately tried to get to his feet and screaming, pulled the scalding gun from his pants. It was Howard Perkins.

The tall man was gone now, instantly disappearing into the darkness of the crowd. People everywhere were screaming and crying. Howard Perkins, waving the gun in the air, stood alone as the crowd backed away from him. A large Hell's Angel came from behind and smashed him across the back of the head, knocking him once again onto the floor. Others immediately took up the war cry and began kicking Perkins in the head and torso. Blood spurted from his mouth and nose as he rolled into a ball, trying in vain to protect himself from the onslaught of crazed vigilantes.

Still holding onto the pistol, Perkins raised it above his head and squeezed the trigger. The explosion was deafening, ringing off the walls in the large auditorium. Through the sudden burst of smoke and flame, Kennedy watched as the bullet made its way directly at him, smashing him in the shoulder and knocking him sideways. He remained standing there, and instinctively reached up in an effort to stop the stabbing pain in his shoulder.

Police officers began to flood the stage area and the crowd broke into a full panic, running and trampling over those who had fallen in front of them. Spontaneous fights broke out and people began to swing blindly at each other regardless of size or sex. Kennedy stood holding his shoulder, numb, watching as several psychotic bikers, high on the taste of blood, continued to kick and spit on an unconscious Howard Perkins. The police rushed forward, swinging their batons and the crowd split apart.

Kennedy looked back up at the stage, empty now except for two police officers standing over the slain body of Lydia Carter, lying there in a pool of her own blood. She was dead.

The bright yellow house lights came up now, yielding an even more gruesome scene of widespread panic and blood.

In the shadows, behind a wall of amplifiers, Kennedy caught sight of Jack Hampton, standing alone, enjoying a cigarette. He just stood there, leaning against the amplifiers, watching, making no effort to help the police, and now paramedics, as they tried unsuccessfully to revive Lydia.

Sucking calmly on his cigarette, Jack flicked the remains in a long arc, up in the air and down into the audience below. He turned to leave the asylum, then spun his head suddenly and looked down directly at Kennedy. He cocked his head slightly to one side, as a smile slowly appeared at the corners of his mouth and spread like an unforgiving disease across his ugly, hate-filled face.

CHAPTER TWENTY-TWO

Kennedy thought Jack Hampton's estate had more than likely been featured in the pages of an *Architectural Digest* magazine. It was three magnificent stories of sheer glamour and fitting for the millionaire he had become. Made almost entirely out of steel and tinted glass, it mirrored the sky around it giving the illusion of clouds floating right through it.

The property was surrounded on three sides by a twelve-foot security wall forming a compound, covered in flowering ivy. The back of the property fell five-hundred and twenty feet off a sheer cliff directly into the ocean, so there was little need for additional security there. Even if a brave thief had attempted to climb the cliff, there were the Dobermans to deal with.

A thick guard wearing black sunglasses and a cheap suit stood by the gate and approached Kennedy as he pulled up, still driving Nash's *Mercedes*.

"Father Kennedy for Mr. Hampton," Kennedy said, rolling down his window. The guard quickly examined Kennedy and the inside of the car, nodded to a security camera watching from the wall and without uttering a word, motioned for Kennedy to proceed as the gate lurched and began to slide open.

A butler stood patiently at the front steps next to several massive iron columns. Kennedy parked the car and climbed out. The butler was made of stone and simply waited for Kennedy to approach. As he did, the butler turned on his heel and led the way into the house, ushering Kennedy into a side library through two towering polished steel doors without exchanging a single word of pleasantry.

Jack Hampton was sitting in a large, maroon leather wingback chair smoking the remains of a cigar. He swirled a glass of cognac in his left hand, shoved the cigar in his jaw and pointed to the matching chair on his right. He did not stand to greet Kennedy nor offer his hand. The butler, taking his cue, left the room closing the doors behind.

"What are you doing with my house?" Jack grumbled.

"Lydia's house."

"My house. Lydia is dead in case you hadn't heard."

"Oh, I know all too well, Jack. I presume that's why you sent some thug to kill me."

"Nash? Don't be ridiculous. Standard procedure. You were trespassing. I should have you arrested."

"But that would involve the police. No sense digging up the past, no pun intended."

Jack stared at Kennedy through the spirals of thick white smoke. He was wrinkled and gray, his eyes drooping and rimmed in red. Dark splotches dotted his head where his hair used to be. A permanent frown had been etched into his jaw. This man was wealthier than could be imagined, but he was far from happy. Especially with Kennedy.

"What exactly do you want?" he barked.

"To set Lydia free. I want the truth."

"Indeed. The truth. Lovely sentiment." Jack stood, groaning under his substantial weight. He lifted a crystal decanter from a small table and refilled his glass. He poured a second and handed it to Kennedy before returning painfully to his chair. He took another cigar from a slender leather case and snapped it shut, offering it to Kennedy but knowing he would refuse. Kennedy shook his head as Jack snipped the end of the brown missile with a small chrome tool that looked like it could have been used to remove someone's finger. He placed the cigar in his mouth and ignited it, sucking repeatedly, lips pushed outward, jowls hanging loose. He resembled a stuffed pig with an apple in its mouth.

"Why should I tell you anything?" Jack said, clearing his throat.

"Because, it's the only way you are ever going to be rid of her. Lydia…"

"Don't be ridiculous. You don't actually buy all that… ghost nonsense," he snapped. Kennedy crossed his leg over the other, sipped his cognac for the first time, smiled at Jack and winked.

"You're a priest, man!" Jack said. "You actually believe in that crap?"

"You wanted her. She didn't want you back. That's gotta hurt. Especially a proud, self-made man such as yourself."

Jack just sat there. Silent. There was simply no viable explanation for how Kennedy knew any of this. His lips began to tremble.

"Get out of my house," he managed.

"Remember, Jack? She laughed at you when you told her… you loved her. So you hit her. You didn't have to hit her, Jack."

"That is ludicrous!"

"You tried to force yourself on her. She was crying."

"How do you know that? Goddamn it, how do you know that?" he yelled, rising from his chair, then slumping back down.

The door opened slightly and one of Jack's security men looked in. "I'm all right, goddamn it!" he screamed. "Go the fuck away!" The door closed again, leaving the two alone. Jack's face was flush. His eyes were brimming with tears.

"Who told you that?" he asked again, gritting his teeth.

"She did Jack. Lydia did."

"That's pure horse shit," he cried. "You expect me to sit here and listen to this crap. Go on, get out of here!" He was shaking now and on the verge of breaking down.

"The truth. The simple truth. It will set her free, Jack. You owe her that."

"I don't owe her a goddamn piece of shit! I made that woman what she was. She had raw talent, that's all! And she threw it all away. Without me, she was nothing."

" Look, you've had the life you wanted," Kennedy said. "And I would guess you don't have a lot of time left. You may not feel you owe her anything, but for almost fifty years she's been tortured, Jack. She didn't deserve that. Don't end life without setting her free."

"I think our time is up here. I want you to leave."

"If you confess your sins, God is willing and able to forgive."

"What is that supposed to mean? What are you talking about?"

"I am a priest, Jack. Confess your sins and she will be free to move on."

"I don't believe in all that Catholic crap."

"You don't want to believe I've seen Lydia either," Kennedy snapped back. "But inside, Jack, you are scared to death. You know I've seen her. You know she told me everything. You know you wanted her and she rejected you."

The tears in Jacks eyes spilled down now, through the creases in his cheeks. He choked and cleared his throat again, gulping at his cognac. He sat silently.

"How would I know these things, Jack? There is no other way. She is in that house. You know the stories. They're true. I have seen it myself. It's her and she's been there, tormented, for all these years. Let her go, Jack. Please. Let her go."

"You have vows," he said finally. "Don't you? You're not allowed to speak of this to anyone?"

"Not a soul. I would be excommunicated."

"That's not bullshit. You can't say anything?"

"I would lose everything."

Drunk now and crying freely, Jack was a tormented man and despite his hardened shell he had obviously carried a tremendous amount of guilt buried deep inside for far too long. The dam was old and brittle and about to burst. Kennedy was moved and almost felt pity for him.

"I'm sorry," Jack blubbered in a wave of heavy sobs. The cigar fell to the floor, he pitched forward and wept openly into his hands. "I did it. I killed her. I killed her." He shook repeatedly gasping for air, allowing the tears to cleanse him.

After a time, he quieted and embarrassed by his childish display, sat back up in his chair. He wiped his eyes with the back of his jacket sleeve and breathed deeply, averting his eyes from Kennedy, trying to regain his composure. He was slightly shocked by his sudden emotional outburst, but pretended that it did not bother him. He had not cried since he was ten years old. But the man in front of him was a priest. Certainly he had seen this sort of thing before. Kennedy picked the cigar off the floor and placed it in the ashtray. Jack took his snifter and filled his mouth, pushing down the pain again.

"She wanted out," he admitted. "She was going to call it quits. I would have lost everything I built. I would have lost her. I didn't know what else to do."

"I don't understand," Kennedy said.

"Think, man! She was a superstar. If she dies...it never ends."

"What never ends?"

"It's true what they say," Jack said sipping his cognac. He was back, in control of his emotions, not weeping anymore, but the pain was still apparent in his eyes. The flood gates had been open, though, a brief mistake, but he spoke easier now, looking up at the ceiling, seeing an entirely different world. He actually smiled.

"A dead rock star is worth ten times as much as a living one," he continued. "But with Lydia, I never dreamed what would happen. She was like this treasure. And I had found her. She was incredible. Back then, rock stars were becoming famous left and right, but few of them had any real talent. They were just grabbed, packaged, and promoted, then tossed aside for the next fool to come along. But Lydia...no, not Lydia. Nobody could believe it. She became a legend. And she was all mine."

Jack gulped at his cognac, relishing the memories.

"But then, she pushed me away," he confessed. "I had to do it. I had no other choice. I realized then it was like… killing the goose that laid the golden egg. Only I got lucky with Lydia. This time, that goose just got stronger and stronger, she kept laying golden eggs, long after she was dead…just like I knew she would."

"The man in prison? Perkins."

"Just a punk."

"But innocent."

"Yes, and stupid. I had people working for me. Poor kid was just the lucky one stupid enough to get in the way. Of course, he told everyone he didn't do it, that someone shoved a gun down the back of his pants, but he was a drug addict. Nobody believed him. Why should they? The police are idiots. They require answers. I simply supplied them with the ones that would satisfy them. Besides, they all loved that she had died. All of them."

The tears had started to flow again, but Jack was in control. He breathed heavily, swirling his glass and stared cold at Kennedy. He was not about to break down again. It dawned on him suddenly, that he was being given a second chance. Kennedy was no real threat to him, in fact, provided a way for him to move on, guilt free without Lydia around his neck another minute. He already was starting to feel better.

"What about the real gunman?" Kennedy asked.

"Gone," Jack said, contemplating the history. "Men like that can be of help, but they can also mess things up after awhile. I needed assurance."

"So you killed him as well."

"It had to be done," Jack whispered, his head hung low on his chest, his eyes puffed and dripping. His transgressions churning in his mind, he processed everything, working it out, justifying it all. He looked up at Kennedy suddenly, eyes narrowing.

"Not a word,' he hissed.

Kennedy made the sign of the cross over Jack. "Your sins are forgiven," he said. "Go in peace and sin no more." He drained the remains of his glass, set it on the table and rose. Jack looked away and did not acknowledge Kennedy as he left the room, quietly closing the door behind him, leaving the bruised old man to his misery.

Outside, Kennedy walked purposefully to his car, scrutinized from several different angles. He climbed into the Porsche, started the engine and shoved it in gear. The Porsche spun around, aggressively and leapt up to the gate. As it slid open, allowing him to leave, he unbuttoned his shirt.

"Hope you got all that, Blakey," he said and with his right hand, ripped the tape and wire from his chest. He rolled down the window and handed the small recording device to the security guard standing there.

"Here," he said, "Make sure the old man gets this. He'll know what it means."

The guard took the wire, and said nothing. Kennedy placed his sunglasses on and drove away, wearing the most-wicked of smiles.

Detective Blakey sat in an unmarked car just down the road with two patrol cars parked directly behind him. He had heard every word and gave the signal to proceed to Jack Hampton's house.

As they pulled out onto the road, Kennedy swept passed them in the opposite direction doing at least 95 miles per hour. Blakey shook his head and laughed.

"Crazy priest," he said.

The wiretap had been his idea, but only after Tony Adams had convinced him to trust Kennedy and give him a little time. Police had found Nash's body at the old mansion along with Kennedy's rented car. Blakey put the pieces together in about two seconds and traced Nash's Porsche. But Tony had realized this from the beginning and knew damn well that Blakey would be banging down his door before the end of the day. He had actually contacted Blakey while Kennedy was sleeping and told him everything, but begged him, as a friend, to give them more time. Blakey, in all of his LA cop hardness, had listened to Tony and against his better judgement, had agreed to work together, for the moment anyway, to see if this whacko priest's theory had an ounce of validity. Who would have known? Thank God for Tony Adams.

The front gate was closed in front of Hampton's place and the guy guarding it, now feeling like a fool, was not sure how to respond as Blakey and the other cops showed up in force, lights flashing. Blakey rolled down his window and grinned sarcastically.

"Yes, I have a warrant. Please open the gate," he said. The guard, suddenly outranked, and wanting to appear compliant, motioned at the cameras rather excitedly, as if to hurry the process. The gates did not budge however, and the guard grew increasingly nervous, waving even more frantically at the cameras.

"I'm really sorry there. Let me make a call," he said, retreating to the safety of a small booth located to the far left of the gate. With the phone to his ear, he lifted his hand apologetically to Blakey, sitting less patiently now in his car.

Inside the house, Jack sat at his desk scribbling a long note on a fresh piece of personalized white linen. The wire recording device, with bits of tape still attached lay next to it on the corner of the desk.

He stood and refilled his glass and held it up emptying it again in several full swallows. He set it down and, opening the double glass doors of a tall wooden cabinet, lifted a single-barrel shotgun from the rack. He used to hunt pheasant in the hills and fields when he was younger, but that had been so long ago. The rifle still felt familiar in his hands as he slipped the shell into the end of the barrel and snapped it shut.

He grabbed the wire from the desk and examined it as he sat down in his winged chair. It was sort of ironic, this little device. Here he had built an entire empire, becoming richer than a king, born from an industry that didn't exist, or at least was is its infancy, in which you recorded other people's voices, their music, their songs. And now, all these years later, it was a simple recording device that would end it all.

He placed the barrel beneath his chin and, hands trembling, fearing the impending blast, squeezed the trigger.

The explosion was heard by everyone outside as they struggled to open the gate. Blakey knew instinctively what had happened. He was too late. But he had been prepared for the possibility. In his experience, he never found an animal that could handle the pressure of being cornered.

Inside, behind the illuminated walls of glass, the smoke still swirled in the middle of the now silent library, joined by the acrid smell of burned powder that would last through the night. The note lay undisturbed on the desk where it had been written, moments before. Jack Hampton hung limp in his chair, like a discarded rag doll, and looked up into the eyes of Lydia, standing there on the thick carpet in front of him.

CHAPTER TWENTY-THREE

Howard Perkins sat on his bunk with his head against the cinder block wall of his cell reading a tattered paperback novel about the Cuban Missile Crisis. He knew the guards were approaching by the sound of the hard-soled click of their footsteps and the sudden quiet, like a noiseless wave cresting, from the cells directly proceeding them. He looked over the top of his book as they stopped at his cell. His heart sank. You never want the guards to stop at your door.

"Perkins, Warden wants a word with you," one of the guards said. The other one yelled out "Number 49!" and the iron bars heaved and slid to the side, ending with a bang that notified everyone on the floors above and below that some sort of new daily drama was unfolding.

Perkins put down his book and swung his legs over the side of the bed and hopped down. His roommate, Ronnie, a young black kid who had served two years so far for armed robbery, looked up at him from the bottom bunk, his eyes searching Perkins for any reason for the visit that he might pass on along the network. Perkins shrugged and fell in between the guards as the cell closed itself automatically with another bang.

He trudged along obediently between the guards on their way down the polished cement corridor, stealing glances at some of his cohorts as they watched from the temporary safety of their cells. His only comfort lay in the fact that he had not been involved in any wrong doing for several years. No fights. Nothing he could think of that would stir the interest of the Warden. He wasn't up for parole again for another ten years.

Benjamin "Mighty" Johnson sat in his tall leather chair behind a rather impressive cherry desk, smoking the first cigarette from his second pack of the day. He smiled warmly as Perkins was ushered in.

"Perkins, please, have a seat," the Warden offered, showing a semblance of hospitality. This couldn't be good. The Warden, known to everyone here as a fair man, was still a Warden. He did not have the reputation as being needlessly brutal as is the case in far too many prisons, but was known to have his way. How he got it was how he got his nickname. He simply won you over, not by force necessarily, but by striking fear into your heart. He could conquer a man by simply looking at him.

The sky was grey and flat outside the wire covered glass behind his desk. Perkins sat down and the Warden slid his own pack of cigarettes across the desk toward him. Perkins looked at them for a second then back up at the

Warden who smiled and nodded his head. He slipped a cigarette from the pack and in a moment joined the Warden as the two of them sat together enjoying a smoke. Two guards stood near the rear of the office, watching, awaiting their orders whatever they might be.

"So, Mr. Perkins," the Warden finally spoke. He seemed different. Almost uncomfortable.

"Prison is a horrible thing," he continued. "Even for a man who has, in his life, done horrible things." Perkins agreed with a gentle nod of his head, trying to determine how he fit into this picture and whether or not it meant he was going to end up on the wrong side of a guard's club. The Warden inhaled his cigarette and contemplated his next words.

"But it is a far worse thing for a man to endure, when that man is innocent. Perkins… myself and the State of California, sir, we owe you the greatest apology there is.

"Sir?" Perkins responded, unsure what was being said.

"You were found innocent this morning, Howard."

Perkins sat there, still, removed the cigarette from his lips and rolled it back and forth between his fingers, studying the shifting directions of the smoke as it twisted up like a snake from the tip. He looked up again at the Warden, then over at the guards, waiting for the cruel joke to finally become apparent in some uncontrollable fit of laughter. But nobody moved. They all just waited in anticipation for Perkins to respond.

"Do you understand what I'm telling you? After having served thirty-four years of a life sentence, as of this moment, you are a free man."

Still Perkins sat there quietly examining his cigarette, the Warden's words bouncing off the insides of his head.

"I'm free," he said, taking the cigarette into his mouth once again as the Warden just sat there grinning like a stupid kid, nodding his head. "I'm free."

"There's also the small matter of…an estate," the Warden continued, trying to suppress his smile. "Evidently, there was some crazy record tycoon that recently killed himself. And for some strange reason, before he did so… he felt compelled to leave you his entire estate. You're not only free Perkins, you're stinkin' rich."

Perkins was the first one to start laughing, immediately joined by the others. One of the guards, Harry, stepped forward and patted Perkins on the back, offering his congratulations. The Warden stood and offered his hand to Perkins. Then, for the first time in forty-eight long, hard years, Howard Perkins began to cry.

Tony Adams sat at his desk, whacking away at his computer for days after Jack Hampton's confession. Unfortunately, the police had arrived at the mansion too late, but it made the story that much better as far as Tony was concerened. Like Tanner, his boss, had always claimed about newspaper sales… "If it bleeds, it leads."

They found Jack Hampton in his library chair soaked in blood, holding the wiretap in his lap, his head blown half off from a single shotgun blast. It was the most incredible story Tony had ever had the opportunity to write and it made him love his job like he did in the beginning. "This is the stuff a reporter lives for," he sang to himself as his fingers made love to the keys. After all this time, justice had been waiting for the right moment to swing her axe, or in this case, a simple priest.

The phone rang and Tony ignored it, trying desperately to quickly get several more words out of his head. Still typing and focused on the screen in front of him, his mouth half full of a picked-over blueberry muffin, he grabbed the phone.

"Tony Adams. LA Times…"

"When's the last time you were in church, young man?"

"Hey! Kennedy!" Tony laughed, turning away from the computer. ""I was just thinking about you. You are unbelievable. This stuff is incredible."

"Well, I seriously could not have done it without you, Tony," Kennedy said. "Seriously."

"Ah, baloney."

"Look, I am leaving, pretty soon here… gonna head back up to St. Augustine's and take advantage of that little rest I was supposed to have before all of this. But, I guess I wanted to say thanks and uh… well, I know you had your doubts… about everything. About me. I know what they say about me. You took a real chance trusting me, Tony. That's what made the difference."

Tony swallowed hard and leaned back in his chair. His eyes were wet and he sat there and grinned like a little boy who had made his father proud. He never felt like he had trusted Kennedy, he just liked him. From the very beginning, they just clicked and he never stopped to ask himself whether or not he had trusted him. It was a gut thing and maybe what made Tony such a good reporter. He didn't judge things up in his head. He instinctively used his heart instead.

"Kennedy, you can thank me all you want, but I have to tell you… what they say…is true. You're fucking crazy, man."

Kennedy laughed hard for a second, then they both fell silent, enjoying the bizarre friendship they had fallen into. They probably would never see each other again, but that was OK. It was good.

"So, do me a favor and go become famous. Win the damn Pulitzer or something, would ya?" Kennedy said. "One of us has to do something with their life."

"Hey, come on. What you did… nobody does shit like that. Nobody cares. It's too much work. You almost got killed, man. See that's the difference between you and all the other people in this freaking world. Me, I want to be famous, yeah, sure. Everybody does. We all want everyone else to notice us, pat us on the head and tell us we're great. Be more, do more, make more than the next guy. But you… your life is not about you. You do shit for other people, man. Even people who died a long time ago. Where does that come from? That's cool shit. And I can't touch that. So seriously, shuttup… Father."

Kennedy laughed again, allowing Tony's words to affect him. But Tony was wrong about one thing. It felt really good to be recognized. They made the obvious commitment to keep in touch, genuine, but knowing that, like so many things in life, it would fade with time.

"Oh, Kennedy," Tony said, as they were about to hang up. "I forgot…talk about bizarre. You know what day this is, don't you?"

"Ash Wednesday?"

"Dude, it's the day she died, man. Lydia. Is that freaky, or what?"

"Whoah. OK, that is a little freaky," Kennedy said. "Extremely freaky." They said goodbye to each other and hung up. Tony sat back and thought about Kennedy. It all could have so easily gone the other direction. He could have ended up in jail as well, at the hands of Jack Hampton, another innocent man, serving a sentence for crimes he didn't commit. Damn, it was a good story. He wondered what would become of Kennedy and if he ever really would see him again. He hoped he would and sat back up, facing his monitor.

Tanner approached him from the side of the office, walking down the crowded isle, desks packed on either side of him. He was shaking his head and smiling, something Tony could not remember ever seeing before. He strutted up to Tony's desk and as the other writers in the department pretended not to look on, he did a little jig and sat down on the corner of Tony's desk and patted him on the back.

"I owe you an apology, son," he said. "It's been a long, long time since I've had the pleasure of working with a reporter who follows his instincts, despite threats and pressure from those who are supposed to encourage him. I guess I sort of forgot what it was like, being in your shoes. You did the right thing, Tony, and I am impressed.

"Thanks, I did almost give up."

"But you didn't. And the result… this stuff you've been pumping out is huge. It's not just national. You're about to rock the world, so to speak. You're going to be famous, Tony."

"You think?"

"Damn straight. Journalists dream of stories like this. It only happens to a rare few. I'm going to have to fight to keep you, now. Every newspaper in the goddamn world is going to be knocking on your door. Which I guess is the other thing that I wanted to talk to you about. How about you and I have lunch today? Talk about a few things?"

Tony laughed, then caught himself. He suddenly realized the full weight of his story. It wasn't just a great piece in and of itself, it had tossed him into the limelight. Like Lydia herself, he was about to become a star overnight. There might even be a book or two in the deal. Maybe a movie.

"You know, I'd really love to," Tony said, "But I have this previous date."

"Anyone I know?" Tanner said with a wink. "Maybe tomorrow?"

"Tomorrow's great," Tony said, and the two shook hands there in front of an entire newsroom of shocked reporters. Little Tony Adams had just been pat on the back, asked to lunch, said no, and shook hands with the head news Natzi.

But nobody was more proud of him than Alice, sitting back at her desk across the isle, watching, grinning from ear to ear.

"Wanna have lunch with me?" Tony whispered loudly. One reporter, then another and another, all around him began crumpling sheets of paper into balls, until everyone joined in, throwing them rapid fire at Tony. In a hailstorm of paper bombs, Alice shook her head and could not stop laughing.

––––––––

Kennedy thought about Lydia. He needed to say his final goodbye to her, too. He wanted to leave her with a few words that he had been unable to share before. Words he hadn't even known existed inside him. Feelings.

As bizarre as it sounds, he felt his vow of celibacy was in question. He had given himself completely to the woman. But the vow was meant specifically for the living. Lydia was dead. Perhaps then, some sin far worse had been committed. He didn't care. Only God could say.

In breaking his vow of silence, divulging information received during the Sacrament of Confession, the church would be forced to release him. He knew he was on his own now, alone to deal God. But something had changed, in his heart. The faith that had somehow always eluded him, now seemed to have turned and humbly accepted him. He laughed at the irony. It was in breaking his vows that he caught his first real glimpse of God.

He had visited the huge house one last time, but it had been empty, just as he knew it would be. As he wandered through it, room after empty room, calling her name, the sound of his voice had echoed back to him, disappearing down dark hallways and bouncing off unseen walls. The place seemed even bigger than he had realized as he took his time wandering around it, looking into rooms he never would have had the courage to open before. It felt a little less cold as well and he was not afraid. She was gone now. Forever. Free.

He saved her bedroom for last and, standing outside her door, hesitated, then knocked before gently turning the knob opening it. The light from outside flooded warmly through the dirty windows. The familiar smell of must and mold greeted him. He stood in the center of the room and looked at all the old rotting furniture and at the bed on the far wall.

Laying directly in the center of the bed was an old Gibson acoustic guitar. A guitar purchased one day, long ago at Parker's Music in Tacoma, Washington. Once a gift to her, now a gift to him. But her real gift to him, was a love he had never known before and a growing sense of freedom deep inside his heart. In life, she had touched countless souls. But it was in death, that she had left her deepest mark… on his.

CHAPTER TWENTY-FOUR

He had several hours to burn before heading to the airport and decided to try and find her grave. He took one last look at the massive structure as he stood below it in the shadows of the courtyard. She had once graced this place. It had been beautiful like her. Perhaps, now that she was free, it too would see better days. Perhaps, someone would grab up this place and cherish it, bring it back to life and it would serve as a standing beacon in her memory. Perhaps.

She was buried in Pierce Brothers Westwood Village Memorial Park, a small, crisply manicured little cemetery tucked away peacefully on the south side of Wilshire Boulevard directly beneath the shadows of the skyscrapers all around it. If you didn't know it was there, you might pass by and never see it. As for being a celebrity, evidently this was the graveyard of choice. It seemed all the stars from yesterday were buried here; Marilyn Monroe, Natalie Wood, Burt Lancaster, Dean Martin, even Janis Joplin. There were plenty more, too, and savvy tourists made it a point to stop in to gawk. It was sort of depressing knowing that someone's final resting place was marked on a Stars Map sold for a couple of dollars on every corner in Hollywood.

Reaching into the back seat of the car, Kennedy picked up the old diary and a bouquet of roses he had purchased from the same corner street vendor, turned off the engine and opened the door. The graveyard was beautiful, trimmed meticulously and dotted with a thousand gray stones, each telling their own story. Some small, bearing a message of love lost, somber angels covered in moss, and some towering high above the rest, competing, tombs of granite and marble, gaudy and ornate, claiming some past importance, real or imagined.

Unfolding the tacky little map, he stepped in between the graves searching for Lydia. He climbed a small grass-covered hill and stopped to catch his breath and look at the map once again. Her grave was just up ahead, a simple headstone and nothing more. As he approached, he bent to lay the roses down and read the inscription cut into the stone.

Lydia Elaine Carter.
1943 – 1971
Your song is forever.

The wind shifted when Kennedy suddenly realized he was not alone. Obscured slightly by the sun setting behind her, he turned and saw Lydia, standing near the grave, watching him. She rose and walked toward him, smiling.

322

She stood directly in front of him and then looked down at the flowers on the grave.

Her familiar beauty tore at Kennedy's heart. He wanted to take her. To hold her. He wanted to be with her forever.

"Are you a fan?" she asked.

"I'm sorry," Kennedy stammered, shaken by the sound of her voice. He had not expected her to talk and did not know how to respond. And her voice, so sweet. So tender.

She wore a red, silk blouse with delicate spaghetti straps over gently tanned shoulders. Her hair was lighter and cut shorter, hanging just below her chin. On her left shoulder, Kennedy noticed a small tattoo of a dove, wings spread wide, and the name Soldier written in the clouds above. He reached out and with two fingers, touched her bare arm. She was warm and real. Cocking her head slightly to one side, she looked up at him, then smiled at his apparent confusion.

"I'm sorry. I'm Susan. She was my mother. I know… we look alike."

Kennedy let the words slowly sink in, then nodded his head. He studied Susan then looked down at the headstone again. "And your father?"

She glanced down at the name tattood on her arm, running her finger over it.

"Nope. Viet Nam," she said. "They never found him. All I really have of him is her grave. I come visit it once a year. Today is the day, you know. October 6th, the day she died."

"I know."

"I don't know why I do it. I guess it's all I have of either of them. I was raised by my uncle Dale. He's not my real uncle, just someone she was close to, someone who cared enough, I guess, to take care of me. He sort of kept me hidden away from the flashing cameras and all. Didn't want the world to destroy me too…"

"Dale raised you?"

"You know uncle Dale?" she asked.

"In a way. Yeah, I think I can say I know him."

She looked down at the grave and bent her knees, reaching to adjust the flowers leaning against the cold stone.

"Did you know her?" she asked.

The sun was dipping quickly away now, painting the clouds in a pastel shower of colors across the sky. It was the beginning of October and the leaves were just now starting to fall. Kennedy smiled up at God, gently took her hand, and placed the diary in it.

Everything was changing now. Nothing would ever be the same.

"I'm Shawn Kennedy," he said, extending his hand.

"I have a lot to tell you."

____

THE END

____

About the Author

Labeled a fanatical writer, D. Michael Flanagan has long been fascinated with religion on the a whole. Growing up in the 60's, steeped in all things Catholic, he entertained the calling of the priesthood, was swept away in the churning world of rock and roll, then fell face first into the Protestant ministry, eventually finding his way through life, leaning on Buddhism, resulting finally in an amiable relationship with his Maker.

He spent much of his adult life pursuing creative passions in the world of independent filmmaking, developing and producing a handful of feature films with box office stars such as Charlize Theron, Michelle Rodriguez, Vivica Fox, Matthew Perry, Rumer Willis, Rob Schneider and many more.

Today, the father of six children, he finds a little time between the cracks to pay attention to his Muse, writing fiction, non-fiction, and the occasional pieces of poetry.

Speaking engagements and book-signings
can be secured by visiting
dflanaganbz@gmail.com